The Desert Store Series

Book # 1

Cowboy Johnson's Desert Oasis

Mama and the 57' Mercury

by Patsy Stanley

© Patsy Stanley 2019

The content of this book is fiction All text, cover art and illustrations by Patsy Stanley and fully protected under copyright law. No portion of this book may be copied or reproduced in any form at any time through any media without the authorized consent of the author or her representatives.

HB IS ISBN 9781734296372

LCCN 2019918860

About the Author

Patsy Stanley is an artist, illustrator and author and a mother, grandmother and great grandmother. She has authored both nonfiction and fiction books including novels, children's books, energy books, art books, and more. She can reached at: patsystanley123@gmail.com for questions, comments and orders.

More books by Patsy Stanley:

Novels:
Addition Jones
An Older Wine
Avalon Blue's Quest
Emerald Hawks Flight
Children and all age readers:
Christmas Stories From the Crone's Castle
The Dreadful Noises of Landoshar
Illustrated by the author
Native American Books:
Red Leaf
The Green Mountain Shaman
Energy books:
The Mental Body
The Spiritual Nature of Atomic Structure
Sound Energies
Shield Energies
Chakras, Meridians, and the Color Energies
The Elements

Series: The Desert Store Series

Cowboy Johnson's Desert Oasis
Mama and the '57 Mercury

The Red Cactus Desert
Geena and the '59 Dodge Lancer

Bud's Garage
The Quest of the Three Magi and Map Girl

Susan Sugar Diamond
Away in a Desert

"The rules of love, they really are severe. If you're giving up everything for something, then give up everything for something and stay with it, with your mind on where you're going."

– Joseph Campbell

> What kind of a sanctuary can a book create?
> The kind within these pages.
> I knew this woman.
> and these people.
> and that place.

The very best thing about being a human being is that we get to tell our stories.

"Throw roses into the abyss and say: here is my thanks to the Monster who didn't succeed in swallowing me alive." -Friedrich Nietzsche

Table of Contents

Chapter 1..............................page 1
Chapter 2........................... page 16
Chapter 3........................... page 33
Chapter 4........................... page 48
Chapter 5........................... page 65
Chapter 6........................... page 84
Chapter 7........................... page 101
Chapter 8........................... page 108
Chapter 9........................... page122
Chapter 10......................... page139
Chapter 11......................... page156
Chapter 12......................... page178
Chapter 13......................... page192
Chapter 14......................... page 210
Chapter 15......................... page 226
Chapter 16......................... page 242
Chapter 17......................... page 253
Chapter 18......................... page 271
Chapter 19......................... page 280
Chapter 20......................... page 292
Chapter 21......................... page 297

Chapter One

Justified travelers,
wedded to a fate,
gittin' on the road,
'fore' it's too damn late!

It was a perfect summer day. The sun was shining. Birds chirped as though nothing was amiss, as though the sky was going to stay gloriously blue without a cloud on the horizon forever, while fragrant loaves of bread roasted in early morning ovens and small children sighed sweetly in their innocent sleep, dreaming of new bikes or velvet and chiffon dresses. Uh huh. Yeah. Right. Sure.

The Merc' was loaded and waiting. The last thing I had to do was to dig up the tin can buried under the only tree in our tiny back yard. I ran across the grass that stayed bumpy and patchy like it had acne, even though I mowed and watered it faithfully every summer.

I dropped to my knees under the tree and dug as fast as I could, terrified that the Monster would come home and catch me. The chill of familiar fear the Monster had instilled in me over the years, stayed alert. I jerked out the tin can, emptied it, tossed the can over the neighbor's back fence. I smoothed the dirt back into place, jumped up, and ran out front. Geena was waiting in the back seat of the car. I reached through the open window and shoved the handful of crumpled money into the purse squatting like a giant toad on the passenger side of the front seat. The purse looked like a Civil War carpet bagger's prize. Superiorly ugly and amazingly floral, it hurt to look at it, but it was exactly what I needed. I figured I was safe in my purchase, since all the men I knew, bar none, never ventured into the land of women's purses—not even the most evil of them. They'd rather be hung like in those old western movies, hung from a weird, tall, badly trimmed or naked tree somewhere while a lonesome cowboy warbled an off key tune about misery in the background, or endure major emergency surgery performed on their nether regions by a sleep-deprived doctor than to be forced to voice an opinion on a purse.

The money went in next to the folded map I'd bought from Bud Spinner last week. The map was folded neatly, like an accordion, snugged up against the inside lining of the toad purse. Unfolded, the map was as big as a small tablecloth. It was worth its weight in gold, for it mapped out the United States of America and all its roads. Now was the time for further unfolding, I hoped.

Bud Spinner had kept that map pinned up on the office wall in his gas station out on the edge of town. I'd stopped there and traced the roads on the map many times with my fingers over the years. I could tell Bud Spinner hoped he might escape Ardenville, too. But Bud knew my situation, and sold the map to me without hesitation.

I cocked my head to the side. My Sight informed me not to feel guilty about buying Bud's map. Bud knew he might sell the map to me someday, and he had a replacement map ready. Maybe we'd both escape.

"Come on, Mama!, Stop daydreaming!" Geena shouted impatiently, fear in her voice.

I stopped my snoopy, psychic investigation of Bud Spinner's private life. Now wasn't the time. I nodded and raced around the mile of shiny chrome gleaming off the Merc'.

I hopped in and pulled away from the curb. I took one quick last glance at the small white house we lived in. The short, white picket fence I'd put up bordered the postage-stamp front lawn, making it look like a happy family lived there. Not so. Never. Sparse shrubs, permanently stubby from previous owners neglect, pressed up tight against the two thin, long windows facing the tiny lawn, as though trying to get inside to get a drink of water. A thin, wandering concrete walk wound its tired, broken way up to the front porch. It wandered like old man Vickers weaving his way home from the bars on Saturday night. The warped, faded front door was spattered with flakes of gray and white tracking their weary across it. I left it that way because it spoke the truth about the erosion of misery living inside there.

Geena and I tiptoed the Merc' carefully through the nasty little town of Ardenville. I watched Geena stick her tongue out at her school in the rearview mirror when we passed it. Mrs. Barberrys porch was empty. She was the proud purveyor of fruitcake and righteous bellowing of the town's front porch citizen's rights. Her roses were in full bloom. They stood bright red, haughty, proud in the sunshine. I hated red roses. The Monster always brought me red roses after one of his binges. They usually came from her.

My Sight, which I could count on to activate all my psychic circuits when I was scared, informed me that Mrs. Barberry was hiding in the backroom of her house, indulging in a Camel cigarette.

Now, you may need to know that my Sight was an errant, unreliable companion back in those early days of my life. It had noisily companioned me through the perils of a childhood fraught with survival, utilizing any means, including gossip and bird calls.

My Sight tends to babble. It lights up like a light bulb at the most inopportune moments, handing me bits and particles of information along with odd facts having nothing to do with what is going on. Since I couldn't always give my Sight notice in advance of when I was going to be in a situation so it could behave sedately and stay on target, we both just made the best of it.

I glanced at Geena in the rearview mirror. She had the Sight too, though hers was better organized. But hers was a scientific blabbermouth, always going on about smells and odd facts about bugs.

Geena used her Sight to survive back then, just like me. I wish I could have provided safety for her, but I wasn't able to—not and stay in Ardenville with her father. It was his town. That's why we left. Again.

I turned on to Main Street, the only street out of town, and headed south. If I went north, I'd pass the factory where my husband worked. I edged past Ruby's Diner out on the edge of town. The windows were dark and blank as I crept by in the Merc'. There were no cars in the parking lot. I'd timed it just right.

I bet my husband's three mean old bitch aunts who owned Ruby's, were home resting. This time they wouldn't be there to pick up the phone and call him and tell him I was heading out of town yet again.

The three old bitches reveled in the misery he caused me and Geena. But what they didn't know, was that I never gave up. I'm a damn snail. I learn, slow but sure. Timing is everything. Maybe I'm a turtle. Thay way, I don't leave a chem. trail.

I passed through Ardenville's border of tidy farms and prim, sharp edged houses and headed south. Past the farms lay gravel roads and two-lane blacktopped highways leading to places Geena and I had only heard of.

I glanced in the rear-view mirror. Tall, lanky, with long brown hair, Geena was busy spreading her stuff around back there. Next time I looked, she was hand surfing with the window down, freckles sharp, green eyes emerald in the wind. Geena turned twelve a few days ago. She got out of school for the summer yesterday. It was past time to move on.

We sped south on the first two-lane blacktop we came to, moving steadily away from Monster Town. Away from the determined overlooking of hidden doings going on behind closed doors and other things going on in that little town. I planned to find cheap, out of the way motels we could sleep sweetly in without worry.

Yes, we were headed south, searching for a new place to live. A place where we could begin a secret, safe, happy new life. A place where none of the people we knew could find us.

The Merc's whitewall tires spun smoothly across the dusty back roads and over blacktopped highways. The purposeful quiet held steady, so I let my mind drift. I started thinking about my mother. A mother is the final person you give up when you leave home for good. This time you won't be back, and you may never see her again. I sighed heavily.

My tendency toward mournful thinking is a genetic part of my Irish heritage, and the assortment of other groups I sprang from.

The state line sign came into view. The sign informed all drivers in huge, formal letters that they were leaving this state and entering a new one, and there may be new rules to be obeyed.

I pulled into the rest area just beneath the state line sign. I parked the Merc', got out, and looked around. This would be the first state line I crossed since my family moved us north to Ardenville. That was back when I was a little wisp of a thing with freckles and a pug nose, crammed in the back of an old green slat sided truck with my large family, a pile of beat-up furniture, and a stale grocery sack of sandwiches made of bologna, mustard, and light bread.

Now I was a married woman, fleeing Ardenville with my daughter. I hoped my plan was solid. That we'd make it out for good this time. But who the hell knew?

I hoped I could do better, but one never knew with me. My unconscious or whatever, was tougher than a boiled owl. Self-sabotage was a war I waged every day with myself. My Sight was strong too. It had to be. It gabbled on about this and that. In self-defense. To protect me from myself. To trick myself into not making another mistake. I was a screwed up unit, and my own worst enemy. I never knew if life was tricking me, or me tricking me.

I tended to forget the most obvious things. I was always going back to finish what I started, what I'd forgotten. Like running away from Ardenville. This was not my first attempt; planning and leaving nothing to chance was always a miracle for me.

Self-sabotage is how I ended up living with the Monster. I specialized in running off good men. As soon as a good man showed even a spark of interest in me, my mental body packed its suitcase and left town, leaving me speechless, giggling, and mindless.

I tried to make it stay present, but it insisted on heading for Bora Bora or some such place, to admire the turquoise coral reefs and get a suntan at the first whiff of male hormones. Upon hearing a deep voice, or seeing a smile on a male face, particularly a hairy one, my mental body swiftly packed up and took a one-way flight out of town.

I bargained with it when I discovered it didn't like hairy faces. Not to get psychological or anything, but I told it that watching too many werewolf movies can cause that phobic condition. Soothingly I said I would only date barefaced men if it would stick around. It didn't buy my wooing. No dice. And it wouldn't give up werewolf movies, either.

As soon as the latest guy left, revolted by whatever my mental body was doing to get rid of him, drooling, giggling, whatever, my mind returned. I immediately came to my senses and fell into an endless sea of remorse. Each time, my blabbermouth mental body tried to give me its line of BS. It said that I was just giving them the "Test." They needed to witness the nut job parts of me all rolled into one, and if they ever came back, we would sally forth into a glorious whole new beginning that included all the parts of me. But none of the good ones ever came back.

I paced the rest area parking lot. My Sight, having kicked in some time ago, kept pestering me, blabbing about unfinished business. It insisted that there was something important I better pay attention to before I crossed the state line.

I sighed and blew out a harried breath before I concentrated. My Sight informed me pompously that I had been on the road before, but never made it this far because of that same unfinished business. Yada Yada. I listened only because I never wanted to go back to Ardenville and the Monster because of unfinished business.

I stopped pacing and looked around. The rest area was located in a farmer's field. There were miles of empty sidewalks nobody used. Why? The people came, they peed, they crapped, they tossed garbage at the many garbage cans. Some garbage went in. Some not. They left. The air was full of the scent of allergy-causing wildflowers, fried stubby brown grass that smelled angry about having just been mowed, and aged, wrinkled, dried up trees.

Geena was watching me. She knew how I was when my Sight kicked in. She knew it was trying its best to help me solve a problem obvious to my angels, but as usual, not to me. She climbed out of the Merc', yawned and stretched. She studied me with steady green eyes.

"I'm going to the restroom."

I nodded. She grinned and skipped away. I started pacing again. Memories of my mother began racing through my mind. I recalled being a little girl. I was extremely sensitive to smells and textures and tones and light back then. I could throw up just from smelling a drunk. And did. Because of my father's friends, mainly.

Mother. She always fixed me crispy side pork, salty, fried golden brown, and brickle. When I broke a piece in two, it snapped and flung tiny, brown, salty showers everywhere. She fixed it for me when I got sick, which was quite often back then. She fed me the cooked brains of squirrels and certain parts of the wild game we lived on when I was growing up.

She did it to woo my mental body and soul into staying here, because I owned a vacationing mind and a skinny, hollow soul in those days. Touchy and easily killed off. Melancholy. She knew it and watched over me, lending me some of her strength so I could make it without anybody else in the bunch noticing.

I watched Geena pull the restroom door open. She was built like my mother, tall, only more slender. My mother was tall and large-boned, a capable Amazon with intense hazel eyes, shoulder length coal-black hair, and a full, generous mouth. Her energy was large. It stood out from her. It was natural and strong with weak, but good instincts. My drunken, mouthy, little father tried to beat it out of her because she was bigger than he was. Time and again, he tried to break her. But he couldn't.

My father, who was not a molester, just a really stupid man, didn't seem to see the evil in his buddies who scattered their spurious seed around like unwanted rabbits. Year after year, he and the drunken bums he surrounded himself with tried to make my mother small. They all hated her large Goodness. They failed in most ways, but not all. Though God allowed her to keep some large, good ways, there were other things she was forced to give in on.

Mother. Her soul was less sensitive than mine. Hers was a mighty oak, while mine was a whiny, weeping willow because I had inherited both the Sight and the melancholy of her father's Irish immigrant family. Mother missed out on that, so she didn't understand it.

My Sight and nature was inherited from the branch of mother's family that spent their lives being full-time mourners. They avidly followed every tragedy they ever heard about to its bitter end. Like those same damp ancestors, I could stroll down Melancholy Lane at the drop of a hat, and mourn near to death over a dark cloud or an innocent drop of rain. I intuited mournfully and was drawn to, as they were, to the misunderstood strengths nesting in the dark side of our family, usually laying fallow in their fields, because of the erring ways of a goodly clutch of ancestors.

Mother was always afraid for me because she knew that branch of her family carried the terrible, doomed, dark, troublesome Sight. She wanted me to be happy instead of mournful. Unlike me, she stayed content, bobbing along like a cork on the surface of life, simply counting her blessings each day. She stayed large, hollow, and bright, just being there, without any need to search out meanings, never feeling the need to weave any part of life into a darker fabric like I yearned to do. She was like the water, her natural habitat. Never bitter or beaten down, she bobbed along, going whichever way the water flowed.

Daily pieces of happiness randomly slipped into her life. She said they were surprise gifts from angels on high. A tiny, bright yellow flower discovered on the bank of the noisy little creek in the field behind our old house could renew her awe of life for days. We children felt the shine in her, and responded to it with our own innocent awe. Our souls grew from it.

She stayed out in nature when she was troubled. She sniffed the air and held private, lengthy conversations with the wind, rain, sunshine, trees, snow, flowers, animals. Eventually, she came back inside, calm, and internally organized again. She was so big natured, Nature itself helped her.

Sometimes it took a while before she came back, having accepted that her life wasn't good or fair, but knowing she sure as hell did have certain powers to make a few things better, and those things worked damn well. She was hell with a gravy skillet. On the surface, she was limited to cleaning and cooking, biscuit and gravy making, hanging sheets on the clothesline so the meanest of sinners could sleep under snowy white linens smelling of innocent sunshine.

I knew she was an innocent healer, one who carried the Light, for I washed a lot of those same white sheets myself. I watched her clean game and kill chickens and forage for mushrooms and pick mustard greens and gather dandelion greens. She could not drink booze, and she did not like wine or beer. She always grinned at me. She knew what I was thinking.

"Wanna' help?"

I nodded. I already knew she would give me something I could do and learn from. I willingly learned from her, but she could never offer me the protection I needed from the darkness. I had to figure that out for myself. She offered me an orange soda once when I refused to come back to the house one day. I finally gave in and took it from her. It was so sweet! But I resented her not protecting me anyway.

I learned very little about the Sight I carried, and even less about God, because mother did not explain life or anything else to us kids. She didn't feel the need to. When we got sick, we knew she wouldn't tell us if was the flu we were dealing with, or a cold or an illness that could mean our demise any minute. She'd just shake her head and scoff at us.

"Ahhh, you ain't that bad off."

Then she would begin curing our ailments with no explanation. Salves and peroxide or alcohol. When I questioned mother about God, she always looked worried and said,

"Go ask somebody else."

She'd look away.

"Ain't the sky blue today?"
She'd roll her eyes upwards.
"I think you'll live through it."
Scoffing, harried, and downcast.
"There's hot rolls in the kitchen."

Mother's moods had their times and places. I was familiar with all of them. I have lived alone in my own internal world all my life, where my moods come and go as they please. Moods have run my show all my life, with only my Sight stepping in to interrupt them now and then.

I knew my mother lived alone in her own interior world, too. She let me be alone and indicated spending time alone in my interior home was good for me, like it was for her. She stepped out of her personal reserve and hugged me every now and then when I was small. She told me to never marry when I grew up, that she'd be proud of me if I didn't. But life didn't go the way either one of us hoped it would. Instead, I got shoved out of the nest too early by jealous, unsighted siblings, and ended up married to the Monster. He was friends with others like him, and before long, I learned there were many kinds of Monster lurking in groups in this old world.

Mother. I gave a soft moan as I realized what was going on. My Sight was having the problem, not me, for a change! It didn't want to leave her. If I got away this time, I would have to leave her behind because she never stopped trying to give herself away, even though it never worked. And I couldn't give myself away any longer and stay alive, to save her. I loved her so much, but I couldn't return to Ardenville this time. Geena had to be saved.

At last, I understood why I wasn't able to get away from the Monster before, though I tried plenty of times. My mother had held me back with both of our Sight-loves and longings. With me gone, there would be no one to "see" her, to recognize the great value of her large, gorgeous inner spirit. And it was through her family that the Sight was bequeathed to me.

I took a deep breath and looked out over the sea of smelly, dried brown stubble surrounding the park, and coughed. Damned allergies! Short of living by the ocean or in a desert, I was stuck with the miserable drooling things!

I coughed again and cocked my head to the side. Maybe another reason I was running away was to better my health. I envisioned myself in a sleeveless blue dress, strolling casually along a sandy beach. The waves roared while my sinus cavities drained and stayed clean and clear. The desert? Nah. Too damn hot for me, although I briefly pictured myself thin and bronzed.

I knew that random speculations and short sideshows were given to me by my Sight angels out of kindness to interrupt, to buffer the rawness of an impending epiphany I might miss out on anyway. They seemed to want me to have plenty of them. Epiphanies, I mean. My angels were merciful to me, because I was a slow learner, with Sight. I was a spiritual dummy in countless ways. They stayed gentle with me, steering me away from too much hurt at one time.

Life puts all of us to the test at one time or another. I learned to run away from it. That's why the Merc' is so important to me. I sighed and turned back towards the Merc'. Geena was leaning against the back door, chewing gum, blowing pink bubbles. Popping them with glee. I frowned. Where did the damn bubble gum come from this time? Geena seemed to have a never-ending supply from an endless source I could never ferret out.

"Spit it out," I ordered.

I had a hard and fast rule about no chewing gum in the Merc' because it stuck to the leather seats and left white spots. Geena grinned at me. She never took a scolding from me any other way. From birth, she acted like I was a silly kid giving silly orders, but she would put up with me anyway. That's what I get for having an old soul for a daughter. I waited.

"Okay," she said. She took aim and spit the pink wad of gum toward the black rubber trash can carefully placed near the curb in an effort to encourage roadside offenders to deposit their trash. The gum flew inside. I looked around. The place was spotless. Either everybody that stopped at this rest area paid attention to the "No Littering" signs, or the county cleaning crew had just left. People just weren't that concerned about looking out for others. How did I miss noticing it? I missed so much, and it kept me eternally nervous. Spirit or God or whatever people call the big boss who runs the show, was a hell of a prankster in my book.

Chapter Two

Born to a crib, wedded to a' fate,
come on baby, sugar pie, honey, darlin',
let's run quick
ya' know it's not too late!

We climbed back in the Merc' and headed out. We crossed the state line. I smiled and settled further back into the Merc's spacious driving seat.

In a while, a horn blew behind me. I moved to the shoulder of the road to let them pass. I guess I was going too slow to suit some people. But I chose to err on the side of caution. No speeding tickets for me, or we might have to face the Monster again, and I'd already gone back too many times.

Twelve years ago, I made a wish to the angels when I lay in a hospital room late at night, holding my newborn baby, listening to her thin, weak cry. She was born three weeks early because of the Monster's sexual attack on us. I almost bled to death. Not knowing what to do with her or me, I prayed, though I didn't believe much in God. I knew we were both alone in this world with the Monster, and needed somebody's help. The angels have helped us ever since.

For the next few years, I was kept busy coping and trying to find a way to get away from the Monster while working to keep us surviving his daily attacks on our vulnerabilities. He wanted us both dead, but he couldn't figure out a way to do it and stay out of jail. He tried to influence Geena against me, to teach her how to kill me so he wouldn't be blamed, but Geena was filled with Sight and Goodness that kept winning out over his evil.

It took almost too long for me to get us away from him. Partly because Geena and I were both susceptible and sensitive to life in general, and we needed to recuperate from the shocks he dealt to our psychic systems every day.

I glanced at Geena in the rear-view mirror. I watched what I was thinking around her because she had the Sight, too. She was like a little psychic bulldog when it came to knowing what I was thinking.

She was napping, her mouth open in innocent, trusting repose. New strength and purpose poured through me. I shifted my eyes to the road ahead. Geena trusted me. I couldn't keep putting her through hell. I had to succeed this time.

I remember the first day my father drove our family into Ardenville. My Sight had raised holy hell. It informed me that this was a bad place. It ordered me to get out. But a kid has no control over that, do they?

In fifth grade, I started walking by the old garage out on the edge of town so I could pore over the tiny map pinned up on Old Bill Addison's front office wall. I discovered the map on my way home from school one day. Nobody much bothered with Old Bill's garage, but I'd noticed his bubble gum machine when I was wandering around one Saturday morning to keep away from home.

There were cars and tires and gasoline at Old Bill's garage. I got the gum and saw the map. It was my first physical proof that people could leave Ardenville for another destination. Day after day, I stepped up to the small, glossy map and traced out the tiny threads of roads. Ornery Old Bill ignored me. I guess that was his way of being kind.

Then Bud Spinner bought the garage from Old Bill. He replaced Old Bill's tiny green map with a big green and white map with thousands of roads on it with names large enough to read.

My plan to flee Ardenville kept getting put off because of the Monster and having to work in a factory where most of the married men acted like dogs in heat during the day, meekly going home to their wives after their shifts were over, pretending they had been good little neutered boys all day.

If I hadn't worked for Will Parton before I got the job at the factory, I wouldn't have been able to stand my life. It would have killed me.

Will Parton hired me to paint his house. The inside of it and the front porch. His house was the former Baptist Church before he bought it and renovated it. Me and a couple of schoolboys worked on his place the whole summer after Geena was born. I healed and painted with baby Geena by my side. The Monster allowed me to work because the pay was better than average.

Will Parton was a Good man. He was my first encounter with an Eternal Reader. He read books all the time. They were all over his house. The Eternal Reader was my hero, not a singing cowboy or Dale

Evans or Batman. I made the Eternal Reader up when I first learned to read. When I grew up, I planned to meet an Eternal Reader somehow. We would get married and live a good life and read together every night. That was the plan. I believed it was just a childhood fantasy until I met Will Parton.

It was Will's Goodness I fell in love with. I happily carted Geena off to his house each morning to bathe in his Goodness. I drove to the little church in the willows and oaks just outside of town and went to work. I intended to make the place so beautiful he would be dazzled by it and quit his girlfriend of many years and take up with me and Geena. That way, I could get me and Geena away from the Monster. I imagined him turning to me in recognition and saying, "There you are, my love!"

I worked while he tackled stacks of papers and went out for a few hours every afternoon. Sometimes we talked about books. I'm sure my admiration and longing for him was obvious, but he treated me with kindness, advised me of books I should read, and kept his distance.

I basked in his Goodness, and he let me. He was a living umbrella I stood under to keep hell at bay for two and a half sunny months while Geena and I healed. Then the job ended. He had no family in Ardenville. He sold the renovated church, married his girlfriend, and moved away. I was bereft, but grateful for the short reprieve. My Sight had grown stronger in the light of his Goodness. Maybe that's why Spirit, or whatever you call the Big Boss of us all, brought the gift of him to me. I certainly needed him.

I got a job at the factory under the water tower. But I never forgot Will Parton's Goodness. He was an angel in my life. He saved me and Geena. So did some others.

In spite of my troubles, I still gassed up once a week at Bud Spinner's garage and pored over the big map pinned on his office wall. The dirty factory men and the Monster could not stop me from hoping and dreaming, just like my father couldn't stop my mother from being who she was.

I knew Good men were out there. I had already met three men filled with Goodness in Ardenville, and I was still young. Will Parton, Bud Spinner, and Old Bill.

Like my mother, I was filled with hope, but hers was permanently caged in by my father. My Sight wouldn't let hopelessness happen to me. My Sight was a tough customer. It nagged at me until I gave in and accepted its larger philosophical bent.

"Everything is cool in school." it chanted when I was young. It played mournful dirges and sent me pictures of death and dying when I rebelled and married the Monster. After it chastised me real good, it started sending me old rock and roll songs to get me through the traumas the Monster inflicted on me. After a few years, it chanted, "Get in the groove and get on the move!" over and over. It didn't like the Monster.

I was still in school when Bud Spinner insisted on instructing me on how to repair a carburetor and a fuel pump. We both knew why he wanted me to learn about cars, but neither of us said it. I listened and learned when I wasn't poring over the map pinned up on the wall.

One day Bud was working on a sky-blue Cadillac parked in the sunshine outside the car bays. It was so shiny my eyes couldn't look at it straight on, so I danced sideways in a circle around it. Bud watched me.

"Notice the fins."

He pointed to the back of the luscious, light blue Cadillac. I danced sideways towards the back of it, admiring the reflections of the sun and sky on the shiny surface. The rear of the Caddy was long and sleek. The gleaming blue fins were so sharp, I was afraid I might cut my fingers on them.

"It's a beauty," Bud said. "Belongs to old Mr. Mayberth. He wanted it checked out. First time out of his garage this year."

I nodded.

"It's gorgeous."

"Let me show you the engine."

He lifted the hood. We grinned at each other. We were both crazy about fine land yachts. The longer, the better. The shinier, the better. The more miles of chrome, the better. Whitewall tires. Tender leather. Fender skirts. Oh yeah.

There was no cozy chitchat between us. I never chitchatted with my family or anyone else in my life, and I didn't plan on starting now. I suspected Bud never did either. The words bottled up inside of us held generation gaps and sad experiences that stopped them from coming out. But there was a silent communication between us, and our hidden words fell into a place of rapport that smoothed out into a deeper understanding of life we shared.

"Maybe you'll get out of here someday."

Bud said this a lot, so I knew he understood about my growing up and about the Monster. He was hoping I would get a move on. He knew I was wrong for this place, for this life. He wanted me to leave and not have to come back again.

Bud had sold me the map a week ago when I walked in and asked, "How much for the map?"

That was my way of telling him I was going to hit the road again. He caught on and stared at me. We held a long, unspoken conversation.

"Five dollars," he finally said, giving me a challenging look. It was a ridiculously high price. The map was worth a couple dollars at most. But that was Bud's way of telling me I better have plenty of money, not just enough to get to the next town like last time. And the time before.

"No problem," I answered jauntily, blushing. He didn't need to know the details, that I'd sold a few things of the Monster's, and they should all be gone and the money collected by the time he got home the day I planned to leave. After all, it was my money that had paid for everything all these long, tiresome years.

"Soon," Bud said.

I nodded and handed him a five-dollar bill. I took the map down myself and carefully folded it down to a letter-sized accordion-pleated piece of paper while he went out and gassed up the Merc'. I strolled out of the gas station and over to the Merc'. I lifted the trunk and hid the map underneath the gray carpet while Bud watched. He nodded and waved. I got in the Merc' and drove off. I never waved or looked back. I couldn't, or I would have cried and turned back to continue living on the short moments of predictable safety that Good people like Bud Spinner offered me.

I drove on. If we made it, I would watch for the Monster to show up, but I figured I was holding three aces in the hole this time.

Number One: The Monster went nuts any time he left Monster Town. He wouldn't leave the state even though the state line was just a hundred miles away. When I ran away before, I stayed in the state. Stupid me.

Number Two: The Monster was terrified of being put in jail. Between his traveling problem and his extreme paranoia of jail, maybe we could disappear successfully this time.

Number Three: The Monster was a coward around able-bodied men. He was terrified of them hurting him. If I ever ran across a man that would stick up for us, he would have to leave us alone.

Number three was just wishful thinking, but at least it was one more to add. I'd got a late start on escaping due to my stupidity, but maybe it would work out for us this time. Let's face it. It had to.

Just then, my troublesome Sight informed me that I needed to make a detour, that there was still unfinished business to tend to. I drove steadily southeast until we reached the foot of the mountains where my parents had grown up. We climbed the tired old mountains slowly.

I never worried about the Merc' breaking down. I could fix it after Bud's training.

The Monster let me keep a car because I worked to support us. He was stone lazy except when it came to certain things. I shuddered. I didn't want to think about those things.

I smoothed my hands over the large, round steering wheel with the clear glass knob on it that looked like an oversized diamond. The Merc' always made me feel better. Through all my troubles, I always managed to keep a reliable land yacht. As soon as I got my first driver's license, I bought one on time. One after the other, they served me well until I had to sell them to make my way a little farther down the line.

The Merc' was used to smooth, paved, small town streets instead of rugged, thin roads that wound around mountains high enough to give a person a nosebleed, but I knew she wouldn't give me any trouble.

The Merc's a turquoise and white 57' Turnpike Cruiser, a four-door hardtop with a fine hood ornament and tender, turquoise leather seats the size of small sofas. Yep, she's a land yacht. Big as a small boat. A lead sled. A Yank Tank. As large as a small barge. That's what people say about "land yachts."

Her trunk is as big as a small bedroom. Just right for storage of all we needed for running away. Maybe it was just as much space as we might ever need again. I could live with that, easy. The Merc' is an easy ride, her powerful V8 engine purring smoothly along, like hauling the weight of our problems and belongings was nothing. No big deal. Every time I stepped out of her, I automatically posed, feeling like a thin, anorexic car model in a slick, glossy magazine. She was my home on wheels. My ticket to freedom.

I never named the Merc' more than "The Merc'." If I had shown affection for her, the Monster would have sold her out from under me. She was a bargain sale, and I hid my excitement from him. That's how I got to keep her.

I wound my way up through the mountains, headed for Spellbind, my parents' birthplace. I figured my Sight was sending me back there to try to find their Philosopher's Stone, so to speak. My girl had never been there. I was born in Spellbind, but we moved north when I was too young to remember.

Geena woke up. I drove into Spellbind with my psychic circuits wide open. Oh, I could just tell this was going to be fun! I gave a short bark of bitter laugher, then shut up.

Warily, I looked around. The little town looked old and grim, lost in a never-ending past. The few cube-shaped, newish red brick buildings on Main Street bore sharp edges with gray utility lines stretched between them. By contrast, the three-story courthouse on the little town square looked like a crooked, much too tall wedding cake gone wrong.

I settled the Merc' into an empty parking spot and pointed across the street. I would make the best of it. I tried to pump up some enthusiasm.

"Look, Geena, there's The Coffee Pot Restaurant! Your grandma said they have the best chicken and dumplings she ever tasted!"

A wave of fear washed over me. I looked away from Geena's bright, expectant face. I didn't know this place. It felt brutal and scary. What the hell was I doing here? I took a deep breath and expelled the fear. Well, I figured I'd blow hot and cold until my Sight let me off the hook again.

I climbed out, posed, and ran my hand over the hood of the Mercury and admired her hood ornament. The Merc' was wearing a broken hood ornament when I first got her. The Monster hadn't seen her yet, so I drove straight to the junkyard and searched until I discovered a silver hood ornament of a running woman. She was six inches in length, naked, with long hair streaming behind her. I hired the junkyard man to weld her on to the hood of the Merc' on the spot. The Monster assumed the hood ornament was already on the Merc' when I bought her. I never told him any different. It was easy to fool him; he barely knew one end of a car from another. That wasn't where his interests lay.

I guided Geena across the street with false bravado, opened the door of the restaurant, and swaggered in. The Coffee Pot Restaurant was empty, warm, and welcoming. The comforting fragrance of lemon pie and hot coffee floated in the air. The portly waitress wore a white apron over a flowered dress that stopped just above her ankles. Her full figure swayed smartly across the room toward us while she looked us up and down.

"You one of them Smith's from over Farthing Way?" she questioned.

"Don't know them."

Her smile grew cautious.

"You one of them Campbells?"

"Nope."

I didn't feel like volunteering any information. Her smile disappeared. She jerked her head at a front window booth and whipped out her order pad. We slid into the booth and ordered chicken and dumplings with milk to drink. The waitress brought the food and set it just far enough away on the red and white plastic tablecloth so we'd have to reach for it and pull it to us. I didn't mind. I've been made to do that most of my life anyway.

I must have mood swings when it comes to food because as usual, I got happy while I was eating. In between bites of delicious chicken and dumplings, I said, "Me and my girl here, her name is Geena, we're trying to look up some relatives."

The waitress got interested in us again.

"Who are you looking for?"

"Well, my mama was a Kingsley from here."

Her face brightened, and she nodded.

"Most a' them Kingsley's live up in Big Bear Holler."

I nodded and grinned.

"Kin' you give us directions on how to git' there?" I asked, using my most twangy southern accent. It felt natural to use it, seeing as how I was here in my birthplace.

After we ate, we moseyed over to the library. It was housed in another gothic monstrosity just around the corner from the courthouse. The soaring heights of the tall, thin building threatened to make me dizzy as I gazed toward the top of it, trying to discover where it ended. It seemed the generations were still trying to outdo each other with feast or jail house architecture.

I tried to look my mother's family up, but there was nothing. No maps. No histories. The librarian strolled by and glanced over my shoulder.

"You won't find them that a' away. You'll jist' have to git' out and drive."

She gave me a few skimpy directions, and I set out. I drove the Merc' up dozens of hollers, climbed hills, and walked up and down rickety porch steps. I sampled white lightning, chicory, and Ginseng tea, and didn't like any of them. After three days of sleeping in a crummy little motel that cost too much and meeting rude people who stared at me suspiciously and asked what I was doing in town without a man, I discovered an old aunt and a few cousins who told stories about how stupid and bad our family was. After the traditional negative Shadow stories about our family that had been passed down for generations were over, we left.

Geena was fine with all of it. She fiddled with her hair and smiled distantly at our long lost relatives like she wasn't too bright so they wouldn't ask her questions or try to chum up to her.

The last thing we did was visit a cousin's funeral home. While cousin Maudie was showing us the caskets, her husband planted his hand on my ass for a good feel while her back was turned. That did it. I jabbed him in the ribs, grabbed Geena's hand, and shouted goodbye to cousin Maudie.

She just smiled at me, never questioning my odd behavior, and in that instant, I realized she knew exactly what was going on. Another little Ardenville. Horrified, I rushed back to the motel, packed, and got the hell out of there.

As I drove, I remembered my mother laboring over letters of love to her mother back home. Letters packed with lies. Letters telling my grandmother that we were prospering, that my father was a kind, good, wise man. Her family went along with her lies, but now I understood that they'd always known better. They knew what my father was. He grew up there. My parents lived in Spellbind for years before they moved north. My mother's people had hung her out to dry. Not one of them ever came north to visit us.

I'd listened to her lies and believed her. I didn't get to stand under a railroad trestle in tall grass swaying in the sunshine while a train roared overhead like she said she did as a child. I didn't discover my true love in this place and damn glad of it. Mostly I wished I could have trained a forty-five on the few men I met here and shot them between their buttercups.

We were on the road again. But now I knew. Two and two had finally made four. I'd found their Philosopher's Stone. It was a hardened negative stone, covered in Shadow, made of lies. I'd tried to find the strengths in my family so I could lean on them when I started my new life. Now I knew.

There wasn't anything to look upon with favor in Spellbind except the Coffee Pot Restaurant, where we'd eaten chicken and dumplings. I glanced over at Geena. She grinned back at me.

My Sight kicked in and informed me that getting the hell out of town with my new knowledge wasn't enough. I was to leave something behind, to return something that had always belonged here. Something my spirit would not allow me to carry with me into my new life.

Suddenly I was dead tired of a nameless old something. I felt a part of my heart start breaking slow like an old dirge played broken claw hammer style on a thin, tired dulcimer, or something like that.

I slowed the Merc' down a few miles out of Spellbind and pulled off the road. I asked Geena for a sheet of paper and a red crayon. Then I drew the tired, broken part of my heart on the piece of paper and claimed it by signing my name to it. I got out of the Merc' and laid the paper down on the ground. That part of me belonged back here. It needed to stay here. It was finally home. It could rest easy from now on. It couldn't go on with me. I laid a small rock on the paper to hold it down.

I thought about drawing a heart for my mother. Maybe someday one of our relatives would tell her about us being here, and maybe she would understand that I came here for her too.

I borrowed another sheet of paper from Geena and drew a strong, steady heart full of good memories of a young girl's ways. I laid my mother's wild young heart paper down beside mine, placed a rock and some tiny wildflowers on it. A little roadside funeral for two sad, tired pieces of two broken hearts.

I didn't grow up here. I would never understand the limits or freedoms my family experienced while living here.

I studied the thick trees on the hillside. The green grass rippled down in the valley below. Shadows stand tall in these ancient mountains. I sensed the darkness and the heaviness of them. Elementals of Shadowed Natures lived here. This place was a big city to them, full of different kinds of Elemental immigrants from all over, some visiting, some staying. They owned these mountains, and it was not given to any human to think differently about it.

Mountain people accepted their presence, and took with them the things they learned from them when they crossed over. A human soul needed to dwell here lengthily to earn that kind of knowing. I chose not to.

I sighed. Well, I was nobody, and I'd never wear the finest clothes in town, and I owned a bad fear from being knocked down in life too many times to count, but I also owned imagination and grit, and the determination to take me and my girl into a better life.

I got some of that grit from being born here, right along with the other things that make each person up. Like genetics and the right kind of food. That knowing is what I came here for. That knowing is what I would carry away from here.

There had to be a place, a sacred place, a home for wounded, misfits like me and Geena. A place where Good men dwelt, too.

I'd got a gift given to me here. It stunk and was slippery and cold. I finally understood that all Shadows were affected by where they lived.

"Mama!" Geena called me, "let's go!"

I would explore more of that thinking later. Right now, it was time to move on.

I climbed back in the Merc' and gunned the motor. The Merc' fishtailed, then swayed its way down out of the old green mountains filled with ancient Shadows and sacred, secret ways. Some nasty. Some divine.

I breathed a sigh of relief as I headed back into the mainstream of life waiting below. I had cut the ties holding us back. We were on our way!

Chapter Three

You knows ever' thaing' changes, honey baby,
for better or worse,
jist' roll dat' car winda' down
and pass right on by dat' bad ol' curse!

The flow of cars increased steadily as the land grew flatter. I sped up as I rejoined the faster moving world I was heading into. Quiet settled over the Merc' as we both retreated into the familiar inner places we each hid out in.

Both were places where we didn't have a care or give a damn. They were places where we were beautiful and treasured and couldn't be spit on or hurt. Places where there was plenty of money and food. A place where books could be read and night lamps enjoyed. A place where the heat of the day sloped gently into cool, clean nights under sun-blessed clean sheets.

We stopped for gas. I bought us two Nehi Strawberry Crème sodas just because they were pink and pretty and cold. The glass bottles were beaded with sweat. Back on the road again, I got to thinking about an ancestor of mine that made his own hell of a road trip.

A hundred years ago, one of my ancestors, a hale and hearty seventy-four-year-old, left Tennessee and move south. Him and his wife and most of their seventeen kids, and a few offhand others, built rafts and floated down the river with the intention of starting a new life. They passed along three rivers, including the Mississippi, before they headed inland and started a new town in Arkansas. They were pioneers on a raft.

Geena and I were pioneers too. Roadies in a '57 Mercury land yacht, our modern version of their raft. Me and my girl were headed south too. I figured there were some big adventures waiting up ahead. Good ones. With more good learning.

That's my inspiration story. I wanted it to be more like the story of the settlers who traveled to Missouri from Tennessee, and today, brag about still having the same fire burning on their hearth they carried with them from their old homestead eighty years ago. A family fire more than eighty years old warming all their generations, providing light to scare off the boogeyman and make their food safe by cooking it.

Well. I was still learning. So was Geena. I would buy books filled with beautiful illustrations for her to read. She would learn about grace and higher thinking and dancing with the universe. After all, I read that the Earth partakes in at least fourteen movements all at the same time, so we humans were taken along on a dancing, spinning, universal road trip mostly without even knowing it.

I would buy Geena pretty clothes and good shoes and coats with cheerful colors. Coats that is, if we ever lived in a cold place in the winter again. I didn't plan to. I was headed south, to an island in the Bahamas or somewhere else warm. Maybe an island no one could get to except by boat. Not being able to swim didn't bother me. I'd just wear a life jacket—something in lime green.

Short of that, we'd find a cheap apartment somewhere—cheap being the operative word—and I would get a job. I'd always worked. I couldn't waitress. I was lousy at it. That was too bad because I was cute in my waitress's uniform and made a lot of tips the two days I was one. Well, I was young enough and healthy enough to find another manual labor job. There were jobs available every place in the country that were hard to do, that paid very little.

I took whatever road headed southwest, driving along, thinking about life. We traveled over two-lane black-topped roads intersecting in small towns with one blinking red stoplight. We bumped across washboard avenues and gravel roads running along farm fences out in the middle of nowhere. I didn't see any rhyme or reason to the road planning, and I didn't care just as long as we kept moving farther away from Ardenville and Spellbind.

The sunset was putting out orange and gold rays when I saw a small motel just off the highway. I swung into the parking lot. We'd been on the road a few days now and were becoming veterans of motel living. This little motel looked safe. Old and clean and cheerful. I crawled out of the Merc' and stretched.

The time flew by on the road because the past stayed busy trying to catch up with me. But I wouldn't let it. We were going to partake of cheeseburgers and fries and drink chocolate shakes if I could find the right place to eat.

Geena woke up, rubbed her eyes, and yawned. She pushed the door open and got out.

"Dad says you can run, but you can't hide."

She stood there, watching me with eyes like sharp green razors. I studied her a minute.

"Oh, yes, you can."

She looked me up and down. There was an edge of hope in her voice, just a tiny thread, but I heard it.

"Yep. You sure can. We've done it before. Only this time, it's for good."

I stated that fact again on a stronger note because Ardenville and Spellbind were behind us. What lay in front of us had to be better than either one of them. She studied me while time stood still and I prayed inside with all my might.

"Okay."

I grinned at her and posed by the Merc' before I headed to the faded blue motel office. She closed the distance between us, and I sighed with relief.

I checked in for the night while Geena charmed the old white-haired gentleman out of a soda. He motioned to the right when I asked him about a restaurant.

"It's over there. No fast food places in these parts."

I nodded and backed out the screen door. It slammed shut behind me. I wiped my face with my hand. There was a fine film of dust on it. We trudged a few steps and pulled open another screen door. The smell of ancient grease coupled with the mouthwatering fragrance of fries and pies wafted over us like the finest perfume. We looked around. The walls were covered with sun-faded pictures of mountain streams.

"Wishful thinking," I thought. The booth seats and backs were covered with creased and faded maroon leather. Tabletops held simple menus under thick, cloudy sheets of plexiglass. The waitress smiled at us. I could tell she was the other half of this Mom and Pop operation. I smiled back.

People tended to walk straight up to me and tell me their stories and secrets because I'm psychic. They were always surprised at themselves, but I never was. It was always that way. My mother said it was from having the Sight and being a Sensitive. I hoped this lady wouldn't want something from me tonight, because I was so hungry I could eat a side of beef with an order of fries!

I felt Geena looking at me. She knew what I was thinking. The lady pointed to a window booth and turned away. We trailed each other over to the booth and slid in. The seats were slick with wear, comfortable. The window looked out over the parking lot. It was almost dark. Night was coming on fast.

My appetite was legendary when I went a long time without eating. So was Geena's. We ordered double cheeseburgers, large fries, pie, and Seven Ups. The old lady stared at us, puzzled. She'd already written down the standard Cokes instead of Seven Ups. Geena and I don't drink caffeine. It speeds us up too much. Makes our hearts pound. We eat chocolate sometimes. And salads. But not tonight. We worked our way through huge, well-done cheeseburgers layered on buttered, crispy grilled buns, juicy, loaded with mayo, onions, and tomatoes. Mine was, that is. Geena's was loaded with pickles, mustard, ketchup, sweet relish, no onions. The French fries were rippled, big, brown, and crisp outside, with hot, soft white insides. Perfect. The ketchup was homemade.

By the time the waitress placed two gorgeous slabs of pie on the table, chocolate for Geena and apple for me, our appetites were not so desperate. When we finished, I asked for the bill. The waitress said, "No checks. Cash only. Four dollars."

I stood up and searched through my purse and peeled a five from the wad of cash stashed in a corner. I handed it to her and said, "Keep the change."

She nodded and smiled at me. "Thanks."

We both understood what I was saying. That it doesn't get any better than the eating was here tonight.

We went back to our motel room and turned in for the night. We slept like babies. Not a worry in the world. In the morning, after a huge breakfast of bacon, biscuits, gravy, fried potatoes, eggs, and milk, we got on the road again. It's a wonder the Merc' didn't sink to the ground when we got in it.

Before I drove away, I bragged to the old couple on the old woman's cooking and the cleanliness of the cozy little motel room. The old couple looked at us with wise eyes that had seen just about everything. She shoved a folded piece of white paper at me with an old, shaky hand.

"Here's our phone number and address in case you need anything."

"Thank you," I mumbled, not looking at her. I didn't want her to see the start of tears in my eyes. I took the paper and put it in my purse. I felt fat and surprised and loved. We all hugged each other real good without blabbing or saying anything smarmy.

Geena and I had just met Angels in a diner, and they'd given us a piece of comfort we'd never found anywhere else. Sometimes it takes a road trip to find a grandma and grandpa just when you need them most.

*

We rode all day until we found ourselves winding our way down through yellow and orange boulders boldly draped in thin red velvet dust. Geena kept exclaiming over them.

"Oh, look! Another one!" she kept shouting like I was a few states away.

"That one is smiling at us!"

I liked it when she was happy. Geena's delight made the boulder people happy. We rode through them without scraping a fender or denting the songs we sang. We were purely melted, both by the heat of the sun and delight at their faces and colors. It became an extra-Elemental experience of a higher nature. I stepped into an altered space where I knew beyond a doubt we were protected, we could relax—a place where I turned into limp, rubbery atoms bouncing along like rubber balls along my fated path with smiley faces on 'em, making my way under the impetus of a higher universal decree, just being and not fighting it.

Saturated with just being, I glanced back in the rearview mirror at Geena. She was riding airwaves with her hand out the open window, her freckles alert and knowing, her hand dancing with the breeze created by the Merc's motion.

I studied the landscape. Flat and mostly brown. Dry beds of old dust mixed with tufts of vegetation straining to stay alive. We were coming into a little burg sporting a tall sign that looked ninety feet high. The sign read, "Dinosaur Park Ahead!" I guess they wanted everybody clear back in Philadelphia to see that sign, too.

I pulled into the gas station, stepped out, posed, and ran one hand over the Merc's hood. One thing about the Merc', it was good on gas, contrary to most of its kin, who it was said of, they passed everything on the road except a gas station. Geena didn't seem inclined to get out of the car. I gave her a questioning look. She smiled at me.

"I'm waiting to see the dinosaur park."

I studied her a few seconds. Evidently, she thought we were on a vacation of some sort. Well, it was true that we were heading someplace with the hope we might stay there and maybe be loved just a little bit by somebody, sometime. Oh well. Justice was never served in either of our cases, so to hell with it. We could play a little along the way. Take a break. Enjoy life for a change.

"No problem, kiddo."

I wanted to see it myself.

We strolled through the entrance to the tiny park. Two giant rubber dinosaurs flanked each side of the entry. I stopped dead still and shaded my eyes. Open-mouthed, I stared up at the dinosaurs while Geena stepped experimentally on one's dusty, green rubber foot.

A middle-aged woman wandered out of a tin lean-to and strolled unhurriedly towards us.

"Good Year Rubber Company made em'."

She spoke in a slow drawl. Then she waved her arm at the tin building, baking in the hot sun behind her. Waves of heat poured off it.

"Tours are a dollar apiece."

I nodded and closed my dry mouth. We left the park wearing two necklaces made of rubber "dinosaur teeth." Geena thought they might be real, and I didn't discourage her with the truth.

We headed southwest. I wasn't following a plan, just my instincts. Right now, I felt an urge to see orange and yellow sand and watch red waves of heat rising into the air. I needed Nature's sauna to cleanse me, to burn out some of the toxic waste from the previous environment.

I pulled over, picked the map up off the passenger seat, got out, and spread it out on the hood of the Merc'. Squinting in the hot sun, I ran my finger over it until I found "Twin Pistols". Once upon a time, there was a motel and a gas station in Twin Pistols. But no longer. Now there was just a bunch of dust and ruins. There'd been a nasty confrontation between two bunches of killer outlaws there long ago. All of them had killed each other off. It was said that their angry ghosts still roamed Twin Pistols. A curse was put on the place after the burial. The place had burned down twice since then.

There was a job I needed to do there, if it was the right place, that is. I folded the map and laid it back on the front passenger seat. I got in and drove on through the afternoon, the wheels on the Merc' spinning through the dust-laden borders of time until I felt a tap on my shoulder.

Geena tapped my shoulder. I came back to myself with a start. I was daydreaming about a white picket fence and an apple pie life with a man. I couldn't tell anything about him, but I had the fence and house and freshly mowed green grass down just fine. And sunny bedrooms that smelled of white, fresh, all-cotton sheets and of ironing starched clothes to perfection while a turquoise and white radio played sedate music in the background, and of shelves filled with new hardback books waiting to be read in front of my cozy fireplace when it was chilly outside.

"It's time to find a place to eat!" Geena announced firmly before sitting back in her seat. I stared at her in the mirror. She stared back at me. She knew all about my daydreaming ways.

Luckily, she had the patience of Job with me over it. No complaints from her. I suspected that even at her early age, she knew she might get stuck with the same problem when she grew up. Oh well. We are what we are.

I stopped for the night. Twin Pistols was just a few miles away. We checked into a cheap motel and ate at the greasy spoon beside it. The bed was lumpy. The sheets and blankets hadn't been washed in this century. I shuddered at the film of grease on the tiny, faded bathroom mirror.

I showered before Geena to find out if it was safe for her. After, she watched television before she went to sleep beside me. She'd slept in the back seat of the Merc' and wasn't tired like I was. I was out like a light.

Early the next morning before anybody was up, we laid the room key on the empty motel office desk and got the hell out of there. I had a case of indigestion from the bad food, and the creepy shudders from staying in that dumpy, negative room.

We started feeling better when we were on the road again. Geena rode shotgun. We were both reactive to any environment we were cast into. We stopped for doughnuts and milk at a clean gas station. Life was good again.

We rode through desert, through flat yellow and orange dust, with few plants and shrubs.

Then the air began to change. A psychic darkness began building up around us. The closer we got to the ruins of Twin Pistols, the worse the darkness got. Geena stopped talking and clenched her fists. She shouted at me, her voice filled with fear.

"Bad choice. Drive away from here, Mama!"

I ignored her and tried to stop at the town ruins. No go. The energy there was too damn negative. Those outlaw ghosts were mean! I sped up and drove away. I drove for awhile. Until the bad energy was gone.

Then I pulled off the side of the road and got out of the Merc', posed, and ran my hand across her hood ornament.

We were in sweet, clean desert again, a place innocent and alive and not plagued by deadly ghosts. Geena got out and stood beside me.

"I don't know why you went there, but I'm not going to a place like that again on purpose, Mama! It's bad enough to live the way we do!"

Remorse washed over me. I stared at her. She was right. She usually was. She was an old soul living in a young girl's body. She had acted like an old woman all her life. I was the perpetually stupid, childish one.

"Sorry, kiddo. It was a mistake."

"It could have been a big one."

She spoke with a hard edge to her voice. We sized each other up. I knew I would never get off easy for choosing the Monster to father her and letting him take over our lives.

But to be practical about it, here we were, two worked over females, one old and one young, one stupid and the other one a wise old kid. Maybe there wasn't much left to us, but here we stood, out in a desert in the sunlight surrounded by emptiness big enough to expand our souls in without bumping into anybody else, good or bad.

I decided to do it here.

"Geena, I got something I need to do."

She looked at me sharply.

"You're not going to try and hurt my dad, are you?"

"No, but I would like to!"

She turned away from me and trudged the million miles down to the Merc's tail lights, keeping her back to me.

Sometimes we were okay with each other, sometimes we weren't. I wished I hadn't said it out loud, but it was the truth.

I got down to business. There were still a few last ties holding us back that had to be cut. I turned away and concentrated, asking the Angels, Guides, and Beings that worked with me for help and guidance. They were all I ever had to turn to.

I let the memories come. The hurt and bitterness and anger washed over me for what I hoped was the last time. Memories of the reunion. My hate filled, self righteous brother and his bitter wife drove two hours just to ambush me. My vindictive sister was in on it. My brother would never drive that far for love—only hate. Hate sure was powerful. I waited for them in love at a family reunion and got ambushed with their hate. It hurt a hell of a lot.

When I was growing up, people looked the other way when I desperately needed help. My father and most of my family included. My mother helped me once in a while. Bud Spinner, too. Will Parton. That was it.

Now it was finally time for me to deliver some comeuppances. I stood straight, held out my hands, closed my eyes. I watched the dead who'd ignored my existence pass by me. Grandparents and aunts and uncles. A no-good white-headed cousin. I had no bones to pick with them.

Just the living ones, the ones I gave a final chance to by hosting a small family reunion. I'd hoped against hope, and failed big time. An easy little failure would have been better for me, but I suppose the Unseens that look out for me figured they needed to keep me enrolled in the School of Hard Knocks before I could catch on to anything. I sighed and filled with new resolve as my Sight agreed that this was the right place and time to do it.

I opened my eyes. I walked out into the desert and stood still, letting the sun bake me until I was as hot as I could stand. Then using my Sight, I formed a sphere, stepped inside it, and spun it to the right. Outside of the sphere flashed holy, righteous, sharp swords of every color, cutting away every attachment the three ambushers had formed with or to me. White Light surrounded us. The sphere of two-edged, sharp swords whirled above and below and all around. They were holy swords and did what was fated to be right for all of us. Outside the sphere stood my next oldest brother, his wife, my sister, along with the Monster, two old boyfriends, and some others I once was attached to, and who once was attached to me.

And this is what I said to them:

"I cancel all soul contracts on every energy plane with the Monster, my brother Blend, my sister-in-law Surly, sister Penny, two old boyfriends, and the rest of these souls. Let this be done in the highest good of all. If it is not supposed to be, it shall not happen."

"I go on the energy planes and undo my karmic agreements and any commitments to and with all of them. Let each one of them process their own karma from now on without my help. I cut all energy ties to each one of them that is not in my highest good, right now. I cancel, null, and void all energetic ties per karmic contract and other energy and relationship agreements that occurred in our past lives right now."

The sphere I stood in spun and flashed while the swords cut and shredded, removing the old relationships. Anything new would have to be agreed on, and built from scratch. I felt relieved and lighter. The old was leaving.

I needed this separation ceremony to rid myself of the people who hated me before I lived any further, and began a new life.

I was damn tired of being shunned and cursed through my old relationships, and I would not stand in my old, helpless endurance before them in my new endeavors.

The innocence of my new life would be mine to hold, cherish, and protect. I wouldn't have to try to be someone I wasn't anymore. Someone wiser and smarter and not silly. I didn't want my enemies to know about my good future and any successes I might have. They would try to take it away from me. In the past, they always succeeded.

I never figured out why they hated me so much, but I would not spend any more of this lifetime wondering. That time was past. I would change my name and start over, far away from all of them.

Sweating and elated, I trudged back to the Merc'. Geena searched my face but didn't say anything. She climbed in the backseat. I got in and drove away. The process I'd started kept on going. The sphere came and went, surrounding me as needed, cutting off the others who were harmful to my life force and its forms. I asked them to help Geena too. And she knew it. I watched her sad little face in the rearview mirror and felt no remorse.

Chapter Four

Build it up, little darlin',
Build it up, ya' knows how,
then jis' take it on down the road wit' ya'
Don't go quarrelin', now

We rode west. We were getting close to California. I really needed to say I'd been there. It was a bragger thing. California may as well have been living on the Moon when I was growing up. California was the land of sophisticated, rich, beautiful people who handled the world easily. California was the home of Disneyland, the Beach Boys, and Annette.

There were just a handful of people back in Monster town that had ever been to California. They were envied, and looked up to by everyone in town.

Every wife in Ardenville dreamed of being Beaver's mother or Donna Reed or Hazel. The men wanted to be Beaver's father or to have fathered the Brady Bunch, or to be Robert Young in Father Knows Best.

I thought just the town kids wanted to be like the kids on those fake shows. It took some time for me to catch on that the parents wanted to be like the mothers and fathers on those shows too.

I stopped, got out the map, and found Blythe, California, a small town just across the border. We headed there, singing every California song we knew. Fifty was the speed limit, but I took it a little faster. We flew like birds, carefree and a little too warm, making a dream coming true. We would be California braggers. No matter where we ended up, even if worst came to worst, and we were forced to go back and live in Monster town, we would still have been to California, and that alone would make us stronger.

We crossed the California border at sunset. The Border Patrol waved us on through. I heard later they check for fruits, vegetables, and birds. But we were two cute tomatoes touring the world in that fine, four-door cruising machine, my fabulous 1957 turquoise and white hardtop Mercury Turnpike Cruiser, trimmed with at least a mile of chrome. Maybe California was the Merc's dream too, because she sure was shining.

We cruised Blythe until we saw a decent looking motel with a restaurant. We stepped out of the Merc' and posed. Geena didn't pose very often, but victory over anything tended to give us both the big head. We swaggered into the motel office and paid a mid-range price for a room.

Tonight wasn't the time to skimp. We showered, using the shampoo and soap the motel provided. The towels were blinding white, thin, and soft, just the way we liked them. I could smell Clorox. Yes!

We didn't have to be out of the room until noon the next day, so we took our time and wandered over to the restaurant and ate California salads, pasta, and dishes of ice cream.

We slept in the next morning, then dressed and drove the Merc' around Blythe until just the before noon check-out time. The Merc' got a lot of admiring glances while she was visiting California. She ran smooth as a top. I wiped down her shiny chrome before we set out to cross the border. All three of us liked being in California. There is nothing like being in a good, clean energy place to make you want to gussy yourself up.

Geena wore a questioning look while we loaded our skimpy luggage into the Merc's trunk. I knew what she wanted. But we couldn't stay. We had to move on. I was too intimidated by the concept, the idea that we were actually in California. It was an event we could live on the rest of our lives. I wanted to carry that truth back across the state line before something went wrong, and it somehow got taken away from us. It was in us now, and we were already different.

We crossed the border again without any mishaps. I drove sedately and cautiously through the checkpoint. When we got out of sight of the border patrol, we whooped and laughed, the fear of losing our California adventure, gone.

We headed towards Roswell, New Mexico in the heat, traveling the back roads, feeling out our new confidence. It felt plush and lush. Expandable.

It was time to go find the aliens I read about in magazines and newspapers. Maybe they were walking this Earth alone too, now that they had crashed here and been seen.

"Roswell, here we come!" I shouted.

I didn't have time to speculate on base energy practices anymore if I wanted to survive. Like reliving the rage I once felt at Ardenville's religious zealots insisting I stay married to the Monster because the Bible said so. I let that thought flow out the window and moved on to thinking about my new choices. That was better.

There were rules about what a woman in my situation should do. Number one was to find a nice man to be forever grateful to, to live in a little white house with a picket fence awaiting his every wish while Geena went to school and became a nurse so she could help men, too. I could cook delicious meals, mainly casseroles, and wash and iron in high heels and pearls, kept company by a Siamese cat named Mabel and a cute little dog named Hullabaloo. But given that my trust level in men because of my past experiences with the Monster and my family was lower than the well I would have to dig to get to China, I guessed the picket fence dream probably wouldn't come true.

I once dreamed of becoming a teacher, single and alone, a professor who taught college and lived in an enormous four-story brick fortress, grim and unapproachable. I was stern and gray, and portly, and Geena lived with me, and I had lots of money my family applied to me for. I would pay their way if they stayed extremely respectful of me for a very long time. Geena wore shirtwaist dresses over the finest of silk slips, her feet shod in Mary Jane shoes. I was dry and dusty and brief in speech, wearing pearl gray business suits with pleats at the bottom of the skirts for comfort when sitting.

I looked out the window and snorted at my silly, familiar daydreams. They would not work out here in the wild, wild, west! That's where we were now. The old dreams were too small, demanding a rigidity that wouldn't work in this vast unknown place.

We would have to expand ourselves and our dreams to fill any space out here. This desert was worn and bare, a dusty, ancient place filled with space and time. A reminder from the Earth that people returned to dust no matter what they did. Better this vast unknown, unfilled space than anything else I had dreamed of so far.

I squared my shoulders. There were no voices to advise me now. I had fled beyond what they knew—beyond my old dreams. New dreams were waiting to be made. I was on my own, flying like a bird. It was time to move into a new space to live and provide protection for Geena.

I wandered down the highway, studying the desert. Red and yellow sand, the dust of eons of time settled horizontally into restless layers under a cloudless blue sky. Probably made of dinosaurs, human remains, a few clam shells, maybe a few fish skeletons.

At noon, we passed through Pistachio Pico, a tiny town with a funny name. A couple of small dried up streets and a few dusty cubes of buildings fronted the highway.

The Merc' ate up about thirty more miles of empty desert highway before I spied a lone white building off in the distance. On its top was a peaked roof with a spire. When I got closer, I could see the building was once a little church that had been renovated into a gas station and grocery store.

Two orange and green gas pumps stood under a large, dark green shade roof. A large, whiteboard nailed to the side of the former church read "Gas and Groceries" in big, hand-painted black letters. A car repair garage shed was attached to the side of the store.

So, gas was served here now instead of religion? I rolled the Merc' to a stop underneath the shade roof covering the gas pumps, climbed out and posed. I studied the store. My guess was the screen door on the shaded front porch led into the store part of this establishment.

I was almost to the porch steps when the sobbing started. I glanced towards the side of the building. A woman sat in her car just around the corner, squalling loud enough to stop a freight train in its tracks. I stopped and sighed. I squinted up at the clear, cobalt blue sky, searching. No clouds with signs in them, nothing pointing to the Trouble I suspected was coming. Where the hell was God right now? Why wasn't He taking care of the bawling woman? Was He taking yet another nap in the shade-filled interior of a condominium with soothing air conditioning? How old was He? Did He really need naps? Or was He off playing golf again like Ike, leaving the problems of mankind behind, like Walter Cronkite said? Why didn't HE put an "out of order" sign up each time HE dozed off, to warn us that we little humans were once again on our own?

Was I going to have to help that howling woman? Was she yet another of the ones the universe sent to me for help because of my Sight, when I couldn't even help myself using it?

My Sight was a little left of center and liked to quarrel with me. And being a Sensitive and breaking out in rashes when exposed to potential fates, mine and others, didn't help either. Well, I just wouldn't do it!

Besides, there was no time for anyone else right now. I was helping me and Geena. I reminded the universe that Geena and I were on the lam. On the run. Incognito.

I decided to ignore the howling woman. I started toward the store steps again before I realized what it was it was I'd seen when I glanced at the woman. I stopped dead in my tracks.

Not because of the woman. With lungs like that, she could crumble monasteries with a single breath, like I read the monks in Buddha land did when they warred with each other. She was a lethal weapon! I could hear in her voice that she had her own special kind of crazy going on. I was unerring in sensing that kind of thing.

But that howling, crazy woman was sitting in a pink 1959 Cadillac Special convertible, an endangered species at least a mile long, featuring elongated tail fins, mounted teardrop taillight pods, whitewalls, and a side-mounted dummy air filter on the rear fender. It was a divine piece of metal sculpture, a fabulous, perfect, luscious pink work of mobile art and that fool sitting in it was bawling as loud as a lost calf.

I huffed, offended. How sacrilegious of her! Why couldn't she bawl somewhere else? Who could possibly be unhappy sitting inside that mile long, beautiful, holy iron and steel temple with its attendant miles of shining chrome, lush carpeting, and plush seats the size of sofas? A preacher could hold a revival in the spacious interior, a six-room motel could get built and never noticed. Why, that Cadillac was one of the holy grails of road travel! That pink Cadillac was a striking monument of the highest order, one of the wonders of the automobile world, and here it sat, strategically positioned around the corner of a little desert store out in the middle of nowhere, formerly a church, under the skimpy shade of the only miserable little scrub tree within miles.

Did the bawling woman steal the Caddy from a movie set in Santa Fe? Did she borrow that gorgeous, stately ride from a traveling salesman in a hurry to cross the state line so he couldn't be extradited and have to return the Cadillac to its owner, who, no doubt, lived on a posh, secluded estate somewhere? Was she traveling incognito and weeping about the loneliness of the road? Because she couldn't have been weeping about that gorgeous pink Cadillac. I looked around. Well, after all, we were in a desert, and that might make some people weep.

I stood there, admiring the Cadillac, ignoring the bawling woman until Geena nudged me out of my stunned reverie with her sharp little elbow. I stared at her in surprise. With one hand on her hip and one foot tapping desert dust in exasperation, she pointed to the wailing woman sitting in the pink Cadillac.

I nodded and started circling the Cadillac, touching it lovingly. The woman kept on bawling. She didn't seem to notice me. I figured she could wait until my love affair with the pink Cadillac ended. That wouldn't happen until the first of Never. So, tough for her!

I traced the thin chrome bead running from the front fender back to the rear bumper and back to the front wheel well with a delicate, loving finger. I was getting ready to run a slow hand over the buttery looking leather seats on the passenger side when Geena "ahemmed!" loudly behind me.

I turned and stared at her. I tilted my head in puzzlement. She didn't seem to be impressed by this fabulous monument, this amazing temple on wheels. Or by most vehicles, for that matter. Oh, she loved the Merc', all right, but not like I did.

I sighed. Fine. Fabulous, grand, monumental vehicles holding the spaciousness of a palace, the luxurious trappings of royalty, the best of blessings from an auto industry who understood the psychology of Needs on Wheels, of nomadic tribes, of roadies, of travelers and hitchhikers, were just not her thing.

If it was a kid sitting in this amazing piece of living, moveable art, she would be all over them, ignoring the car and hugging them, wiping their eyes, and saying, "There, there." But because it was a woman and not a kid, she expected me to handle it. I shook my head. Self-pity washed over me. I felt like a bucket of water just got thrown over me. I sighed and stared down at the desert dust. The kid would never let me off the hook. I had to be the parent. The person who took the blame when things didn't go right. The one who never got any help, but had to give it all the time.

"Damn Karma!" I muttered under my breath. Geena glared at me and squinted hard. She knew what I was thinking. Suddenly, I felt ashamed. I looked up and jerked my hand back from the smooth, inviting surface of the Cadillac to study the hefty woman sitting in the divine pink temple. Her face was partially hidden in her hands while long, black, unkempt, straight hair covered the rest of it.

Suddenly, a man's voice startled me. I knew that voice. It was familiar like heat and light, and love are familiar to all species, especially women. Doves took flight, and started flying around my heart and head.

I turned around to see a stocky, middle-aged cowboy, about five feet eight, standing at the corner of the refurbished church as though hesitant to get too close to any of us women. His stance was wide like he owned this piece of desert and on his head sat a battered, yellowed, straw-colored cowboy hat. Straight brown hair poked out from underneath. The cowboy watched me with steady green eyes from a weathered face bearing traces of a disillusioned soul—a very old soul.

I knew he was a cowboy because of the cowboy hat. Astonished, I recoiled. I hated cowboys. The Monster used being a cowboy as way to get to his victims. The western theme of rugged goodness. He wore white, too. This guy better watch out for me.

"Do you want the Mercury gassed up?"

The man spoke in a deep, slow voice, a voice steady and warm with nuances as tender and slow as molasses while he locked eyes with me. My Sight kicked in. I was meeting an old flame, an old friend and much, much more. Now my world would be okay.

Many people wouldn't notice this man twice. He wasn't particularly good looking, but his spiritual bearing was elegant and refined. His inner soul was filled with a vast, sweet strength making him stunningly beautiful. Soothing gentleness poured through his voice like cool drops of rain. His square, mild face held the wind and sun and the force of aware goodness in it. His chin was stubborn, his nose straight. His upper lip dimpled in the middle. He had a strong jawline, indicating a weighty and proud will. He had a neck a lumberjack would envy, and the brows of a Zeus. He was a thinker, too. All the joys and travails of his many lifetimes had gilded his being with a profound and timeless dignity.

    I edged closer without thinking about what I was doing. He wasn't that much taller than me. I could easily fit under his chin and wanted to. He would make a hell of a shade tree for me. He stood patiently waiting while I took his measure, drawing closer and closer. Eventually, after an eon of time passed, I realized I had closed in on him until I was standing just inches from him. And he let me. I was sniffing him like a stray dog, getting ready to throw my arms around him and never let him go. My eyes swept over his hat, and I realized again that he was a cowboy. I froze. I wanted to touch him in the worst way but my caution won out. No more cowboys! I came out of my brown study to find Geena holding my hand. We were both standing right in front of him, staring at him with our mouths open.

    "Damn it! Oh, why, oh, why, does he have to be a cowboy?" I whimpered under my breath with painful regret. Geena nodded sadly in agreement.

    "Do you want the car gassed up?"

    He questioned me again, amusement lighting his rugged face into a sudden, startling beauty. I snapped my mouth shut and nodded. He started to turn away and then stopped.

"That's Normaine Red Deer." He pointed at the Cadillac.

"She's just keening over killing one of the worst bastards in these parts. Her husband. You being nice ladies, you might want to tarry with her a bit so justice might finish its course."

"What?" I asked. The cowboy started to turn back toward the Merc'. Like all good gas station attendants, he would clean the windshield, check the water and oil, and the hoses after he gassed up the Merc'. "What?" I muttered again. I looked out at the desert and the few dried frizzes of hopeful plants trying to grow near the store. He stopped.

"I can't afford a gardener," he said, following my glance. "Nor do I want one. Hearts are often broken in the midst of the flora and fauna growing in the better residential areas, but never here."

"What?" I asked again. I stared at his retreating back, astonished.

"Oh, God. Two Nuts in one place!" I muttered to myself. I turned back to deal with Normaine Red Deer, the first Nut. I hoped I wouldn't have to deal with the nutty cowboy too. Maybe I could just pay him and get the hell out of here even though I sensed that he could talk to angels. And did.

The woman had stopped crying. She was leaning back in her seat, staring up at the sky. I looked up to see what she was staring at. There were no clouds to make ducks out of or other things. Just a hot, empty blue sky.

I wandered closer to the Cadillac, taking my time. I didn't know what to do or think. I knew a few women who secretly wanted to kill a man, but I had never known one who actually did it. I stopped. Now that she was a killer, would she be willing to kill again? Become a contract killer? Could I impose on her long enough to persuade her to travel north and kill a Monster or two for me? If she showed up in Ardenville, the town would be wasted.

I scolded myself for my thoughts. Grudgingly, I did the right thing. I stepped into a role I knew well. Spontaneously, I posed by the Cadillac.

"Anything I can do to help you?" I asked half-heartedly, with the hope that she would spurn any help I could offer and still tell me every single juicy detail of the kill.

The woman didn't answer. I sucked in my lip and started feeling sorry for myself again. I didn't have much to offer because I'd mostly been used up too, I whined to myself. What little I had left was supposed to be used to help me and Geena, right? And where was MY pity party being held? Not in this county, I bet. I glared at Geena resentfully.

Evidently, she didn't agree with me. She stood to the side, expecting me to handle it, an inexorable, waiting boulder of single-minded, tough young judgment.

I slipped over to the mirror on the driver's door of the Cadillac and stopped where the woman could see my face. I held myself back as long as I could before I found myself stroking the smooth, warm metal of the pink Cadillac again.

I was thinking of pink flamingos wading in cool water when the woman finally stirred. She was watching me pet her car. She shoved her hair back out of her face while a slow, wide, gap-toothed smile with two front teeth missing spread over her broad, flat face. Black hair and scars. Ravaged skin. Desperate. Used violently. Seen a lot of misery. Eyes that had seen much ugliness. No favor. No grace. The words slapped me, hard. I looked away, but her voice brought me back.

"You like her, huh?"

Her voice was guttural, coarse and ragged, filled with false bravado used to cover many bad experiences. It also held a deep well of remorse for things I hoped never to know about, including the killing of her husband. There were a bunch of men I didn't like, but there were some I did. Like Bud Spinner. I sighed. I had to admit it. I didn't really want to kill off a bunch of men. Maybe just the Monster? I ruminated on this familiar dilemma while she rummaged around and came up with a cigarette and lit it. I sniffed deeply as I fought the urge to turn and run to the Merc'. I lusted to jump in it and spin out in a cloud of dust. I imagined the dust plumes rising from the Merc's back tires as I raced away from this little godforsaken outpost of ragged, nutty, hurting humanity.

The woman dragged in a deep puff and blew it out. I watched with envy and glanced over at Geena. I wanted to ask the woman for a drag, but I couldn't smoke with "Junior" around. She was big on quoting death statistics from smoking to me. Hard to get much enjoyment inhaling "death" with Geena watching me.

"Her name's Esmerelda."

I nodded. So, she knew to name cars too. After another deep, cleansing puff, which I envied with all my heart, she waved the hand holding her cigarette in our general direction.

"Who are you, and who's the kid?" she asked.

I decided to go for it. After all, she was in worse shape than us, for we hadn't killed anybody yet.

"This is Geena. My daughter. We're on the road, looking for a new place to live."

I couldn't say "running from the Monster" because Geena was standing right there. The woman studied me. I waited while she figured it out.

"The man said your name is Normaine Red Deer?"

She nodded and yawned real big.

"A.M. Judson. He owns this place."

I nodded, not listening. My mind was on Esmerelda. The gas man was Number Two Nut to me, and I was too busy communing with the hot pink beauty of Esmerelda to pay much attention to her words. She said something about the cowboy's name. Johnson? Yeah, Johnson. That was it. Cowboy Johnson. The second Nut. I'd never been good with names, anyway. I really didn't care about them—only about the essence of a person, which usually presented itself to me before their name because of my Sight. That's why I had trouble remembering names. After a long silence, during which I caressed the pink and beautiful Esmerelda's contours and evolution with busy eyes and hands, Normaine spoke.

"Go pay him for your gas while I get some ice and food, then follow me."

I bristled for just a second at the brashness of her words and the harshness in her voice. Then I sighed.

"Okay," I answered mildly, accepting the fate before us. I guess Geena and I could spend a few hours helping somebody else.

"Only because you love Esmerelda," she explained. I didn't know what that was supposed to mean, but I followed her instructions. I paid Cowboy Johnson and waited in the Merc' for Normaine. She went into the store and came back out, tapping a pack of cigarettes, got in Esmerelda, and drove behind the store. I followed her a quarter mile or so and parked the Merc' beside Esmerelda under a large green shade roof covering a little pink trailer.

I could see the back porch of the store from here. It didn't look much like a former church, even though it boasted a white railed, large back porch. Rusted cans hung from nails on the back-porch posts. Maybe the cans once held plants.

Standing alone on a little rise a strategic distance from the store and us, stood a beige Duke's Hardware Economy Readymade Shed with a worn path leading to it. It was made of wood. No doubt a metal shed would have been too hot to use as an outhouse in the desert. A small moon-shaped window was cut in the door of the shed.

"That's the outhouse."

Normaine jerked her thumb toward it. Between the little pink trailer and the store was a much used campfire area with wood stumps and logs squaring off around it and a few faded umbrellas for shade.

We followed Normaine into the trailer. The place was dirty. Ground in dirt carrying the stench of hopeless and crazy in it. She brought out a whiskey bottle, poured some in a glass, sat down, and took a drink. I looked at Geena. We should leave. What the hell was I doing with this portly, deranged Native American woman who just happened to be a mankiller, standing in a little pink trailer out in the middle of nowhere in a desert watching her while she sat drinking whiskey out of a dirty glass?

"This isn't fitting my pictures!" I muttered under my breath, informing the "Unseens" of the situation, in case they didn't notice, while I watched Geena. Craziness. It followed me everywhere. Why me, God? I rolled my eyes upward and held a quick, private conversation with God the Dude.

"You should know better, Dude! I do!" I scolded Him under my breath.

"It isn't proper or good for Geena to be here, and we should leave right now!"

As usual, I didn't get an answer from God. I'd been hung out to dry as usual. He probably thought that was especially apt out here in the desert where it would be a quick dry. He probably thought that idea was funny. Maybe He was off somewhere laughing about it.

Chapter Five

Put him in the car
and take him for a ride
he's a bad un'
so take along a jug of bleach
and Tide

I couldn't decide what to do, so I watched Geena for a cue. She was listening hard to Normaine, but I didn't hear a word because of my own thoughts. I was too nervous to sit down and listen, so I rummaged around the tiny trailer and discovered a box of Tide and a large bottle of Clorox under the tiny sink. I poured a few drops of bleach into a large plastic bowl, added Tide and water, and started scrubbing everything in sight. They ignored me. Normaine stared off in the distance like she was watching a movie and reading the subtitles to it in a monotone.

"You are women, too," she intoned, sounding like a judge sitting on a high bench, looking down on prospective prisoners bowed heads, "so you both know some of the abuse men can inflict on women."

She waited, watching us to see if we were willing to defend bad men. Geena and I looked at each other. The answer to what we were doing in this situation was becoming all too clear.

All of us are obligated to pay at least some of our emotional debts back during each lifetime. And I, for one, never wanted to. But I had wanted to kill the

Monster and a few other men many times, so maybe I was sticking around so I could hear firsthand how it could be done, just in case.

Normaine continued her monologue.

"I was born on a prairie reservation. I was happy as a child, but always hungry. Never enough food."

A long silence ensued.

"Now, I got this little trailer that my friend lets me live in."

More silence.

"It sure gets hot on the rez."

She shifted in her chair and looked at Geena. "Why don't you go outside awhile? I don't know if you should hear this."

"No way," Geena announced firmly. "I'm staying."

Normaine studied her.

"I guess you've had your own troubles, haven't you? Young as you are."

She shook her head sadly, looking from Geena to me.

"It's on you, Mama."

A minute passed.

I said, "Get on with it."

Normaine heaved a deep sigh and stared past us out the tiny, curved trailer window. I glanced at Geena. We both busied ourselves so we wouldn't be staring at her. She deserved that privacy no matter what she had done. I cleaned while Geena pleated the red skirt hanging across the back of her chair with long, slim, nervous fingers.

Normaine's voice hurried into words, quick and fast. To get it over with, I supposed.

"We got married after he forced himself on me a whole bunch of times, and nobody stopped him. He made me marry him, and we had a son. My son was six years old when I killed his father. That was just over two years ago."

She let out a long breath before she spoke again.

"My mother lived in a little frame house on the rez. She was old when she had me, but she raised me as best she could. You know how some men are. They make the babies and leave."

"My husband was a drinker and a wife beater and a child molester. I was scared to death of him, but I tried not to let on. It becomes a way of life, the years pass, and he knocks out your teeth, and you have his babies and cook for him and dread to see him come in the door. That was the way it was supposed to be. I had my son and no more babies."

"My man kept his violence limited to me for a long time. Then he started beating up other people. He kept getting worse, and I knew he would kill us if we didn't leave. When I told him I was leaving, he tied me up and beat me, but I got loose and took my son and ran away after he passed out from the booze."

I glanced at Geena. She had stopped pleating the red skirt. She sat perfectly still, her hands in her lap. I stared at her hands. Sadness washed over me. Long, tan, thin girl's hands. Innocent hands. Too young to hear this. She didn't notice. She was staring at Normaine, waiting. I sighed.

"Geena, go outside for a while. You are too young to hear this."

She swiveled her head and gave me her flinty, old soul look. The one that said, "Don't tell me what to do. I know best." From experience, I knew she couldn't be swayed when she got this way.

"No!"

A wave of sadness swept over me. For whatever reason, Karma had brought us both here to listen to this story. I wished it was just me and not an innocent like Geena too. Normaine watched us.

"Okay, Normaine. Go on," I said wearily, while my soul cried for Geena.

"We hid out from him for a long time. I got work as a waitress in a truck stop in the little town we were hiding in. That's where I met Eddy."

She smiled a wide, gap-toothed smile and jerked her thumb at the window.

"Eddy is how I got Esmerelda. He's a truck driver—drives an eighteen-wheeler. He wants to marry me. He got her for me."

She grew sad again and stared off in the distance. The heat in the little trailer had us sweating rivers, but we stayed put.

"I couldn't start a divorce because I didn't have any money."

Bitterness filled her voice. Then she brightened and smiled her gap-toothed smile.

"I'm going to meet Eddy. We're supposed to meet in Wyoming and get married. I been in the pen for two years and he's been waiting for me. It's just that I got to settle something first, and I can't figure out how to do it."

I interrupted her.

"You said your husband found you?"

She sighed and looked down at her hands. I could tell she didn't want to tell us the whole story, but I needed it.

"Yep. I left my boy with my neighbor when I went to work. One day he forced his way in, beat her up, and stole my boy. She called the police, but they said he had the right to visit his son because he was the boy's father."

"She got a ride over here, and we went to the cop shop. She filed a complaint against him for beating her up, even though they told her it wouldn't do any good. I tried to file on him for kidnapping, but they said I was still married to him and that was that."

"I found some reservation people he done bad stuff to and got them to watch his mother's house. We stole my boy back. I took him to my mother's house and she hid him. I went back to work. I was trying to get enough money to move to Wyoming and stay with relatives off the rez, so I could divorce him. He went to my mother's place and busted the door down while she was there by herself. He dragged her upstairs and beat her almost to death and..." She glanced at Geena, "...and more. Then he worked my son over too."

She glanced at Geena again, then back at me.

"Thanks," I said. She nodded. She knew I was glad she was choosing easier words because of Geena.

"My mother was in the hospital for two months. My son was hospitalized for a week, and he started seeing a therapist. I went to the cops, but they let me file an assault charge only on my mother's behalf. I couldn't act for my son. They took that legal right away from me. They said I never protected him."

She started shoving her words together, tossing them out in a fast and breathless voice. I watched Geena. She seemed calm, but two angry red spots were blooming on her cheeks.

"Geena! Are you okay?"

"Yes!" she hissed the word out, low and urgent. I shut up, a lump as big as a boulder in my throat. Damn Sight and Damn Karma!

"All of this happened on the rez. They were reservation police. All of them were related to my husband. Then some of the rez people that had trouble with him slipped me a loaded pistol. They said he was a wild animal that was out of control and it was time to put him out of his misery.

The law let me have my son back. He went to school while I worked. My husband kept trying to steal my son from school. He said he was his property. The school always called the police, but I knew he would never stop trying to get my son, so I gave my son to the people who had given me the gun. They left the rez with him. My mind was made up.

It was time to stop the mad dog in his tracks. He beat my mother and sent her to the hospital. She used a walker and took all kinds of medicine from then on. He molested our little child. He had no regrets, and he would keep on, and nobody else would stop him.

The people who gave me the gun spread the word and found out where he was for me. I borrowed an old car and took the gun and went straight to the little bar he liked to hang out at. It was in a long metal building with a pool table. It's not far from here. I went in and held the gun on everybody and told him to come with me. He said he'd been waiting for me to show up. I backed out the door and told the rest of them to call the police and tell them that I was going to kill him.

We got in his old car. I made him drive. We went down a couple of dirt roads and stopped. We got out. He put his hands in the air and started backing away from me. He was finally scared. He realized that I was really going to kill him. He thought I was joking. That I was just mad at him. I could see he was thinking about begging."

He said, "I'm scared. I don't want to die."

Then he stopped.

"Go ahead. There isn't anything else to be done anyway."

Normaine stopped and looked at both us with the saddest eyes I have ever seen.

"So, I shot him. Three times before he laid still. An evil demon had took a hold of his spirit. It made its life strong in him, so it took three shots to rid him of it. The police showed up and took me to jail and give me two years in the pen after all the other people went in and told the judge all the bad things he did to them. Two years ain't very long. But I'll have to live with being a murderer the rest of my life."

Her shoulders slumped.

"Should I have done it? I believe I did the only thing there was left to do. I made my boy and my mother safe. I might never see my boy again, but he is safe now. I wish someone else had locked that man up or killed him, but nobody would. They just turned their backs on him. So I had to do it. I had to do it, and I am damned forever because of it."

I studied her. I wondered what her "unfinished business" was. She waited in the hot silence in the little pink trailer for our verdict.

Instead of answering, I stumbled and smacked my hand hard against the tabletop. It made a funny sound. Normaine jumped up and grabbed me. I chuckled bitterly. She let me go. Dumbfounded, she sat back down. I lifted my top lip in a churlish sneer, pulled my glasses out of my shirt pocket and put them on. I was supposed to wear them all the time, but mostly I used them as a prop. I depended more on my Sight than on my glasses because I never liked seeing life too clearly anyway. I peered over their frame at her, lifted my leg, and plopped my foot on the tiny table beneath her nose.

"I stubbed my toe. See how bad I hurt it, okay?"

I would buy time as long as I could. I rolled my eyes at Geena while Normaine examined my toe. Geena knew my ways were weird, but she knew it always came out right in the end. She trusted me more than I trusted me. She just sat there, a young, solid, solemn mass of waiting. Well, hell, what next? My eyes lit on the bottle of Clorox. The little trailer reeked of it from my cleaning efforts. The fumes would turn us into bleached, dead albinos if we stayed in here much longer.

I jerked my foot off the table, sprang for the bleach bottle, and grabbed it in a death grip. Daintily, I minced over the two feet between me and the bowl of soapy water, measured out several cups, and poured them into the bowl. That's a lot of bleach. Then, as though I was a professor teaching a university class, I began instructing Normaine and Geena on the use of cleaners to eradicate germs and bacteria of all kinds. Which subject led to the eradication of filth. At that point, I knew I had come full circle.

Geena knew I was a profound nut until I found the doorway to my psychic organizing abilities. A psychic orangutan. Which explained why I hadn't had a lot of success in my endeavors to assist others utilizing my psychic platform. Most people didn't stick around until I found the gateway. Finding the path that opened to the Way to do it was always a challenge for me. Well, I'd found it once again. I always did. Eventually.

"Okay, Normaine. We're going to do a ritual, okay? Since you're Native and probably used to more rituals than I could ever understand anyway, just go along with me, okay?"

By this time, the little trailer was beginning to reek of Clorox. The fumes were spreading rapidly, assisting in the persuasion of Normaine's immediate departure with us. She nodded. I searched through the kitchen, found a large plastic Tupperware pitcher, poured the bowl of bleach water into it and, secured the lid.

"Okay. Here's what we're gonna' do. Normaine, take the sheet off your bed and bring it. That's the sheet you been sleeping on?"

She nodded.

"Geena, you carry the pitcher and don't spill it. I gotta' drive."

We hurried out of the hot, furiously fumy little trailer, propped the door open, and piled into the Merc'. I gave Esmerelda a longing glance before I burned out of there. I would ask Normaine for more of the love story of Esmerelda later. Where was Esmerelda from? Was she birthed on an assembly line in Detroit? Waco? From a mansion in Beverly Hills? Did she have siblings? Were they pink, too?

Normaine said her sweetheart was a semi-truck driver. That meant he'd probably been everywhere. Did Esmerelda have relatives parked in dusty, silent warehouses in strategic locations all across the country, waiting and yearning to be claimed by a roadie, a traveler, a gypsy?

We were heading out to take care of Normaine's unfinished business. I snorted as I realized there was going to be a later. I was committed. I sighed and yearned for a cigarette as I made a wide U-turn in the dust behind the back of the store.

Suddenly Cowboy Johnson stepped in front of us. I skidded the Merc' to a swaying stop.

"Well, Cowboy Johnson, what do you want?"

I questioned expansively, looking him up and down with painful yearning. I felt like a suction cup wanting to be glued to him forever. I wanted to knock his cowboy hat off, crush it under my feet in a wild tango wearing something red and tight, and forget he ever wore it. I whimpered. Why, oh why, did he have to be a cowboy? Normaine and Geena giggled. He ignored me and shoved his hat back on his head, folded his arms, and took a wide-legged, unhurried stance.

"You okay, Normaine? Where you going in such a hurry?"

"Everything's okay, but I need a pack of cigarettes."

"Get me some, too!" I wanted to yell but kept my mouth shut because of Geena. I could feel her green eyes, hard as marbles, boring into me from the back seat. Normaine got out of the car, and they strolled toward the store. As I watched them, I remembered there was something else we needed.

"Normaine, bring back the biggest box of salt you can find!" I shouted.

After the cigarettes, salt and Normaine were safely ensconced in the Merc' once again, Normaine asked, "Where are we going?"

I turned to her with another churlish sneer and said, "We're going to where you killed him. All you gotta' do is tell me how to get there."

She sat in stunned silence, thinking it over while I put the Merc in gear, gripped the diamond-shaped steering knob, and climbed onto the two-lane blacktop running straight as an arrow in front of Cowboy Johnson's store.

"One piece at a time, Normaine. Am I going in the right direction?"

"Yes."

A few miles later, the blacktop passed between a few metal buildings scattered carelessly like dice under the hot sun, their windows darkened with aluminum foil. I slowed to a crawl as we drove past them. Normaine pointed her finger at a long, low building with one door and a few tiny windows.

"That's where he liked to drink. That's where I picked him up."

I glanced over at her. She rode heavy and distant in the passenger seat. Geena leaned forward in the backseat and put her hands on Normaine's shoulders. Normaine had gone to another place to handle this. Like me and Geena, she was adept at moving in and out of altered states as needed for survival. The Merc' crawled past the buildings. Just past them, she pointed a finger.

"Take that road."

I turned onto what amounted to a wide, dusty path. We rode awhile.

"Stop here."

I stopped the Merc' and looked around. Flat red and yellow desert surrounded the dusty road. The three of us sat silent for a moment. "Where, Normaine?" I asked.

"There."

She pointed a stubby, fat brown finger at a dark red spot on the ground on the other side of the dusty road.

"Get out and show me, okay?"

We got out. "There," she said, stopping a few feet away from the dark stain, pointing at it. She studied it with narrowed eyes.

"Two years, and it still isn't gone."

I nodded, examining the spot with my Sight.

"There's a reason for that. You stay here. I'll do the rest."

I turned back to the Merc'. Geena stayed by Normaine's side. I opened the back door of the Merc' and took out the pitcher of Tide and Clorox water. I carried it over and set it down beside them and went back for the box of salt and the sheet. Iodized salt. Good. It makes all the difference.

It helped that Normaine, being Native American, was used to rituals. Me and Geena, being the natural pagans we were, had no problem with improvised rituals.

We three females were all strong in our principles of inner equality as souls that gave no gender the right to rule another gender. Spiritually speaking, that put us on the same page. Three women just starting out on new paths of freedom from terrible gender bondage. Though Geena already owned the rights to her old soul, we were three females who kept on going, drawn inexorably past the ugliness we encountered towards the beauty and awe life held.

I shook out the sheet. Geena hunted up scissors and cut eye holes in it. I opened the box of salt, removed the lid from the pitcher of soapy bleach water. It was time.

"Okay, Normaine. Show me exactly where the body laid."

She shuddered but did as I asked. I outlined the body shape with a layer of salt. Then I asked her to pull the sheet over her head and stand at the head of the outline.

She looked like a Halloween ghost with one black eye staring at us while the other eye stared off to the right at a small ridge. I poured half of the Tide and Clorox water into the outline.

"State your full name first, then repeat after me."

She stated her name. Now state, "I revoke this bastard's right to remain here on this Earth in any form."

The ghost in the sheet stared at me for a few seconds before it repeated what I said.

"Now tell him off, Normaine!'

The ghost looked around and swayed silently. Then it shouted and ranted until it ran down. It took a ghost to do this part, to get rid of an evil that wouldn't let go of its hold on a dead human being on this Earth. A human couldn't get it to leave. But a ghost could. It was Trickster magic. Trickster power.

When the thing started leaving, I intoned, "May the Spirit of Creation take this Ugly Being into its Keeping so that it does no more harm using memory, life on Earth, Karmic ties, soul connections, or any other methods or agreements to reach out with any of its evil intentions. From this moment on, the water and the emotional content of this entity can no longer use Normaine's man or any other human to stay here.

All things have a place waiting for them when they leave this Earth, for better or worse. It is the Law. Let this entity go to the place waiting for it as it passes from this Earth and go forth from there into its new future, not allowing a returning to harm another on Earth. Let as much of this as can be done, be done in the highest good of all involved. What is not in the highest good of all, shall not take place here today."

I set the pitcher down. Tide and Clorox. A half-empty pitcher of two powerful cleaners, their names known and trusted by almost every woman in the country. A cleansing formula most women knew about and used to cleanse the clothes and much more of many men as well as their children and themselves. Down through centuries, women eradicated germs and evils and sent men and children and themselves off to places such as school and church and work, clean and ready to sparkle in this world. We were following that age-old practice, sending an evil off to a better place today, using the ways women have always used.

"Take the sheet off and throw it in the center of the outline, Normaine." I ordered. She did. "It is now the ghost of the sheets of your sexual past with him."

"What about my boy and my mother?"

"You have to go first before you can help them."

I stated this matter-of-factly, but my heart was pounding. I looked at Geena with tears in my eyes but she wasn't watching me. She was staring at the dark red circle on the ground. A quick sadness swept over me. My girl was growing up too fast in many ways. I placed the half-empty box of salt in Normaine's hands.

"Pour the salt just like I did, around the outline. Then salt the inside."

She walked the outline slowly, carefully pouring the salt, and then she salted the inside of the outline. Next, I had her pour the bleach and soap water inside the outline to cleanse and purify it to make sure her man and the entity were on their way to the places waiting for them over two years.

When the pitcher was empty, Normaine dropped it on the ground and stood there, staring at the outline. I knew it wouldn't stay wet for long. We watched the dark red dust as it began to fade back to yellow.

Suddenly a hot ochre wind blew over us, restless, wanting to carry its new discovery elsewhere. The wind wanted to carry the contaminated dust away and mix it with other dust until it became anonymous. My Sight had taught me about the Wind's Nature when I was a child. The Wind's Nature was drawn to concentrations, and it liked to thin and spread them out.

I turned to Geena. "Go get the broom out of the trunk."

She brought the broom to me, and I swept the angry wet dirt toward the center of the outline, covering the sheet, lifting the dirt up into the air with each sweep so the hungry, yellow wind could carry more of it away. I knew that if you helped the wind, it would help you breathe better. Maybe it would help me stop yearning for cigarettes. But I stopped smoking to save money to leave on, and it worked, so I couldn't really regret it. But I still yearned for them. I handed the broom to Normaine. She swept the dirt up into the air—an unholy offering to the hot wind. Then she passed the broom to Geena and she swept the last few remnants up into the air.

When Geena finished, Normaine sang a song in her Native language. We bowed our heads and thanked the Creator for the opportunity the Wind and Sun and Clorox and Tide and a box of salt and a white sheet had given us three women to eradicate the remnants of one man's evil from the Earth.

Where those energies went, we didn't give a damn, just that they were gone. None of us trusted men's stories about sky Gods and their silly stories about the Hereafter. We were pagans who believed that God was both male and female and resided in everything in balance. But after we speculated on it awhile, we chose to believe Normaine's husband had been carried off to the Christian Hell men insisted on. It was a matter of religious convenience and a greatly comforting thought.

We left the pitcher and the sheet and the salt box lying inside the outline. The elements would send them on their way. Nothing would ever grow where salt had been seeded. I learned that from reading about the Dead Sea, which is located somewhere in Europe, a place I would like to visit someday, but probably never will. We got in the Merc' and headed back to the trailer.

Cowboy Johnson, with his eternal cowboy hat on his head, was standing on the front porch of the store. I whimpered again as I slowed the Merc' down and edged slowly past him, looking him up and down. He stared back at me with steady eyes. Did he wear his cowboy hat when he was sleeping? While he was cooking? Showering? Was he born with it on? I knew he wore it when he pumped gas. Oh, why, oh, why did he have to be a cowboy? I whimpered again. Geena and Normaine started giggling. I realized that they were onto my lust for Cowboy Johnson. To cover my embarrassment, I flipped on the radio, and out came a blast of Doo Wop.

I gunned the motor, and he watched as we swooped past on our way back to Normaine's trailer. We waved and hooted at him as he disappeared back into the store. I parked the Merc' up tight against Esmerelda, and we got out. I was rummaging through the trunk of the Merc' when I heard his voice behind me.

"Anyone up for a cold one?"

I located the new, still wrapped, fabulously marbled pink sheet by Ralph Lauren I was searching for and drew it out of one of the neatly stacked piles of stuff stored in the Merc's trunk. I shut the trunk lid and handed the package to Normaine.

Cowboy Johnson deftly slid a cold Pabst Blue Ribbon into my empty hand. Geena was standing beside him, holding a Pabst Blue Ribbon in her hand. She was waiting for me to say "No," but I didn't. I nodded and grinned at her. What could I say? She'd grown up a little bit more today anyway.

Normaine whooped over the sheet.

"It matches Esmerelda!"

Cowboy Johnson watched Normaine open the package and shake out the sheet. It was a gorgeous, large piece of pink marbled, soft fabric, dreamed up by a fabulous designer who thoroughly understood the deep, true pinks of passion and romance.

She shook it out and flapped it in the air, twirling in circles under the sun.

"Ooh, my Eddy's gonna' love this!"

She shouted off-color words of lovemaking into the air.

Suddenly, I realized Cowboy Johnson was studying me with a look in his eyes that said he knew exactly why I carried a brand-new pink marbled designer sheet in the trunk of my Mercury clear across the country. He recognized this form of hope. I blushed so deep, I felt like a fireball trying to find an Arctic iceberg to cling to.

"Take a drink, it'll help."

He offered his comforting words in a deep, slow drawl. I heard the humor in his voice. I turned and looked him up and down, imagining him in a pink marbled shirt. I liked that image a lot. However, I wasn't going to take any chances. Besides, I was still feeling holy, and I didn't want to start feeling smutty again.

Chapter Six

Cain't live with em',
Cain't live without em',
just give em' some room,
and try not to crowd em'.
dat's' what I say
dat's smart, yeah

Of course, that left out the angry part of me riding with me night and day. There wasn't a man alive that could take the wrath or grief I felt about men. They'd run for cover at the first glimpse of it. Or look for an opportunity to use it to hurt me. Some men were very creative that way. I learned a lot from the Monster, and I didn't intend to forget the lessons. Cowboy Johnson watched me with steady eyes.

"What you ladies been out doing?"

"Well, he's asking for it now!" I thought. "Let's see what he's made of."

"Didn't Normaine tell you?"

"Nope."

With a churlish sneer a medieval lout would envy, I said, "We been out rekillin' Normaine's man, Cowboy Johnson."

"Oh?"

"Ooh, yes."

He didn't speak. I batted my eyes at him and lisped the next words out.

"We went to where he was killed. We made an outline of his body and poured Clorox and Tide water inside it, salted the ground, and tossed Normaine's old sheet in the middle, so she would never have to sleep with him again in this lifetime or any other. That's why she needed a new sheet. Then we did a bunch more stuff to get him gone for good! All three of us carry an extremely Pure Hate for certain kinds of men, and probably will forever!"

I swept out my arm to include Geena and Normaine, who were dancing with that fine pink sheet, each of them holding up two corners and whooping. I watched him intently, figuring he would run. But he stood his ground.

After studying me for a minute, he said, "You should have let me go with you. I could have helped you with it. I got a couple of men I hate, too. And I despised Normaine's man."

"So you're refusing to be in the hated men's circle we have going on here, Cowboy Johnson?"

He looked around.

"I don't see one. But then, I'm not as organized as I could be. I like big, empty spaces."

He studied me for another minute.

"I can't take away whatever it is that's happened to any of you. Hell, I got my own problems, or I wouldn't be living out here in the middle of a desert. All I can do is offer you supper after a while. And maybe a campfire for the girl? Want to call it a draw? And yeah, you can call me Cowboy Johnson if you want to. It's all right with me."

I peered back through eons of time, back to the memory of the first caveman offering me berries on a leaf or a slab of raw meat or some other not very viable delicacy to chew on while I sat on an animal skin in a cave. This was not a new pattern for me. I could handle this.

"Okay. It's a draw, Cowboy Johnson."

He grinned and raised his voice to include Normaine and Geena.

"Come and set on the front porch. It's cooler there."

Geena and Normaine stopped dancing, folded up the sheet and put it in the trailer. Then the three of us trudged single file through the sand behind him, just like a bunch of baby ducks following their mama to water. We followed him around the store and up the wide steps of the front porch.

An assortment of beat-up rocking chairs, tree stumps, and a couple of rusty metal milk crates turned upside down were scattered across the porch. It wouldn't win a contest for "Best Decorated Desert Porch" in The Ladies Good Housekeeping Journal, but it lay in deep shade under the green peaked porch roof. That was enough to recommend it.

I parked myself in a curved back rocking chair with straight arms and crooked legs that tilted to the left. It was surprisingly comfortable after Cowboy Johnson handed me a cushion. Normaine claimed a faded rocker, and Geena draped her long length into a white wicker chair with a high back.

Cowboy Johnson disappeared through the screen door and came back carrying a metal jug of cold water. We each took a drink, then he carried the jug back in the store. I glanced over at Normaine and Geena. We'd accomplished a hell of a lot this day.

I dozed off while scolding myself for not thinking twice before stopping at a gas station that was obviously a former church. From now on, I would curb my curiosity and stop only at newly built gas stations. I would watch out for crosses and other religious paraphernalia and rush past them.

My curiosity got the best of me once again. And, to top it off, even though there was no cross at this former church, now a gas station and store, there were two Nuts—one Nut hollering clear to Canada, and the other Nut wearing a cowboy hat. One Nut was already fixed, so maybe I could get out of here before the other Nut needed fixing. I dozed off.

I woke up quick and easy. I'd refined the skill of pretending I was still asleep after I woke up, a skill developed from living with the Monster. I kept my eyes shut and listened as Geena explained to Normaine and Cowboy Johnson that I was tired because we never got to sleep safe because some sort of Monster kept throwing itself through our windows after we went to sleep in our rooms and shattered glass would fall all over us. Tiny little teardrop sized glass sprays. She said the glass cut and hurt, and the Monster made huge noises. That's why we ran away. I remembered when that happened. It was one time when the Monster, high on drugs, found us after we ran away.

She jumped up and ran off the porch. I jumped out of the rocker and ran after her. I grabbed her and pulled her to a stop, wrapped my arms around her. She was already taller than me at twelve years old. She laid her head on my shoulder and hid her face. Neither one of us said anything. We both hid in her long brown hair awhile before we went back up the porch steps and sat down again. I rocked awhile, then to change the deafening silence around us, I asked Normaine if she liked to cook. She laughed her big, hearty laugh.

"Hell no, Dumbass! When I got put in the Pen, they tried to make me cook. They put me in the kitchen and told me to clean and stuff a bunch of cheap assed tom turkeys, then the dumbasses handed me a large butcher knife. Well, I started out okay, but it wasn't long before I was stabbing every one of those damn turkeys for all it was worth. It felt real good!

They caught me and took that beautiful butcher knife away from me. They dragged me out of the kitchen and put me in lockdown, but the other girls told them I was just tenderizing those tough old tom turkeys to make them edible, so they let me out and sent me to the laundry to work."

Cowboy Johnson stood up and went into the store. After a while, he came back out.

"Come in and eat," he ordered. We stood up and filed into the store behind him just like baby ducks following their mother again.

It was noticeably cooler inside. I looked around. The little white renovated church had no cross or pews inside it, which would have caused me to run. Instead, it was one long, wide room, much larger than it looked from the outside. We stood on aged planks varnished to a shine. The walls were fine, golden whorled wood. Shelves holding rows of canned and dry goods, fresh bread, and other groceries lined the walls. Barrels of pickles and other stuff lined up like soldiers under a long white sales counter.

A couple of white glass-topped freezers, long enough to place a body in without having to bend it, stood against a wall. An upright drink cooler with a glass door stood at the end of the freezers. The cooler was lit up. It was filled with beer and soda bottles. A wood-handled broom and dustpan leaned against the wall behind the checkout counter. Behind the cash register were boxes of cigarettes, papers, whiskey, and other goods on shelves.

A couple of colorful beach calendars with girls in bathing suits hung on nails behind the counter. One was current, the other was dated March nineteen thirty-seven. Old wishful thinking and new wishful thinking, I thought.

I looked toward the back of the store. Books. Shelves of them, books in stacks everywhere. Shock threw a memory into my mind. God is always joking—look at my life. It's a joke. I learned to fast early on. Especially up until I was nine. Until my father quit drinking and food became available more than once or twice a week. My father and oldest brother drank together. That's where every bit of their money went. Not to beer, but to whiskey. Ten Roses. The cheapest. The most for the least. They used to drive by and toss us hungry kids a jar of pickled pig's feet or a Nehi orange soda once in a while when we hadn't eaten in days. They weren't hungry because of the booze. They thought it was funny. We thought it was heaven. So I was already an old hand at fasting and familiar with drawing nearer to God than I wanted to be.

Being a healer with a great deal of Sight that bosses you around until you give it whatever it is after, is not always easy or explainable. Somebody here was a Reader. Maybe an Eternal Reader.

"Whose books? Do they actually read them?' I croaked the words out.

"They are mine. Yes, I read them," he answered briefly, a note of both possession and annoyance in his voice.

Perfect. He was "The Reader?" In a cowboy hat? NO way! Most kids grow up looking for heroes: Batman, Mr. Atlas, Ginger Rogers, Hop Along Cassidy, Roy or Dale, the list is endless. But I turned to books and created my own hero in my book world. My hero was named The Eternal Reader. When I grew up, I was going to meet him, and we were going to marry and have a huge home library and two children and travel to find rare books. Our children would wear glasses and learn about magic worlds. The library would be our sanctuary every evening after we dealt with our day. We would read together and sometimes to each other.

That's how we would get by in this world where we were misunderstood misfits. Our books would be our defense against the world. To escape into for survival. To escape into to not see or feel the hurt or loud noises and the chaos in the world and many more reasons. The list goes on. I knew I would always love "The Eternal Reader" staunchly and readily if I ever found him. I whimpered. I'd already met one "Reader". He lived in a little white church, too. But he would never wear a cowboy hat! This scenario was all wrong! "The Reader" would never wear a cowboy hat! Astounded, my thoughts screeched to a stop.

By this time, we were at the back of the store. Cowboy Johnson led the way past floor to ceiling tan drapes pushed to the sides. Behind them stood wall to wall sliding glass doors partitioning off Cowboy Johnson's living quarters. They were open.

I sniffed the air. It held a lovely, meaty smell. Suddenly I was starving. Following the bait, we meekly stepped into his lair.

Cowboy Johnson's quarters was one large room sharing the same wood floors and walls with the store. To the left, a long, sky blue counter ran beneath white cupboards with a stove and refrigerator at one end. A window framed with blue and white checked curtains stood above a large, deep sink in the middle of the counter. A simple open kitchen. More shelves holding books. A beat-up wood table with mismatched chairs centered in the room. I eyed them doubtfully. Handmade by a manly, muscled, homesteader who could yodel and swing an ax in some freezing northern woods somewhere? A trapper or log cabin builder who had run out of nails? Pulling out one of those heavy chairs could give a person a hernia! I briefly pictured a rugged, square-jawed, heavily bearded woodsman lying in a hospital bed, his privates trussed in white from lifting one of those chairs.

To the right of a closet door on the other side of the room stood a single army cot with ugly, plain black iron railing. A chest of drawers, rife with badly carved wood angels atop its outermost rims stood next to the cot. A rifle was propped against the chest of drawers. One of the angels was staring down at the end of the rifle barrel, holding his hands to his chest. Was the angel afraid of getting shot? I took the opportunity to nudge my bossy Sight, making sure it got the picture.

The ugly cot beside the dresser squared off to an ugly green sofa. Geena and I stared at the sofa and whispered to each other in agreement. It definitely qualified as the Most Hideous Green Sofa we'd ever seen.

"Good thing he's got big porches!" I thought. Then my eyes lit on the platter towering with sandwiches sitting in the middle of the ugly table. The bait. I watched Cowboy Johnson go to the stove and move the coffee pot off a burner. The pot was aluminum, the same kind my father used. There was a clear glass knob on top so the expectant coffee drinkers could watch the coffee change color as it perked to just the right shade of rich brown, fragrantly signaling when it was ready to pour in their cups.

"Spam sandwiches. Thick sliced and fried until crisp." Cowboy Johnson stated this fact calmly, his back to us. I almost swooned. One of my favorite things in the whole world! How did he know? I rushed the table, pulled out one of the heavy chairs with the ease of a three hundred pound, heavily muscled weightlifter, sat down, and did a quick mental review.

A former church filled with good energy and much bigger inside than it looked from the outside. One long building with wood floors so shiny they could easily inspire a spontaneous dance contest, wood walls shelved with goods, a long white counter, and plenty of freezers. Living quarters in the back partitioned off with sliding glass doors and floor-length drapes for privacy.

"Not bad!" I muttered to myself. No assaults on furniture in this place, even though some of it was far uglier than necessary. No cursing of furniture here. No men throwing themselves down on sofas until they broke and were carried outside to molder away in the front yard. No kitchen table weaving back and forth on tottery legs so loose no one passed the bowls of food, they just grabbed them when they swayed by, took what they wanted, then set the bowl back on the table when it swayed by again.

I glanced at the trim, neat, ugly army cot. It was covered with a tucked in blanket bearing a geometric southwest motif. It was so neat, I bet a quarter would bounce on it. I bet Cowboy Johnson didn't have any busted bed springs, either. I glanced at him. He was watching me. I bet he already knew that his Hideous Green Sofa was so ugly it was safe from any of us.

I blushed involuntarily and shrugged at him. I didn't have time to think about him. I reached out a hand and grabbed a sandwich. It was years since I ate a Spam sandwich on soft, fresh light bread.

The platter of Spam sandwiches disappeared quicker than grains of sand sucked up in a hot, whirling desert wind, along with cold Cokes and hot coffee.

"I'm impressed!" Cowboy Johnson said.

We were still licking our fingers and smacking our lips when he announced cautiously, "I have a Pepperidge Farm Frozen Devil's Food Cake in the freezer."

We gasped. He stayed calm and watched us warily.

"But you can't have it until the campfire...later."

We groaned.

"Just a sample?" Geena whined.

"Nope. Go set on the front porch and let your food digest."

We wandered back out to the front porch and sat down. I dozed off again until Normaine prodded me awake with one finger. She pushed her face close to mine. I watched groggily as one of her eyes slid to the left while the other one stayed focused on me. I just wanted to go back into my food-induced coma. To hell with everything else.

"He's a good man, Avery Judson."

"Cowboy Johnson?" I asked sleepily as I traced the long scar that ran down her right cheek with my eyes. Why couldn't she say his name right? She ruminated a minute.

"Okay. Cowboy Johnson. I like that."

"Who?"

"Dumbass!"

She laughed at me, and I grinned back at her. The same old game women have played forever about men, no matter the hurts inflicted by them. It just came natural. I dozed off.

My snoring jerked me awake. I looked around. Geena was missing. It was almost dark. I jumped up and ran into the store. It was empty. I ran through Cowboy Johnson's living quarters, rushed out on the back porch, and skidded to a stop. The two of them were sitting on a log out by the campfire, laughing and talking. I headed back to the front porch and nudged Normaine awake.

"Get up, Lazybones!" I shouted at her. I laughed and stepped back when she flung out an arm, trying to hit me. She crawled to her feet, and we trudged up the path leading to the Duke's Hardware Emporium on the hill before we crossed the sand to the campfire. Conveniently, it was a double seater.

Geena and Cowboy Johnson ignored us. They were engaged in an earnest discussion of the merits of desert lizards, snakes, frogs, and geckos versus salamanders. We sat down on logs and admired the glowing fire. When the world of lizards was taken apart, examined, and resolved, the two of them turned toward us.

I grinned at them. This whole day had been ridiculously weird so far. I suspected it might prove even weirder later, but my Sight stayed mum on the subject. Geena narrowed her eyes at me in disapproval. She knew what I was thinking.

"Don't act too flighty, Mama. It is dreadfully destabilizing for me."

I watched surprised, curious expressions come over Cowboy Johnson and Normaine's face. I looked at Geena. She was still glaring at me in disapproval. Back and forth from her to them. I watched their expressions until I couldn't hold it in any longer.

Oh, Geez! I'd made more mistakes than all the harlots and prophets and sling shotters and nay sayers, and all the ark riders in the Bible put together! And it looked like there was more in front of me to make. But the Universe, in its unfathomable wisdom, somehow saw fit to give me a break.

It had evicted my sorry ass out of my former life, kicked me out of my worn-thin misery, and sent me south to a desert store in the middle of nowhere to eat fried Spam sandwiches and Pepperidge Farm cake at a campfire held behind a little church—one that most likely had seen its share of sinners, penitents and miracles long before it became a gas station and store with a couple of Nuts living at it.

No more Universe faithfully providing predictable Monster predator misery for me and my daughter day and night. Especially night. We'd been kicked out, evicted, and right now, we were hanging out somewhere in a big old desert around a campfire without the Monster.

I burst out laughing and fell backward over the log. I lay on my back in the sand and laughed it out. After the whoops were gone and the hiccups started, I struggled to a sitting position on the log. Immediately, small white missiles started hitting me. I grabbed one and stuck it in my mouth.

"Marshmallows!" I shouted.

I was deliberately working to keep it light. To stay off serious subjects. I never minded playing the Fool or the Clown when it was needed. I was one anyway. All of us were wounded warriors playing on the face of this Earth, including young Geena, and we all needed a respite. Each of us had dug ourselves into deep dark holes in life and been forced to live there a long time. None of us could explain the things that happened to us or why. It was just Karma.

Out here in this lonesome, hot desert, amidst us runaways, I sensed that Cowboy Johnson had a story too. I knew some of Normaine, the first Nut's story, but I couldn't stand to hear the second Nut's story tonight. I was filled with Spam and marshmallows, and I needed to stay happy. We fell silent, and I stared into the fire, looking for answers in it. The flames flickered. A piece of wood caved deeper into its red center.

Suddenly Cowboy Johnson stood up. He grabbed a straw broom and a long, painted stick lying against a log.

"Ladies and young lady, do I have your attention?"

We nodded, glad for the relief of any interruption.

"There are many tools of magic. This broom and stick are just two of them. Would you like me to show you some of the ways they can be used?"

We nodded. I didn't care what he did as long as I could listen to his voice. He laid the painted stick down and circled the fire with the broom, sweeping the sand around the fire back and forth until it was clean and bore no prints of anything. Then he leaned the broom against a log and picked up the stick.

"Many moons ago, I undertook the learning of how to be a Fire Keeper in the Native American tradition, since I live here anyway."

He shrugged. Then he began drawing animal images, moons, stars, and elementals in the smooth sand, erasing and drawing as he talked. He could have drawn demons and invoked them for all I cared, just as long as I could listen to him. I watched him through glazed, sleepy eyes. Me and my Sight were hanging out in an altered space, a place well remembered from past lifetimes spent with Cowboy Johnson.

"Fire has a way of finishing what we start, of burning the dross away from the pure. The old, the ugly, and the impure move on to another time of necessary refinement, taken away with dignity by the animals, plants, images, the planets, Elders, and stars. They leave behind the young, the fresh, the new, the beautiful, the learned, and innocence is renewed once again and celebrated. That is why we are having a fire tonight."

"Congratulations, ladies. I don't know what all you did today, and I don't need to know. But you finished a whole bunch of bad old something and started something new. New life is beginning again."

He stopped drawing and shrugged again.

"I would have thought twice if I had known that this kind of understanding was a permanent part of a Fire Keeper's responsibility."

I came out of my voice induced trance in which he and I were holding hands. I tilted my head at him. He understood and applauded us? Now, how many guys did I personally know that would understand what we accomplished today? Try zero. Well, maybe that was my fault.

Then he changed the subject.

"I don't want to sound like I'm complaining, but it's getting late, and I'm ready for some of that Pepperidge Farm cake. How about all of you? Would you go get it, young lady? Second freezer on the left?"

Geena jumped up and ran for the back door of the store.

"Don't forget the cold beers!" Cowboy Johnson shouted after her.

"I won't!" she shouted back importantly.

I watched her proudly while Cowboy Johnson watched me. I could see him out of the corner of my eye. Still waters run deep. He had shared some of his self with us without it hurting us. He had presented himself as a higher grade of man. A man who could make perfect Spam sandwiches while perfecting his philosophies on life all at the same time. Had Spirit given him a bunch of hoo-hah to learn, like it had me while it kept us busy multi-tasking? And while busy being "enlightened," had we missed the boat? Or was it a ship? A Spam Master was in our midst. I wanted to genuflect in front of him.

But what the hell, we were leaving in the morning anyway. Leaving the questions and the attraction for the second Nut far behind. Leaving with the righteousness of having done Normaine, the first Nut, a good deed. On the road again. Heading out to meet aliens.

He was watching me again, so I stopped muttering to myself. Sometimes I looked nuts, too. I bet he was thinking I fit in real well around this Nut camp and was planning to stick around. Well, I could tell him a thing or two about the road to hell. Mostly that it was paved with crap instead of good intentions.

Geena came back, her arms full of cake and Stroh's Beer. We cut the cake and ate it with our fingers and licked the cold gooiness off them. Cowboy Johnson left to get more beer.

"No more beer for Geena!" I called after him. "Can you bring her an orange Nehi?"

He nodded without turning around. Pretty soon, mellow classical music began drifting through the air from the store. The music was full-bodied and kind.

Mozart, maybe? I looked at Normaine and Geena. They were propped against each other, eyes almost closed, sleepy grins on satisfied faces. Full of Spam and Pepperidge Farm chocolate cake and Stroh's and Pabst Blue Ribbon Beer. Time to turn in. But where?

Chapter Seven

Lay that thaing' down baby,
an' let's git' some rest.
Don't cha' know suga'
dis' day's been da' best?

I was contemplating the bedless journey of an endless night in the Merc's front seat when Cowboy Johnson came back carrying a tire pump and something that looked like a rolled-up piece of green rubber. He spread the rubber thing out on the other side of the fire and attached the tire pump to it. Normaine and Geena watched him fill it with air until it almost floated. Then they ran and jumped on it and promptly fell asleep.

"Well, it looks like I'm not going to get a chance to put a clean sheet on the air mattress," he commented dryly, sitting down by me. "How about you? You sleepy?"

I nodded. But I wasn't sleepy at all. In fact, I was intensely awake. Every nerve ending in my body was bent toward him like a field of sunflowers turned toward the sun, tingling, and alert. Of course, I couldn't let him know that. He stood up and held out his hand. I put my hand in his. He drew me up and over to the mattress and released my hand. Then he reached out, smoothed my hair back, and took my face in his hands. Shock and his gentleness allowed me to stand still.

"Goodnight," he murmured.

He gave me a quick, chaste kiss. A peck that a man fastened into the death grip of an iron chastity belt would give. When he let go, I whimpered and dropped to the mattress, graceless as a tossed sack of potatoes. I lay there while he turned and walked away. My first kiss from another man. It felt clean and good, what little there'd been of it. I whimpered. Why, oh why, did he have to be a cowboy?

I lay there staring at the fire, listening to the music floating through the night as long as I could stand it before I gave up and struggled to my feet, purposeful, elated energy running through me. I began the million-mile trek toward the store, slogging through the sand like I was Lawrence of Arabia with the whole Ottoman Empire chasing me. I felt like a thousand years passed before I reached the back porch. Freed at last from the sand sucking at my feet, I nimbly ran up the steps. But as I touched the back-door handle to pull it open, all my courage left me. I leaned my head against the screen door, my heart pounding like a Kentucky Derby loser.

"Hey, you."

His voice caressed me gently.

"Come in."

He reached around the door, took my hand, and drew me in. Darkness and Strauss enveloped us. He pulled me into his arms and held me. He held me like a mother holds a hurt child. Gingerly, with care. Then he held me like I was a silly little girl, then like a blushing teenager with a crush, then like a friend who had plenty to say. I didn't know there were so many ways to hold someone. I knew only my mother's rare hugs when I was very young, and I could count those on one hand. My father never hugged anybody. He didn't think about them needing it. The Monster never hugged anyone. His affection was utility driven by his crotch.

Cowboy Johnson held me many different ways while we slipped in and out of past lives. He protected and calmed me when no one wanted us to be together. He cajoled me into bravery and soothed me into acceptance. He jested and teased me into laughing at life and not being so damn scared of it. He smoothed my hair, and I leaned against him, his words falling like tender rain around us.

He said that I was never lost, that he was waiting for me all this time. That we both just took a few detours along the way. Karma stuff to take care of. There was plenty of time now, for we'd found each other again, and each lifetime the finding grew easier and stronger. I sighed from my soul in agreement and gave in to the magic of what was happening. I was home at last.

I don't know when we started dancing. I do remember Pachelbel's Canon in D was playing. We danced together in wide-open spaces carrying the scents of newly mown grass and wildflowers, at the top of an ornate stairway in a great perfumed palace filled with people and music, and later when we strolled down an empty, winding, rainy night street with no end.

The scents of cinnamon and frankincense and lilac came and went as my Beloved whirled me away in blue gingham then drew me back in calico, with him in coveralls. He laughed with me while I wore fluted silks with high, white powdered hair, and he wore black tails and then a white tuxedo in an island lagoon ablaze with candles and colorful flowers.

We moved around the floor like two glowing, pink crystals encased in wondrous white light with the universe streaming through us. Singing metals and smooth gravel and cool water streamed within us, brought together again to work their wondrous magic upon two lonely human beings whose souls had been waiting all their lives for each other.

Suddenly, it all stopped. I slammed down into deep and dark and tainted, and it hurt. I pushed away from him, tottered to the screen door and shoved it open. I didn't look back at him and he didn't try to stop me. I weaved my way down the porch steps and zigzagged drunkenly toward the safety of the mattress by the dying campfire and fell on it. Cowboy Johnson's movements were gentle, kind, sweet with the fire of banked passion held back. And he hadn't worn his hat. But just as I began to test the heat and depth of his passion with tentative fingertips, opening the doorway to exploring more with him, memories of the Monster shoved their way in, reminding me of how terrible it was to be physical with a man. And that's where this was leading. I ran.

Sleep claimed me almost instantly. I woke up the next morning and sat up. I watched the sun dawn hot and fierce, roaring its way over the edge of the world, swallowing the lingering darkness up in one easy bite.

I was anxious to put everything behind me and head out on the road. The Merc' and the aliens were waiting for us. I refused to think about the night before. Sanity had returned, I thought grimly. Just in time! What the hell was I thinking? I had just got rid of the Monster, I hoped forever, and I didn't need any more man trouble for a long time, if ever. To stop that possibility from happening, I just needed to get the hell out of here! It was that simple.

I fidgeted and drummed my fingers on the tiny table in the little pink trailer while Geena and Normaine casually scrambled eggs, brewed coffee, and made pancakes for their breakfast like there was all the time in the world. Normaine jerked her thumb at me.

"Go walk it off."

"You kickin' me out?"

"Yep. We want some peace and quiet while we eat our breakfast."

I left them to it. I went out and ambled around the dead campfire, then over to the shade under the roof the Merc' and Esmerelda shared. If they could produce offspring together, what would they look like? I smirked at the idea and began to pet them.

Normaine and Geena finally came outside. Normaine was smiling, but Geena wore a look of grim determination on her face. I recognized that look.

"Time to get a move on, kiddo."

"Yep. It sure is."

She spread her feet apart and locked her arms across her chest. That stance was familiar, too.

"We're going to follow Normaine to Wyoming to meet Eddy!" she announced.

"What?"

She looked at me like I wasn't too bright.

"We are going to be her bridesmaids!"

"No way!" I shouted at her.

"We have to! She can't get there without us!"

"Why not?" I asked.

"She's too afraid!" Geena shouted.

"Of what?" I queried.

"She's afraid he won't think she's pretty anymore," Geena answered.

I looked at Normaine. She waited, portly and motionless, her uncombed hair hanging lank and greasy around her moon face, sweat accenting the scars lining it while one black eye watched me steadily and the other one stared at the dead campfire.

"...and he won't want to marry her."

"No!" I said again.

"Think of it as a summer vacation!" she urged.

"No!" I said.

"I'll just have to go alone with her, then! I've never been a bridesmaid before, and I intend to be one!"

Geena strode to the Merc', jerked open the back door, and started rummaging through her stuff. I argued with her while she pulled out a backpack and began to fill it.

"Geena, we're going to see the aliens!" I said.

"Well, I'm not. You can," she said. "I prefer real people!"

We argued until she hefted her filled backpack to her shoulder and said, "Normaine needs us!"

Normaine nodded vigorously and smiled a wide, toothless smile at us. I glared at her, then fell to my knees, knowing it was all over.

"Lord God, help us all!" I clasped my hands together in humble prayer and atonement. Where did

I go wrong this time? Once again, I was not spared. I prayed loudly up at the sky. Geena interrupted me.

"Let's go, Mama! It's getting hot!"

I was beaten. I sighed and got to my feet. We loaded our cars, closed the trailer, and headed for the gas pumps in front of the store.

Cowboy Johnson stepped out of the store. He was wearing black. Llike he was in deep mourning. Black tee-shirt and jeans and reflector sunglasses under his cowboy hat, so I couldn't see his eyes. He filled our gas tanks and checked the oil and fluids without a word while Normaine explained everything to him. Then Normaine hugged him and thanked him for all he'd done for her.

"And they are coming back after I'm married." She stated this expansively, waving her arm in our direction.

"Sure they are," he said, real slow. "Okay. I'm done. Goodbye, Normaine. And Geena. And You."

I left him standing with one hand on his hip, gazing after us as I followed Esmerelda out onto the dusty two-lane blacktop. I never looked back. I couldn't. I had to run. A little pitstop out in the desert. That's where he was located.

Chapter Eight

Rollin' on down de' road
thowed' off ma' load herewhile back
so's it cain't fine' me an' jump and clack
lak' it did back in dat' lil' ol' town
and back in dat' lil' ol' shack.

    Geena rode with Normaine. I followed. We kept to the backroads as we wandered north. I tried to think about Normaine instead of Cowboy Johnson, but I had to fight myself constantly. A big part of me yearned to go back. I kept visualizing doing a U-turn with tires screeching and rubber burning, racing back to the store, and throwing myself into Cowboy Johnson's arms while choruses of angels sang Halleluiah! Yeah, I wanted to run back to Cowboy Johnson real bad, but I reminded myself that he wore a cowboy hat, like my former tormenter did. I tried to convince myself that he was another bad guy hiding behind Goodness, but my Sight knew better. It wanted him real bad, and so the yearning for him never stopped. It made me ornery and testy with Normaine and Geena.
    Every time we stopped for gas, I peppered Normaine with questions.
    "How did you meet Eddy? What's his last name?"
    "I told you. Eddy's last name is Savingo. He's Italian with some Spanish and Native in him. I met him at the restaurant I worked in. We're supposed to meet up in Medicine Bow, Wyoming, and get married.

He owns a trailer on land over there, but he's always on the road, so he wants me to move in and wait for him. He sends me money through Western Union to live on, but once I get there, he can send it through the mail a lot cheaper."

Geena acted like Normaine's defense attorney. She interrupted me every time I asked Normaine a question.

"Lay off, Mama!" she said. "That's enough for now!"

"We gotta' go!" she said.

One day after we had gassed up and our usual exchange was over, Normaine said, "No hurry," in a high, syrupy, soothing drawl to Geena. "Your Mama was just worried."

She smiled at me. I looked at her suspiciously. Something was up. She grinned apologetically and watched the sweat trail beading the cold Coke she was holding with unusual fascination. In a small, casual voice almost an octave higher than her usual voice, she said, "Oh, I just thought maybe we could stop a few places along the way. Maybe see a couple of things."

"Like what?" I asked testily.

She warmed to her subject. "In Loveland, Colorado, they got a giant chair, a Statue of Liberty, and a carving of an Indian. In Manitou Springs, they got The Cave of the Winds, a coffin race, a castle, dinosaurs, and Indian caves. In Estes Park, they got that creepy hotel full of ghosts. Then there's the Giant Chili Pepper and free beer at the Coors beer factory!"

Geena, smiling and nodding, was sitting beside Normaine in Esmerelda, one hand resting on her shoulder. I frowned at Geena. Did she think that we were on a permanent vacation? What about when summer ended and school started? We needed to be settled someplace before then!

I stared down at the Earth I stood on, sorting my thoughts, so I might trod on it in a better way. I had a good stash of cash and a bit more put back. What should I do? Try to find those distant cousins I never met, that no doubt wouldn't like me, and would tell the Monster where I was? Try to find a small town, homeschool Geena, and hide in a meaningless job where no one knew our stories? That was the right thing to do to keep us safe until Geena turned eighteen. Six more years. That had been my plan.

But then, there were earthquakes in this world. Under the Earth I stood on this very instant lay sleeping dragons filled with heat, rumbling under the ground, with people running around above like crazed ants whenever they turned over. I sighed. And there was time, and there were other people to love in this world, though I didn't want to. Besides, Geena was going to do this with or without me. I trusted her freckle-faced intuition. It always came out right. She was an old soul who knew which way the psychic winds blew better than I did. I sighed mightily again, just for effect. I'd already given in, though they didn't know it.

"Okay. I guess I'll have to trust you two on this." I turned and shook my finger at them. "But first of all, we are going to need my road map."

They whooped and jumped out of Esmerelda and hugged me. Normaine hammered my back.

"I got lots of extra money for gas and stuff," she explained magnanimously.

"Yeah, right," I stated sarcastically.

We slept in Esmerelda and the Merc' at night and wandered through New Mexico, Colorado, and elsewhere during the day. We ambled over to the Carlsbad Caverns, then to the Grand Canyon. We sat on the front porch of the Stanley Hotel in tall, white rockers and listened to ghost stories. We saw all the things Normaine thought up and more. We saw a giant metal lizard made of old wrecked cars. One farmer had a horse and wagon made of petrified vegetables standing on his front lawn. He sold apple cider if you wanted to get out and look it over.

We kept to the backroads, letting the dust of ages and old ways sort itself out and settle around us and through us. We passed weathered barns and fragrant, full of life fields and farmhouses and went through little villages of twenty or thirty people where quilts hung on clotheslines and chickens pecked for bugs. The air lay tranquil in those places, where common sense and simple ways of life were followed with contentment. Though we would someday be forced to become too fast for that long ago dusty time before most roads were blacktopped, none of us would ever forget the road trip that made us a part of the universe for a while and gave each of us a strength and a piece of foundation that would endure all our lives.

We ate peanut butter and crackers and bologna sandwiches and warm, runny yellow cheese and potato chips to replenish our salt. We drank water from jugs we filled along the way. We ate stolen watermelon and spit out the seeds and watched the stars come out in high, domed night skies while we huddled below over small campfires. We stopped at R.V. rentals and doled out the change needed to take showers and shampoo our hair. We washed our clothes at Laundromats. Every small town seemed to have one right on Main Street.

I followed Esmerelda in the Merc', watching the sun and wind ply Normaine's black hair, turning it to red-black and lightening Geena's hair to golden brown.

I sobbed and prayed to Jesus and God and Buddha and everyone else I could think of the whole time we were crossing the highest part of the Rocky Mountains. I was awestruck and dumbfounded and stunningly terrified of their heights. I couldn't back out, or I would have; there was no place to turn around. I stared at the thin, high trail partially covered with clouds ahead of me—clouds! I couldn't look left or right. The narrow road was not wide enough for guard rails.

Geena rode with me. She kept her hand on my shoulder and chanted "Om Mani Padme Hum" while I envisioned a million death scenarios, all involving falling from the top of the Rockies. Normaine didn't help matters any. She rode ahead of us, top down, fishtailing Esmerelda, happily and loudly singing and shouting stuff to someone named 'Tuncunchala".

At last, the time came when we crossed into Wyoming. I followed Normaine across the border. Geena was riding with her. As usual, the top was down on Esmerelda. I watched the wind sift through their long hair, playing with it. Soon our spontaneous adventuring would end, along with the days and nights of following teardrop taillights that flashed pink at night and red during the day. Oh, those were golden days! But they were over now.

I looked at the somber, dark green pine forests surrounding us. Normaine's new home lay on the edge of a National Forest. We rode soberly into the town of Medicine Bow and stopped at the local hotel to get directions.

I followed Esmerelda down a couple of dirt roads and bounced along a path leading into a field where a new double-wide trailer rested on a concrete slab. Someone had built a wood porch onto the front of the trailer and planted young pine trees all around it. The trees were small. It would take time for them to grow.

We parked Esmerelda and the Merc' in front of the trailer and got out. Nobody spoke. Normaine looked nervous and downcast. The party was over. She had arrived at her destination. She retrieved the key from its hiding place, and we went inside. The trailer was furnished and pretty with a big kitchen and three bedrooms.

We looked everything over, then drove back to town, called and got the electricity and water turned on, and bought groceries. We went back to the trailer, ate dinner, and sat around. The electricity was still off, so we used the kerosene lamps we carried with us. Geena and I made small talk. We kept saying encouraging things to Normaine.

Bedtime was early and quiet. We all had plenty to think about. What were we going to do next? I tossed and turned endlessly. We never planned a damn thing past each day of travel. We escorted Normaine to her new home, and now we were supposed to leave her, right? That's what I assumed would happen. But I had a funny feeling I was wrong.

The electricity was on the next morning. We got up and made a big country breakfast of scrambled eggs and bacon and biscuits to kill time and to try make up for having no energy from the sleepless night. We ate morosely and watched each other like somber, mean, baggy-eyed raccoons with bad hair. We watched each other while the psychic tension mounted steadily, filling the air all around us, making it heavy and dense. The denseness grew more and more sullen, like a falling barometer predicting rain and storms. We didn't know what was wrong. But we all sensed something serious was building up. And it wasn't good.

I went outside to get away from them and think—down the steps and across the yard. I started walking, circling all I was seeing. That was a thing I did when I needed to get clarity on something.

I looked around. The yard wasn't played in. No simple, dusty paths where happy country children played and shouted and chased each other. No one kept lawns in this part of the world. No solid green grassy squares to be mowed and admired. To hide behind. This was High Plains territory. The climate was cold with a short growing season.

Suddenly, it struck me that Normaine hadn't called Eddy in a long time. Why, we'd played for weeks on the road, and she never called him once!

I hurried back into the trailer. The question of why she never called anyone all this time had been building in the back of my mind, but I ignored it until now. I was too busy having fun on the road.

"Why haven't you called Eddy?" I shouted the question at her. For a second, she looked at me with a weary, impassive look on her face, a look that scared the hell out of me. I hastily improvised a lie so she wouldn't have to say what her look meant.

"You forgot to call him yesterday, Dunderhead!"

The awful look fled, and she shouted. "Okay! Let's go to town!"

Relieved at having something to do to bring down the psychic tension building around us, we headed for town. We dropped Geena off at the laundromat to wash clothes. Normaine and I headed for the hotel. We clomped up the wide board steps and over to the hotel double doors. I opened one of the doors and bowed the bride to be inside. She giggled and headed for the phone booth at the back of the lobby.

I sat down and watched her over the top of the magazine I picked up from the generic hotel coffee table. Something was up with her. My psychic hotline was on red alert. She turned her back to me and rummaged in her purse. After some serious assaults on the interior of the large, red, odd-shaped thing that was supposed to be made of "supple" leather, she came out with a handful of white paper scraps. Some of the white scraps fell. They fluttered to the floor in slow motion, like large snowflakes. She scrambled to collect them, watching me the whole time. By then, I was standing, staring at her, the glossy magazine bearing Sean Connery's name and smiling face on it, forgotten.

She shoved her way into the telephone booth, slammed the door shut, and picked up the phone. I sat down again and stared into space, my mouth opening and closing like I had just grown a set of gills. I remembered.

Ro. She was acting like Ro. Seventy-two-year-old Ro. My friend Ro. Ro was short for Rhoda. Visions of being dressed in a tight canary yellow shirtwaist dress, designed courtesy of the Donna Reed Era, a dress that made me look like a giant, rotund dandelion with arms and a face, floating and rotating down the aisle at Ro's wedding, came back to me.

I was Ro's maid of honor at her wedding to that handsome seventy-four-year-old lad, Jed, the guy she abducted from the grief of his wife's passing a mere six months earlier and carried into new nuptials using the lure of being a devout, religious lady that would mind him and give him companionship and sex, the sex part being the most important to her, and the religious, demure, obeying lady part the most important to him.

Jed never knew what hit him. She saw him and took him by storm while I watched from the sidelines. We once shared backyard fences, meeting there every morning. She explained her plan while I listened, astonished. Her strategy was to keep him with her constantly and to charm him out of his socks and pants.

"Doesn't he need time to grieve his loss? His wife has only been dead a few months. Not even half a year," I asked.

She nodded at me wisely. "Nope, we ain't got no time to spare! That would take him a hundred years if he got started on it. Remember, she was tall and thin and made a lot of money and liked going to bed with him. If he was to realize all that's gone, he'd never be fit for anybody to live with again!" She paused and looked up at the blue sky. "Besides, it's in God's plan for us to marry!"

She laughed her big, raucous laugh, the one that once charmed truck drivers from Philly to San Francisco. And fisherman. And delivery men. And farmers.

Ro was short and small and round as Humpty Dumpty. She had huge, liquid brown eyes, a pert little pug nose, and a little bow mouth. She wore screaming red lipstick and short blond wigs over her thin hair. She had an independent mind and cussed like a sailor and shared personal things about her sex life. Her feet were little, and she knew how to mince and sway and pour on the charm with the best of them. She played pool like a hustler; she drove an eighteen-wheeler at one time. She never discussed any of this history with Jed—he was a very burly, tan, cheap, doughty, and religious Scotsman.

Quickly it came time for them to marry. Jed stood waiting for Ro in the chapel of the little church he and his devout family built. He went there all his life, and his barely dead wife attended that same church with him for many years. Guests at the wedding included a rage-filled ex-mother-in-law, his three angry brothers, four angry children, and a whole bunch of astonished and angry, but faithful, church-going regulars. In the church basement, stood tables skimpy with reluctantly prepared food plus a small, apologetic, demure, beige wedding cake to be cut at their reception.

Ro's family turned out in full force. One son was fresh out of jail. Another was on long term probation. No one wore a suit, tie, or dress. They wore tight jeans and tank tops and chewed gum that cracked like gunshots throughout the acoustically unsound, small church cemented together brick by brick by Jed's frugal, tight-fisted ancestors.

I waited with Ro in a tiny room at the back of the church. I was to stroll out sedately when the music started, parade slowly down the aisle and stand to the left of the altar. Then Ro would make her grand entrance in her pale-yellow "A" line wedding dress and her short veil, carrying a bouquet of yellow tulips laced with canary yellow ribbons.

She was nervous. All her sisters and daughters kissed and hugged her while they applied makeup to her and settled the short veil over her new blond wig. They were sweet and charming and very feminine in spite of their jeans and tops. Then they left, taking the excitement and the vestiges of the old, ancient ritual with them as women always do.

Ro sat there waiting, brown eyes as big as saucers darting around the small room we waited in. Finally, she jumped up and grabbed my hands.

"Get me out of here!" she shouted desperately.

"Ro, you'll be all right. It's just your nerves."

I spoke soothingly and gently, almost in southern belle accents, as though this was a movie we were in. Anything to get through wearing this dandelion shaped dress.

"I mean it! If you don't, I'll leave by myself!"

"Why, Ro?"

She backed up, sat down again, and looked at me in stark fear.

"What's the matter, Ro?"

Suddenly she shoved one small, dainty arm out in front of her and examined her long, lacquered, obviously fake fingernails with her eyes to keep from looking at me.

"Well, it's just that I might not have told Jed everything."

"Like what?"

"Well, like the fact that I've been married three, no, actually, four times he doesn't know about. He knows about the other three." She looked at me with beseeching, frightened brown eyes. "There may be a few more little things I haven't told him about, too."

I didn't dare ask, "What?" again. I staggered over to a chair in the despised but required high heels matching my pumpkin-shaped yellow dress and fell into a chair. Ro sat silent, frozen to her chair. It was obvious she didn't know what to do next.

I did some of the fastest thinking I ever did in my life and drew a swift conclusion. I knew they would be happy together. She desperately needed a rudder to guide the ship of her life, and he was it. And he needed someone to rudder. They could worry about making it to the dock later.

"You're right, Ro. Neither one of you have got time to live in the past or to deal with it. You're both too damn old for many more shenanigans anyway. What Jed doesn't know won't hurt him. I bet he already knows you haven't told him everything. And he is okay with it. Just don't tell him anything more."

"What if my family tells on me?"

"Are you divorced from all of the others?"

"Yes. The ones that aren't dead."

'So, it's not bigamy, and you won't have to go to the pen? You didn't murder any of them?"

"No, But I wanted to. A couple of them, I mean."

"Well, right now you're getting married again. For the seventh time...?"

"Maybe the eighth or more...?" She started counting off on her fingers. "The ones that are dead don't count, right?"

That stopped me cold for a few seconds. I realized I was standing up with a woman I barely knew. A secret keeper. And the stuff I didn't know could involve bigamy and a plethora of other unsavory secrets and characters. But what the hell, how much longer did they have to live? I was young, but Ro and Jed were in their seventies!

Not to mention that Ro was diabetic and ate a large platter mounded high with greasy corned beef hash, three fried eggs, and a half a dozen heavily buttered and jammed biscuits for breakfast every morning. She couldn't see straight nor walk straight much of the time. She had a penchant for singing at odd times, too. Jed limped and talked to himself all the time. He took Ro for long rides in the country in his flame-red muscle truck, during which they munched on ring bologna, and some sort of semi-liquid, evil-smelling cheese. Their diet alone would kill them off soon enough.

I heard the Wedding March begin. I staggered to my feet, grabbed her hands, and pulled her up out of her chair.

"You're going through with it. You can tell him whatever you want to later."

I wobbled to the door on the damn high heels, flung it open, and set sail down the aisle. Ro followed me, and they got married, and we had a chilly reception, with no dancing because the Lord and a few other folks didn't approve of it, in the church basement. Then Ro and Jed roared out of the parking lot in his red, shiny truck. They moved away, and I never did find out what Ro told him or didn't. Sometimes life has secrets it doesn't share. So do people.

Chapter Nine

Some people get's der' comeuppance,
Some's don't,
Sa' jist' moves on, honi' baby, suga' pie,
An ya's neva' lets em' take out another loan

I wondered how many secrets Normaine was holding back from me. Like Ro did. I watched her dial the numbers written on the scraps of paper. She said her son got taken away from her and put in permanent foster care, and her mother wasn't allowed to see her ever again because the Feds had a restraining order on her. After all, she was a murderess and had to pay those kinds of prices. So she couldn't be calling them. I tried to figure it out, but I couldn't. Suddenly I was furious. I'd been left out of the loop again. The emotional pain of that caused me to jump up.

"Let's go!"

I hurled the words across the lobby at her. She talked into the phone a bit longer, then hung up and circled her way around the barn sized empty lobby, humming a little tune and righting every dust-covered plastic flower in the place before she finally reached me. With one eye on the door and the other on me, she said, "What do you want?"

"Did you talk to Eddy?" I asked testily.

"Yup."

I waited, but she didn't say any more.

"Well, what did he say? When is he getting here?"

She didn't answer.

"Who else did you call?"

"I'm going to the grocery store," she announced and turned on her heel. I followed her out of the hotel. At the grocery store, she filled two brown grocery bags with wine and beer. I refused to help her carry them. We picked Geena up at the Laundromat and rode back to the trailer in sullen silence. Geena was puzzled but wisely kept quiet.

Normaine collected the grocery bags in her arms and stalked into the trailer. She stashed her drinks in the refrigerator. I am ashamed to say I followed her to the dining room table, shouting questions, throwing them like missiles at her. She sat down, opened a beer, took a long drink, and nursed it while she ruminated silently, staring out the dining room window at nothing.

The verbal missiles I threw landed and eventually turned the silent Normaine into a soft puddle of grieving humanity. A round-shouldered, flat-footed puddle of silence, padding back and forth between the refrigerator and table, drinking beer noisily, burping and hiccupping now and then. No answers, just misery. I couldn't stop myself. I stayed in freaked out, screaming, crazy mode.

"What the hell, Normaine! Getting drunk isn't going to solve anything! Who the hell did you call? You had a whole bunch of phone numbers you called! I watched you! Who were they? Family? Friends?" I paced the floor and shouted at her. "Talk to me, Normaine!"

She ignored me.

Finally, I looked around. Geena was gone. She'd seen me go into emotional storms before and oh, how she hated them! I hated them, too. They seemed to be brought on with the advent of an epiphany I should have got a long time ago, but didn't, and might not get this time, either. I knew better than anyone that there was no guarantee of my ability to have a successful "aha!" that would help me right my world.

Geena knew it too. She was an old soul who knew all about drawing snowflakes under the Shadows while I was just learning. She knew how to bend over the pure, crystal whiteness of a snowflake to hide the Light she was creating using timeless, sacred geometry; bending to hide it from the Shadow looming above her.

When it snowed during the long winters back in Monster town, I told Geena stories of the White Light Beings who shook the crystal powder of Snowy Goodness down into the dark realms where humanity lived. On her own, during her early childhood, Geena easily mastered the sacred geometry needed to organize the Light into bigger and more Goodness to hold on to, just like people always do when the Shadow gets too large, trying to make it look like there is no way out.

Furthermore, she learned to walk the paths the snowflake crystal people made and thus escape the Shadow. They were her Protectors. All were One, because each snowflake was a protector and small didn't mean not mighty. And I informed her that just like Humpty Dumpty, everybody was supposed to have breaks and cracks in them. That's how the Light gets in.

Unlike Geena, each time I chanced upon one of my cracked or broken places, I became mean and scared, but the scared never showed up until the mean was let out first.

I pounded the table with my fists, pacing back and forth, shouting, a part of me watching, dumbfounded, with no clue as to why I was doing this. Just my innards running the show. They knew something I didn't. Suddenly I stopped. Understanding flooded me. Tortured souls. My soul was calling me out to stand in my own skin. This was not the time for a caesura, a timely pause, a strategic silence that is used in music. This was not the beginning of a light, happy music hour filled with bubbles, smiling singers, accordions, or twirling batons.

Suddenly, my Sight finally decided to show up and help me. I saw myself wearing a mask of my face over my face. The mask was stiff and stayed the same no matter what happened. It stayed worn and tired, dense, and smiling like it was supposed to. But behind it, the real me kept changing. I started out young and grew old behind the mask that never changed. In that moment, I understood how many times I used that mask to either perjure my soul or save my life.

Each smiling mask I'd worn was necessary for my survival, but this one had to go right here and now because it was composed of a rock-hard set of women's survival skills, like smiling back at the Monster during this lifetime. That smiling mask had held back a thousand fear-filled miseries lived through alone, without recourse to anyone's help but my own.

    I moaned. What would my new mask look like? Surely, I would have to have one. Everyone in the world has one. I didn't remember until this instant that when change came, old masks were exchanged for new ones whether we liked it or not, and we didn't get to consciously pick the time it was going to happen, either.

    I blew out a breath. Meeting Cowboy Johnson was the final reason I could now change my old mask for a new one. My years of not giving up, of getting practice in on being a roadie in a fine machine, had finally paid off by leading me to him and Normaine—Angels waiting in a desert.

    Normaine and I were moving steadily toward this moment in time from the moment we met. I remembered the yowling woman sitting in her gorgeous pink Cadillac. I realized I'd driven thousands of miles to get to her. It was no accident we were here.

    I didn't know I needed the company of another woman who'd dealt with a true Monster of her own, without help from God or country or anyone else, to do this. Morally evolved humans? Were we? Ha! It was time to take a tour and introduce some new things to each other.

    The old familiar things I'd held on to forever and the worn-out mask clattered to the floor and shattered. I tottered over to the table and sat down in a chair across from the amazing warrior woman who been forced by God and law to kill her Monster. But he wasn't completely dead to her-yet.

I got up and went to the door and looked outside. Esmerelda was gone. Geena was gone. She'd left before. She'd seen me get so full in my internal being that I was forced to let it out. No baking soda made could ever cure an emotional bellyache.

She'd watched me stop strangers over the years and give them odd suggestions that saved their lives or restored their health if they took them. Some of them laughed at me, others got offended, but all of them avoided me. Some of them needed life to be hard and painful. But a few of them listened and did the silly, painless things that made perfect sense when viewed in a certain way, and were healed. But they stayed away from me, too. I was only led to help certain people. I didn't get to pick and choose who.

Now it was time for me and Normaine to help heal each other. Geena disappeared so she wouldn't be a part of it, because she knew her father was my Monster as well as hers. I looked at Normaine. She was staring out the dining room window, numb and wordless. I sat down and started talking. The words poured out. I glanced down at the old, broken mask pieces lying on the floor. It was okay to speak this now. I told her what I'd never told anyone else.

"I met the monster when I was seventeen. I was a schoolgirl without a home. There was an ice storm. I dropped a bag of groceries I just picked up for the old people I was living with, and they spilled out on the ice. I grabbed a parking meter to keep from sliding into the icy street and under the front of his car. He stopped and got out and helped me pick up the groceries and offered me a ride home. He stood there, grinning at me in the cold winter sun, short, blond, and wiry. He was wearing a cowboy hat. I hate cowboys to this day, especially cowboy hats."

She didn't answer or look at me. I shrugged. It didn't matter.

"It was the era of the western on television, and he knew that people believed that cowboys were good guys. His eyes were blue and cold as ice, calculating, and watchful. Everything in me warned me to not have anything to do with him—there was something bad wrong with him. But when you have nobody, you'll date the devil. So I took the ride he offered. Then he started following me around. I worked a weekly babysitting job I made survival money at, and I paid fifteen dollars a month to stay with some old folks. I had to quit school to go to work. My family never came near me. A brother and a sister were glad I was gone. They spread filthy lies about me all over town. I was at a dead-end and too young to know what to do. And there was nobody to ask."

I shuddered.

"A whole bunch of people's loud voices have insisted for most of my life that the Monster I lived with was a good man. Those people deliberately used every means to bury my voice, to bury the truth of what he is. But there were others, amen, that knew better.

Regardless of any of them, today I am telling on him, and I am heard and believed, at last. The truth has risen up through the lies, cruelty, and denial, up past the mask."

I had Normaine's attention now. She was staring at me. I kept talking. I couldn't stop once I got started.

"He stalked me and kept getting into every corner of my life that he could. I was dumb, and he was sly as a fox. He was in his twenties, way older than me, a mama's boy, evil and petted. He lived at home with his mother."

I sneered at the word "Mother."

She nodded.

I said, "He hid who he really was and worked me for a couple of months. By then, I was riding around in his car with him. One day, he took me out to a field outside of town and forced himself on me. He told me I had asked for it and drove me back to town and dumped me off at my girlfriend's apartment. I was a bloody mess. She took care of me. She wanted me to report him to the cops, but I was too ashamed. Besides, like your man, the cops were friends of his."

We grabbed each other and wobbled over to the living room sofa. There were large red and blue floral throw pillows at each end. We held each other and touched foreheads and cried and let the scared pieces that stayed hid forever in our darkest places step out into the light with our words. That was their safe passage, at last. They poured out. At other times, they crawled out or tiredly whispered their way out.

"He came to my babysitting job and took me in the bathroom and closed the door and held me up against the wall, and forced himself on me. I lost that job because of it. I was so stressed, I missed a period and thought I was pregnant and married him. Every intuition I owned, every part of my being, didn't want that marriage. Even the angels cried out against it.

But I was mad at God and scared and stubborn, and there was no place to turn for a young girl, so I did it. But I wasn't pregnant. The night we got married, he locked the door after his friends left and told me he was going to show me who the boss was. And he did just that."

Our words went on, intermingling sentences that waiting to come out in the open.

"He choked me."

"He drove on the wrong side of the road and ran four cars in the ditch to scare me because I got a haircut without asking him."

"He got on top of me and threatened to kill me and our unborn baby."

"He forced himself on me three weeks before the baby was due, and I started hemorrhaging and that's why the baby was born early."

"He told me not to leave the house while he was gone, that he'd be watching me and know if I left."

Horror after horror poured out of us as we fought our way with halting words past the thousands of taboos the outraged people that had stood for them and against us had put in place.

Most sexual predators are men. That has remained true down through time. Sexual predators have patterns that have stayed the same throughout history. Their victim's stories, if they ever get heard, all describe similar patterns of victimization. When people look the other way, sexual predators just keep exploring new and worse ways of exploiting innocents. There were many people that protected our predators from justice by refusing to look at the truth. I never liked or understood the women and men who knew and still protected them.

Yet we had loved some of the people that took up for the predators even though there were no protectors of us among any of them. We were called liars. We went to court and lost. No family stood by us. Odd thing was, many of them were assaulted, too, but put on like they were shocked and called us liars.

In that trailer, parked in a field by a national forest in Wyoming, we gained painful inches of ground with our words because we'd finally found somebody strong enough to share our truths with. Someone who believed us.

"He set in the doorway of my hospital room and wouldn't move and moaned and said he was having sympathy pains every time the nurses wanted to check on me. They thought he was endearing at first, then a nurse was looking past him into the room when I dropped my leg, and she saw my top sheet get soaked with blood instantly.

I was so weak I couldn't talk. I was still hemorrhaging from his attack on us hours earlier, and he knew it. He wanted me and the baby to die. I knew what he was up to, but I was too weak to speak.

The nurse tried to get past him, but he wouldn't let her through the doorway where he was sitting on the floor. She ran to the nurse's station and put in an alarm, and the security guards came, and he made them pick him up and carry him out. He was giving us more time to die.

They moved me to a gurney and wheeled me away. I asked the green-eyed nurse looking down on me if I was going to die. I said the words in slow motion, and she said no, you have to live and take care of your baby. They told me later that I didn't have much time left, and it was a good thing my leg dropped just the way it did."

I wept bitterly. The tears felt like ancient battery acid running down my face.

"They wouldn't let him see us, thank God! We had two heavenly days without the Monster. But then we had to go home with him. He had to meet us at the front door of the hospital to pick us up because of the way he had acted. They'd figured out real quick what he was up to.

I worked and paid the bills while he stayed home and played at being a cowboy and molested everything that moved. It was years before I realized that besides all the bad things he was, he was also a child molester.

That's when I started making plans to get away from him. I couldn't tell anybody because a lot of people saw him as being a good guy because he wore a white cowboy hat and had a line of talk. Never black for him. He wouldn't wear it."

I sat back, sniffling, waiting for Normaine's verdict. I expected for her to somehow blame me. Everyone always blames the mother instead of the predator. Instead, she jumped to her feet.

"That dirty bastard! He should have had his balls cut off when he was born! He shouldn't have been allowed to live! Damn his fat little dark smilin' mother!"

She ran to the kitchen, grabbed a long butcher knife out of a drawer, and rushed the red chair beside the sofa. She began stabbing it with all her might, as though it was him. I was startled at first, but it looked good to me. Made sense. It was the thing to do. I ran to the kitchen and grabbed a knife and went to work on the other end of the sofa.

Normaine and I called our Monsters every bad name we knew and worse. We upgraded our cussing abilities while accumulating the most ventilation we could on our Monsters. We worked over the pretty new living room sofa, matching upholstered chairs, and everything we could find. We hung the bastards using the living room curtains and deballed them using pinking shears, scissors, and the placemats from the kitchen table. Normaine shouted.

"You beat me your last time, you bastard! Took out my teeth and got me looking in two directions forever! But I can still see, and you can't, can you? I'm glad you're dead! Now you can't hurt anyone else! I'm glad I killed you!"

It took a long time to rid ourselves of the poison we'd held inside for so many years. After we emptied ourselves out, we wound down and eyed each other. I felt thin and clean in a way I never did before. I could see Normaine did too. We both looked around. "Oops!" we both shouted and laughed with pure joy and the relief of an ancient burden gone.

"We should feel SO bad!" Normaine yelled and laughed.

"Yeah!" I shouted back, laughing.

"But we don't!" we yelled in unison, like cheerleaders.

The sofa and chair were stripped down to tattered wood frames, and the windows were bare-but not broken. Busted dishes lay scattered on the floor, and a frozen chicken lay mutilated and tenderized between the dining room and kitchen. It was the closest thing to human flesh we could find to destroy.

The laughing ended abruptly as I looked at Normaine and one of the most knowing, painful moments of stark acceptance I would ever have flooded over me. I plopped down on the floor and howled.

"No matter what I do, I'll never trust a man again! I'm too scared! I'll always be too scared!"

"Me too!" Normaine howled, falling in a heap on the floor. "That's why I can't marry Eddy, even though I want to so bad!"

"And I will hate cowboys forever!" I wailed.

We both began sobbing our hurtful way through the words it took to tell the truth of what our future would be now. Many of our nightmares had been healed, but our dreams of being with a fine, nice man lay shattered. No matter how much we healed, a long, lonesome road lay ahead of us, one without the companionship of a good man.

No man would ever have our back. We couldn't let them, for we were too wounded, too crazy, too scarred by the Monsters we had to deal with. In a way, our bad men had won. We were theirs forever. The beauty of what could have been was gone. All hope left us.

"No more dreams," Normaine said brokenly.

I nodded.

"No more men," I said.

"Normaine, we're gonna' grow old together and we don't have any money to insulate our sorry asses so we're gonna' end up in state run nursing homes, warehoused like all the other old poor people living in tiny rooms with bad food and crazy inmates."

I stopped and thought about it.

"Maybe the overload of drugs they always give old people might compensate for the loss of freedom? Kind of like in some movies I saw years ago? We'll die, drugged out of our minds and alone!"

She looked at me blankly. After a while, she said, "Dumbass!"

I got up and went to the door and looked out.

"Normaine, let's carry the sofa and chair outside and torch 'em! We can pretend they're all the people that stopped us from having a good life and a good man. It'll be a funeral pyre. A real cremation!"

"I'd be happy to fry their sorry asses to ashes!" she shouted and grinned at me.

We dug a hole in the front yard, carried the broken sofa and chair out, piled them in it, and lit them up. Then we added the slashed living room curtains, broken dishes, bent knives, and the crooked potato masher.

I stood before the fire and threw a piece of a kitchen dish in. I have to admit that I am partial to rituals. Solemnly I shouted, "Let the Monster's mother fry in Hell for petting him and looking the other way, and his oaf of a father who taught him to molest, fry in the hottest fires in Hell!"

An empty can followed the broken dish as I announced, "May the Spawn of Satan, the Monster's father, who molested his own girls and taught the monster everything he knows, and sent him out to do more evil than he ever did, fry in hell double twice!"

I shuddered as a new thought hit me. Even though the Monster wouldn't leave where he lived, he might send someone after us.

Normaine stepped forward and yelled a bunch of words in her Native language and threw a full bottle of whiskey into the fire. It broke. Red flames flared up.

"It's a Molotov cocktail!" she explained happily. I looked up at the thousands of stars twinkling in the black sky above us. Hope surrounded us, for an angel was attached to every star.

"It sure is!" I yelled and picked up another dish.

When everything was burned, and our funeral pyre was dead black ashes, we climbed into Esmerelda and headed for town. We parked beside the Merc' and climbed the wide plank steps leading into the cathedral size, empty interior of the hotel. I rang the bell on the check-in desk, and an older woman appeared. The pleasant look disappeared from her face. A careful one replaced it.

"Yes? Can I help you?"

"I think my daughter Geena may have checked in here tonight. Can you tell me what room she is in?"

She pored over her ledger, not looking at us. "No, I can't. But I can call her to come down here."

"Would you do that?"

She called a number and talked for a minute, her back to us.

"She will be right down."

Her voice turned sympathetic as she looked us up and down.

"You've both got black stuff all over you. Did you get caught in a fire?"

Normaine rolled her eyes over at me as though she had just seen me for the first time. She removed the unlit cigarette dangling from her lips and sent me a wide, toothless smile.

"Uhh...Yes!" I said.

"Where?"

Well, we were burning trash out in the back yard," I hastily improvised.

We were saved from more suspicious questions by Geena's regal appearance. She walked down the stairs like a queen, taking her time. She strolled over to us with a proprietary air.

"Madam, I will see to it that my mother and her friend are much more presentable the next time they inhabit your formidable establishment. Come, ladies," she said to us. "It's time for your bubble baths."

I drew Normaine away from the front desk. I could see that she'd stood just about all she could stand. We climbed the stairs quickly before her mutter could rise into a shout.

"We burnt up a bunch of assholes and now we're taking bubble baths?"

Geena marched us into her hotel room. Normaine and I sniffed and looked around. Something smelled wonderful. Then we saw the huge pizza repining in an open box on the coffee table in front of a rundown, ugly brown sofa. A sagging double bed filled the rest of the room. I could see past it into the tiny bathroom on the other side. The whole room was brown—worn brown carpet and walls, a brown bedspread, and the usual generic painting above the bed.

Normaine and I plopped down on the ugly brown sofa, grabbed slices of pizza, and began to shove them into our mouths. We inhaled the loaded pizza in whale-sized bites. It was so heavy I needed to lift each slice with both hands. Geena watched us, shaking her head, hands on her hips. Her long, brown, straight hair swung side to side, squeaky clean and shining.

"When you two finish eating, I want you to take bubble baths. I'll go down and get clean clothes out of the car. You didn't burn the trailer down or hurt anyone, did you?" We shook our heads guiltily, our mouths filled with pizza.

A bottle of expensive bubble bath sat on the edge of the tub in the bathroom. There was a fancy jar of rose-scented, pink skin cream by the sink. Beside the jar sat a box of chocolate-covered cherries. Geena had been shopping. I wondered how much money she'd spent. After we bathed and put on pajamas, we piled into the double bed.

"You okay?" Normaine asked me.

"Yep. You?'

"Yep."

Chapter Ten

Come on honey chile'
we gots ta' git' a move on"
rise and shine!
time's a wastin'
sun be a' settin'
'fore we gone!

We fell asleep. Geena checked us out the next morning while we waited in Esmerelda and the Merc'. She said she might need to come back here someday, and she wasn't going to let us ruin it for her. She insisted on driving the Merc'. I rode shotgun without complaint.

I figured now was probably a good time to explain a few things to her before we got back to the trailer. Like how there was not much furniture left on the place. Or dishes. Or beer. Or placemats, potato mashers, forks, and especially knives. And how there was a charred pit of ashes in the front yard now. But I couldn't bring myself to do it. Somewhere inside of me, I knew this wasn't over yet. There were still life-changing decisions to be made. So I waited. Normaine waited, too.

Geena turned the Merc into the driveway and parked it. She got out, closed the door, and surveyed the ruins of the fire with the little wisp of smoke still curling up from the black ashes in the pit.

She never said a word. She just went to the trunk of the Merc', opened it, and took out the huge container of bubble bath and her sunglasses. She put her sunglasses on and carried the bubble bath into the trailer. The sunglasses were a clear message to leave her alone, she needed her own time and space to think about what we had done. Wisely, we waited outside. After a while, she opened the trailer door.

"This is not going to interfere with me eating a large baked potato with butter later today at the Longhorn Restaurant in town."

After making her statement, the door closed again. Normaine and I wandered over to the fire and poked the ashes into a smaller and neater pile. Conclusions and decisions would set in. We'd just have to wait for them.

After a while, Geena opened the trailer door.

"You two need to get in here and clean up your mess. Right now."

We swept and washed the floor and tidied up. Then we made a list of the things we'd destroyed. Humbly, list in hand, I asked Geena if she would go with us and pick everything out, new and cheap but nice. She stared at me contemplatively through her black sunglasses for a minute.

"Okay."

We headed for town. By the end of the day the trailer was back to a different kind of normal. We went to the local Day Mart and a couple other places where we solemnly trailed Geena around while she picked out things Normaine paid for, using the money Eddy sent her. The new plates were square instead of round, a gentle blue with shiny black edges. The potato masher was now a red-handled antique. The drinking glasses were tall and turquoise, a match for the tropical colored placemats covering the knife marks on the dining room table. Large, colorful bean bag chairs replaced the burnt living room furniture, with round white plastic end tables and a matching coffee table flanking them. Wheat-colored curtains covered the windows of the living room, and a tiny, red portable radio poured soft music into the air.

Normaine and I spent the next two days wandering in and out of the trailer. Mostly out, because of Geena being in the trailer. She watched us with an impassive face, ate a lot of popcorn, listened to her radio, and read.

"A flowerbed of zinnias would have looked pretty over there," Normaine said wistfully, pointing to a corner of the yard. At the end of the second day she gave up the ghost, so to speak, sat down at the kitchen table, and began to write.

Before she got started, I needed to know.

"Who did you call?"

She pulled the scraps of white paper out of her pocket and tossed them on the table. They fell slow, like lazy white snowflakes, and lay there.

"All of them. Relatives. Friends. The number of the store and Eddy and one friend are all that's left. Eddy will be here in a couple of days. Go away. I gotta' finish this letter and get the hell out of here."

She agonized over her letter to Eddy, changing it again and again, folding and refolding it, not asking what we thought or to read it. When she was done, she folded it and placed it under a rock on the kitchen table. Then she announced, "I'm leaving

Esmerelda here. Take me back to the store in the morning."

I gave the letter a longing glance. I wanted to read it, but we just looked at each other. She couldn't have Eddie, and I couldn't have Cowboy Johnson. Letters. Whatever. Nothing would make any difference. That was all there was to it. "Okay." I sighed and turned away.

The next morning, we loaded up the Merc'. Normaine put Esmerelda's top up, rolled up her windows, and locked her doors. She hid the car and house keys. We left, riding slow through the early morning air, steeped in misery, headed south again.

We spent all day on the road. We stopped at a roadside park and slept a few hours that night. We rode on through the next day and spent another night in another rest area. Early the third morning, we started out again, still moving slow. There was no reason to hurry now. It was over for both of us. I bought boxes of chocolates and Kleenex for us at a gas station. Geena was with me. She snorted and tossed a big bag of fresh oranges and a banana on the countertop.

"You need vitamin C more than anything else, Mama!"

Geena played music on her little red battery-operated radio. She kept it low, and it stayed a background noise for our misery. She ignored us and ate and read and napped, stretched out like a young, tawny cat in the back seat.

Normaine and I were solar flares that were burnt out, and there wasn't a damn thing we could do about it. It was inevitable. I could see that now.

Cosmic. We were at this place in our journey. We had the vote, but not a choice. It was supposed to go this way. We needed to open our hearts so the mournful, cosmic cellular debris could be released. Which might take the rest of our lives.

We slept in another roadside park that night. We were awake at daybreak. We were almost home. We used the restrooms and got on our way. Around noon, the roads started looking familiar. We were getting close to the store.

About five miles out, I slowed down, and Normaine got out of the Merc' and walked alongside. She showed no surprise at the fact that I was coasting at almost zero miles an hour without even knowing it.

Finally, I realized what I was doing and looked back in the mirror. Geena was biting her fingernails desperately, her face strained and nervous. Remorse swept over me. I gunned the motor, forgetting all about Normaine. She shouted, and I had to back up.

"Dumbass!' she yelled at me and climbed in the Merc'.

"Yeah!" Geena shouted.

It was only a few more miles to Cowboy Johnson's place, but I couldn't take any more. I pulled over and put the Merc' in park. I got out and started walking, leaving the door open and the motor running. In a few minutes, Geena and Normaine cruised by real slow. Geena was driving. They didn't look at me or offer me a ride.

Since Cain killed Abel back in the Bible days, people have been asking what causes one person to be good and another person to be bad. There are many explanations, but none have ever changed the pattern. It's just the way things are. People, since time out of mind, for some reason, have always loved the bad ones. It was the reality of human life. I looked around. The need to deal with the Dark to assure myself that I was made of Light passed farther from me with each grain of sand that absorbed my Shadow and tickled my nose out here in this desert. A sort of calm began to fill me.

I waved, and Geena backed up. I crawled in the backseat. Before long, we cruised off the two-lane blacktop, bounced across the sand, and jerked to a stop beside Cowboy Johnson's former church, now a gas station and grocery store. Geena parked the Merc' beside his El Camino and shut the engine off.

We sat in frozen silence until Cowboy Johnson ambled out of the store and down the front porch steps. He took his time, coming to a stop not far from us. He was wearing a purple tee-shirt tucked into his jeans, cowboy boots, and a Panama hat. I stared at him, stunned. He was wearing a Panama hat instead of his usual cowboy hat. Why?

Geena shoved the driver's door of the Merc' open, and like an ungainly young Bambi, brown and freckled, she scrambled out. With thin legs wobbling, she ran to Cowboy Johnson, leaped into his arms, and laid her head on his chest. He smoothed her hair and glared at us.

"I suppose you two forgot there was a child with you when you were doing whatever it was you decided to do."

It was not a question. It was a statement.

"And I suppose you made this wise old soul child take care of you two at the expense of herself. And I bet you two thought that was okay."

His eyes were chips of icy green granite. I stared at the stranger in the Panama hat, scolding me about my daughter. Why, he didn't even know us!

"No! No! You don't understand!" Normaine shouted.

"She wasn't in on it! She drove to the motel in town and stayed there while we killed the sofa and chair and burned them. We stabbed them to death, and it felt real good!"

He stared at her for a moment, speechless.

"Then I gave them bubble baths," Geena announced solemnly from his arms, looking up at him. A moment of silence passed. He looked from us to her and back. Finally, he gave up.

"Women!" he muttered.

He turned on his heel and headed into the store, carrying Geena as if she held only the weight of a pure white feather. We climbed out of the Merc' and trudged after him, single file, like those damn ducks again.

Cowboy Johnson carried Geena back into his lair and set her down on the Hideous Green Sofa. We started to sit down by her, but he glared at us like that was a really bad idea, so we sat down at his ugly table.

He tossed his Panama hat on the chest of drawers in the corner. I noticed his straight brown hair was dented where the hat was. He disappeared into the store and came back with milk and cookies for Geena. He sat down beside her and began feeding her cookies and giving her sips of milk and talking to her in soft murmurs. She leaned against him and ate and drank. When she was finished, he pulled her to her feet and guided her to the screen door.

"You know how to use a travel shower?" She looked at him, puzzled. "Okay. At the end of the back porch..." he pointed left, "there is a small building I call the shower room." She giggled. "In it is a tank of water sitting up on a shelf. From that tank runs a garden hose. That hose has settings that allow for the water flow to go fast or slow. Use too much, too fast, and you'll run out of water. Just keep an eye on the water level and go slow. It is set exactly where I want it to be for me, so you don't have to do anything except release the valve. Shut it off while you shampoo and soap down. Turn it back on when you're ready to rinse. Go get clean clothes to change into and take them with you to the shower. There is shampoo, soap, and towels already out there."

She nodded and pranced out the door, glancing back at us. I could tell she thought we needed a good spanking. We stared down at the tabletop like it was the most interesting thing we'd ever seen. There has never been a woman born who has a baby who hasn't at some time felt the guilt of being a bad mother. And Normaine and I were both mothers. He studied us for a minute.

"Why don't you two get yourselves settled into the trailer and take showers when Geena is done?"

He was kicking us out. He turned on his heel and stalked into the front of the store. Meekly, we got up and trailed out the back door, across the porch, down the steps and around the side of the store to the Merc'. We climbed in and rode silently across the sandy distance between the little pink trailer and the store. I parked the Merc' under the tin roof and got out and stood there a minute, remembering the beautiful Esmerelda we left behind.

Normaine went behind the trailer and came back carrying a pair of faded blue plastic chairs. We sat in the shade under the roof and watched the back porch of the store.

We watched Geena cross the porch and go into the store wearing clean clothes. I looked at Normaine. She was greasy-haired, covered with ashes and streaks of dirt and she stunk like a skunk at high noon. I got the feeling that I did too.

Normaine rummaged around in the trunk of the Merc' and found some clean clothes. Then she wandered toward the back of the store, zigzagging across the sand, while I watched Cowboy Johnson carry more water out to the shower. She arrived there just after he filled up the tank again. Normaine always operated on what she called "Indian Time."

The wood "shower room" was a sturdy, six-foot square of blue painted board walls with a couple of feet of airspace at the top and the bottom. A small shade roof overhung the top.

The used water was caught in a large rectangular plastic basin covering the floor of the shower. When it came my turn, I stepped into the basin and turned the shower on. A thin stream of water came out. I got wet fast as I could and turned it off.

I shampooed and washed, turned it back on, and rinsed. When I was done, I hung up the towels and pulled on fresh underwear, a white tee-shirt, and a pair of thin, stretchy black Capri pants. I crossed the back porch, opened the screen door and the solid door, and stepped inside, closing the door behind me because the air conditioner was on.

Geena was sound asleep on his ugly cot, sprawled out with her hair covering her like a brown blanket. Normaine lay sprawled on an air mattress next to the cot. The sliding glass doors to the store were closed. The curtains were pulled. The lights were off. The air conditioner was blowing cool air around the closed room.

On the table lay a sandwich on a plate. I ate the cheese sandwich and drank the water sitting beside it. Then I lay down on the mattress beside Normaine and thought about Cowboy Johnson. Did he sew as well as make sandwiches? Did he sell Avon? Or Tupperware? Encyclopedias? Give survival classes in desert living? Where did the Panama hat come from? Most important of all, where did his cowboy hat disappear to? I fell asleep.

In a while, I woke up. I didn't sleep long. I stood up and tiptoed to the curtains and peeked through them into the store. Cowboy Johnson, that Sage of Sandwiches, sat with his back to me at the counter that ran the length of the store. Now he was wearing a baseball cap. I wondered what the logo on it read. On the counter beside him was an adding machine and a calculator. Stacks of files lay nearby. I turned away, padded to the back door, and opened it. A wave of heat hit me in the face. I closed it hastily.

I studied Normaine and Geena. They were sleeping the kind of sleep angels allow humans to sleep when they've done enough.

I sighed. Here we were again. Back in the former church turned gas station, hanging out with the Earl of Spam Sandwiches. Three women hanging on for dear life to the only good man they knew. I shook my head sorrowfully—three of us needy unto death for a good word and a little respect from a man. We were pitiful. One iota of emotional support from the Lord of Beers and a hot Spam sandwich won us over quicker than a hairy man proposing marriage on a hot, sweaty Friday night in a backwoods bar reeking of stale beer with a band wailing a loud, lonesome country song in the background.

Geena and I were back in the same desert again, still hanging out with the Spam Man and Normaine. God help us! I lay down beside Normaine and closed my eyes.

When I woke up again, Normaine was still asleep, spread out over most of the mattress, snoring loud enough to raise the dead. Geena was gone. I got up, went to the drapes, and peeked through them again. Geena was sitting on a stool next to Cowboy Johnson, eating a strawberry ice cream cone.

The end of the cone looked as sharp as a number two pencil point. It looked crispy and delicious, like those vanilla wafer cookies that crunch into nothingness and melt in your mouth. The ice cream was beautifully rounded in the center, surrounded by edges and remnants of more pink ice cream.

When I was growing up, store-bought ice cream came in one gallon blocks encased in heavy paper squares in strawberry, chocolate, vanilla, or Neapolitan. That was it.

A frozen block of happiness rushed home to be eaten before it melted, off plates, bowls, or if you were socially adept, placed in cut glasses using a real ice cream scoop, with the leftover ice cream stored in a Tupperware container in your freezer.

I flashed back to the few times my mother stood over the table on a hot summer day in the afternoon, slicing thin slabs of quick melting Neapolitan ice cream onto plates for us. Her smile always said that this was a peak moment, one she would recall with pleasure. In those moments, she got to feed her children delight with life instead of misery and dark futures. Everyone's troubles were suspended while the ice cream lasted. I turned away from the memory. The happiness never lasted long enough.

Faint strains of music began drifting through the closed curtains. I watched Geena and Cowboy Johnson sorting through a stack of familiar seventy-eight R.P.M. records. Records from the trunk of the Merc'. I discovered them in the attic of one of the old houses we lived in with the Monster. I hid them from him so he couldn't carry them over to his greedy, fat little mother like he did every other fine thing I ever got my hands on.

I craned my neck and saw the edge of a Victrola in the corner to the left of them. My powers of observation had deserted me completely. I never noticed the Victrola before. Of course, I wasn't looking for one. I ruminated on my ignorance, trying to find an answer. To anything. It didn't take long to give it up.

Spaghetti. The only reliable answer. The only one I could count on. Spaghetti was the one thing I made every time Geena and I escaped from the Monster. We ate spaghetti with ketchup while I paid the bills until he caught up with us again.

Spaghetti meant freedom. I rummaged through Cowboy Johnson's cupboards without mercy until I found spaghetti noodles and Chef Boyardee Spaghetti Sauce. I retrieved butter and Parmesan cheese from the refrigerator. The Parmesan was in a shaker.

A beautiful mound of hamburger covered with foil repined in the refrigerator. I pulled it out and studied it. I could fry it up with diced onions, garlic, and add it to the spaghetti sauce. Or I could make meatballs. I thought about it, then placed the hamburger back in the refrigerator. Meat with spaghetti would indicate something else entirely. It would mean that we were a family enjoying no financial troubles, just eating spaghetti together, with our needs already met.

I found the biggest pot in the kitchen, filled it with water and set it on the stove to boil. I looked around. No bread. I slid one of the glass doors open, shoved the curtain aside and breezed past Cowboy Johnson and Geena. Porgy and Bess was playing. I grabbed a long loaf of bread and hurried back to the kitchen. I made garlic butter, then buttered the bread and filled the bubbling pot with as much spaghetti as it would hold. I opened half dozen cans of Chef Boyardee Spaghetti Sauce and poured the sauce into an empty pot to heat.

When I was done, I strode over to the mattress where Normaine slept, spread out like she was running a race, black hair everywhere. I studied her a minute. Her eyes were closed, her mouth was open, and she was snoring like Godzilla. Her nose ran in at least three directions from being broken so many times. She had a permanent cauliflower ear and a couple of scars from cuts running through her eyebrow, proceeding up into her scalp. She was exceedingly beautiful and beat up, like me.

I nudged her with my foot. I didn't want to get too close, she might sock me or something. I understood that completely. She mumbled something and turned over.

"Get the hell up, Normaine!" I shouted. "Come on, get up! You don't get to sleep your life away, you hear me?"

She didn't move until I said there was spaghetti cooking, and I needed her help with it. Kind of a universal thing, I guess, us women and spaghetti. She sat up and yawned and grinned at me.

"Gotta' make a pee run."

She stood up and stretched and made her way out the back door. I opened the curtains over the little window above the sink, turned off the air conditioner, and toasted the bread. By the time I finished, Normaine shouldered in beside me and took over the spaghetti pot. She found the strainer and put it in the sink. Then she studied the spaghetti.

"We're gonna' have to divide it into at least two batches. Maybe more."

I nodded. She didn't say anything about me overdoing it, and I appreciated that. I stirred the sauce and covered it with a lid. Then I carried the bread to the table while she hunted up bowls and other containers. We oiled a bunch of the spaghetti down and set it out to cool. Then we filled the biggest bowl in the kitchen with spaghetti and hauled it to the table. The sauce went into two large glass bowls. I strode to the sliding glass doors and slid them open.

"It's ready!" I bellowed.

A couple minutes later, Geena strolled in, holding four frosty sodas in her hands. Cowboy Johnson followed her, holding four Pabst Blue Ribbon's in his hands. They set the bottles on the table with satisfying clinks. Cowboy Johnson pushed the curtains and sliding glass doors open so he could keep an eye on the store.

Geena and Cowboy Johnson eyed the bowls and pots of spaghetti sitting everywhere. They seemed overwhelmed by the vast amount of spaghetti, but to their credit, they didn't say one word. Bread, spaghetti, and sauce were all that was on the table. I was happy with that.

We sat down to eat spaghetti off the fancy white plates I discovered in Cowboy Johnson's cupboards. He took off his cap and laid it by his plate. On the front of it was a New York Yankees logo. We finished one big bowl of spaghetti and a small one sitting by the sink. All of us knew what this meal meant.

"Mine was chicken noodle soup and crackers. Watered down until you barely knew what it was," Cowboy Johnson volunteered.

"Mine was light bread and whatever I could find to put on it. Mustard or ketchup samples from diners or stores," Normaine said.

"Mine was spaghetti with ketchup. I bought a bottle of ketchup and watered it down and poured it over spaghetti," I said.

Geena nodded but didn't add anything to our culinary revelations. We sat there, bathed in the comradeship that survivors share.

"Where you from, Cowboy Johnson?" Geena finally asked him.

He grinned at her. "Northern California. Grew up on the beach. I'm here because I wanted to get just as far away from the beach as I could, at least in terms of Elements."

Geena gasped in delight. "Oh, my God! Wow! I've never even seen the ocean!" She looked at me, accusingly.

"They have beaches up north, but I never got to go to one."

I shrugged. "Hey, what can I say?"

Was this the perfect time to explain that we were survivors who'd not yet lived? I thought not. I shrugged again. At least we went to California.

"How about you?" he asked, looking at me.

"Up North. Who cares where?"

"Did you like it?"

"It gets too cold."

"I grew up on a Reservation in Dakota territory. I was sure glad to see the last of it. Too cold and too mean," Normaine said.

Wasn't much more to say. Normaine and I washed the dishes and packed the extra spaghetti into the depths of the refrigerator. Cowboy Johnson and Geena wandered back into the store and changed records on the Victrola. Strains of music floated through the air. Then the bell above the front door of the store chimed, interrupting the spell we were all under.

"We're going to the library tomorrow to look for books on music," Geena announced, coming into the back, sitting down at the table.

Reality hit me quick and hard. I stared at her. What day was this? What hour? Hell, I didn't even know. Geena wasn't in school because it was summer. What was I doing? We were supposed to be on the road, finding a place to settle down so Geena could go to back to school in the fall and I could work at some factory or grocery store. Living with the Monster never opened any avenues of further education, other than what he personally taught. I couldn't get a good paying job that required a normal education.

"Okay." I didn't know what else to say.

Normaine was back on the mattress, snoring softly. We were both worn out. I pulled the curtains, closed the sliding doors, and laid down beside Normaine. I didn't want to, but I felt like a giant weight of inertia was suddenly flattening me.

Chapter Eleven

Papa had a cave
we none knew about
he kept it to himself
and never let himself out

I slept and dreamed of my dad and the few good years after he quit drinking when he began to make atonement for at least some of the lousy things he put us through before he quit drinking.

He planted himself in an old green armchair and suffered like hell the summer he quit. He stayed white as a sheet and held onto the stuffed arms of his ugly green chair like it was an island keeping him from drowning.

I was a kid when he quit, maybe nine or a little older. I learned early on to stay away from him, but I walked by the doors of the silent living room he set in every day, so I could get a glimpse of him suffering. Suited me. He had it coming.

In the fall, he got a job working midnights in a factory. Then he bought a lawnmower and started keeping the yard up. Next, he started chopping wood for the winter, driving to other people's places and turning their unwanted, fallen trees into firewood to keep us warm, something he never cared about doing before. He stacked the wood in neat rows beside the outside cellar doors leading down to the dirt basement at the back of the house. The wood furnace was in the basement, and my mother stored her canned goods down there. Us kids never thought about going down in the basement because it was his territory, just like his car was.

Over the next few years, he built a sturdy chicken coop out by the back fence and added quarters at one end for two pigs. He planted grapevines and sweet peas at the edge of his big garden. Morning glories bloomed all through the garden, intertwined with the tomatoes, climbing the rows of corn.

He did these good things, but he would not talk to us or try to protect us from our brothers or from life. I figured he'd lost his backbone (or something lower) and his voice when he quit the booze.

I ate the food he steadily provided. I strolled through the rows of golden corn and plump red tomatoes and perfectly shaped cucumbers and gorgeous pink marbled fall beans. I helped string green beans and can tomatoes. But I never truly accepted him as the provider of these things until the day I accidentally came across the frog prince he kept in his basement sanctuary.

The Frog Prince was one of his secrets. One day when nobody else was around, I wandered around the back of the house and saw his frog. It was sitting in the sun on his big square bottom shovel, and it was so big it filled the whole shovel. The frog was green and white with leathery-looking wrinkled skin lying in folds and puddles around it. It stared back at me with black and green pop eyes that didn't blink.

It was so big I didn't realize it was just a frog, so I jumped back a couple of steps and stared at the monstrous thing, trying to figure out whether to try to kill it or run. I'd never seen anything like it in the world. I picked up a rock and hefted it in my hand. Just then, my dad climbed up the cellar steps and spoke in a low voice to me.

"Now, don't even think about hurtin' my frog. He keeps me company in the basement. I set him out ever now and then so he can get a little sun. So you jist' leave him alone. I'll take him back downstairs in a few minutes."

He waited until I put the rock down. I leaned over and looked a little closer.

"Don't git' too close," he warned. "He's not used to anybody but me."

I stepped back a safe distance from it and my dad. I already knew his temper. Because I sensed things that other people didn't, I suddenly knew that my father worked with the Elementals; they liked him, and this Frog Prince was there to keep him company, to honor him for some reason. The Elementals had their reasons, and I knew it was none of my business what he earned from them, but I didn't like him being favored. The reasons would mostly remain a mystery, anyway. That's how the Elementals worked.

After a while, from my wise and distant position, I announced, "He's a Frog Prince. Maybe the biggest one in the whole world. Lucky you got him. I won't tell."

He nodded and picked up the shovel with the Frog Prince on it, carried it down the cellar steps, and back into the dark, private Earth domain they shared.

We never spoke of the Frog Prince again, and I never told anyone about it. Since he never invited anyone to go into his cellar, no one else ever knew.

For the first time, I realized that my dad lived with his own kind of incurable loneliness, too.

That day, my thinking about him changed. From that day on, I knew he was well regarded by the Elementals. He worked deep down in the coal mines back in the mountains, and for years, he worked midnights tempering metals in a furnace.

He stayed little and wiry and quiet after he quit the drink. Gone was the noise and stench of his drunken friends. He became addicted to work instead of booze. He worked constantly and stayed away from people. He developed just a couple friendships with non-drinking friends. He drove through life carefully in his good cars and never went near a big city; he couldn't navigate them.

Even though my father lost his backbone and his voice when he quit drinking, he went to work, making the glue that would have held a fine family together. He made a big garden, made enough money, and provided a good home and more.

He did all he could, but the glue could not be accepted without his apology and protection, and he wouldn't give either. He expected his hard work and actions to speak for him, but the older kids were grown and gone by the time he quit drinking, and the younger ones just didn't have enough years left to understand the goodness of what he was finally offering. It would take me until I was very old to understand the immense amount of work my father did on our behalf and the beauty he unfolded for us in our daily lives, and the failure he felt in the last years of his life. There have never been any answers to this kind of thing that I know of. None that would comfort either side of the learning.

I woke up to the smell of fresh coffee and frying potatoes. Normaine was still asleep. I looked at the clock on Cowboy Johnson's wall. I couldn't read the fuzzy-looking numbers. I felt almost drugged.

"Arrgh!" I said desperately, trying to wake up. I turned over and went back to sleep. We both slept for the better part of three days, only getting up to pee or get a drink of water. Gradually and reluctantly, we returned to the world we lived in. A world filled with Monsters, Spam sandwiches, Geena, and Cowboy Johnson. The worst and the best.

After we finally woke up, we were still useless. We wandered from the front porch to the back porch and sat in rockers and stared out at the desert views offered by each porch like we might receive a revelation from them about our crappy lives. No such luck. Not even a lightning strike to wise us up or to hasten our demise.

Normaine's misery over giving up Eddy and mine over not knowing what the hell to do next overcame us. We were officially zombies in a stupor who had to descend all the way to the bottom of the pain and darkness of our losses and dwell there until we could hope to climb out, if ever. There weren't any guarantees when it came to either one of us.

Geena and Cowboy Johnson happily ignored us. They didn't seem worried about our condition at all. Strains of classical music, country, blues, and rock poured from the lovely old Victrola Geena informed me was a "Gramophone Grand," put out by the Columbia Phonograph Company, a gift to Cowboy

Johnson from his grandfather when he was a boy. So, there was a grandpa Cowboy Johnson? Did he wear a cowboy hat? Did he know about Spam? Did he surf?

More stacks of books collected on every table and on the countertop of the store. Cowboy Johnson and Geena went on frequent short trips. He closed the store and locked the gas pumps each time they left. He couldn't leave us to watch the store because he said we were out of commission for the time being. They returned with books and other strange things, like lampshades and odd chairs.

"What's that for?" I asked Geena as she came up the steps with her arms full of more odd things.

"I wanted them, and they are mine, okay?"

I peered at her from my rocking chair as she swept across the wide porch and into the store, letting the door slam shut behind her. After a while, I said, "Okay," even though she wasn't there to hear it. I fell back into my funk, lounging even farther down in the rocking chair.

Normaine and I watched cars and trucks drive in and stop. We watched people get out and stretch and walk around. They were mostly middle-aged men who drove eighteen-wheelers, looking tired and gritty, dusty cars with determinedly silent drivers, and sometimes a tough, badass biker loaded with tattoos and bad hair who obviously romanticized the desert.

We watched Cowboy Johnson, wearing a variety of caps with logos on the front, gas up their vehicles, and chat with them. I wanted to ask Normaine why he didn't wear his cowboy hat anymore, but I couldn't dredge up the energy to speak the required words.

Then there were the store suppliers and the bread truck, the ice cream and frozen foods truck, and the fruits and meats and vegetable trucks. We watched the drivers climb the steps carrying their wares, carefully not looking at us. We watched them go inside the store and come back out with receipts and long neck, cold glass bottles of orange Nesbit or grape Nehi soda, or a cold Pabst beer. Windshields got washed, oil got changed, and tires got aired up. Cowboy Johnson seemed to be tireless, with a good word for everyone. Geena helped him.

Sometimes we moved to the back porch and watched Geena and Cowboy Johnson while they set about erecting two tan square tents the height and size of a bedroom next to Normaine's trailer in their spare time. I knew it was suspicious, but I didn't have any questions yet. I was just a big fat ball of something waiting. I glanced over at Normaine from time to time. We just were.

Days and nights passed. We couldn't respond to the outer world. Our inner world held control over us. Two catatonic zombies watched over by Cowboy Johnson and Geena, a cowboy and a young girl. What a sorry pass we had come to!

Sometimes Geena shoved half a fried bologna sandwich into each of our hands. We ate most of it before our arms grew too tired to lift it to our mouths. She pulled the remains out of our hands and threw them into the yard where the black crows waited.

Then one morning, when we were sitting on the front porch, Cowboy Johnson came out of the store and put his hand on Normaine's shoulder.

"You've got a phone call."

He made this announcement in a firm voice that brooked no argument. She nodded, rose to her feet, and stumbled along behind him in slow motion as he went back into the store. I stood up and followed them. Normaine slowly listed left and right down the length of the store to where the black dial phone sat on the counter. At last, she picked up the receiver lying beside the phone.

"Arrgh?" she said into the mouthpiece. I watched her from halfway down the store and saw the scraps of white paper with her phone numbers on them. They were floating down like snowflakes under a bending Shadow that could not stop them. This one was hers. She would have this one, whoever it was.

I moved closer until I was right beside her. I heard the voice on the phone and said, "Arghhh?" to it. Normaine nodded and tried to give me the phone. The voice kept on talking, and we both listened. We understood some of it, but not much. We understood the parts about traveling and hotels and burnt sofas and the sign in the yard that said, "All Men Can Go to Hell." We couldn't understand nor go near the parts about true love, or any other smarmy feelings. We couldn't decide that part for the voice. It was on its own.

"Arghh!" we said into the receiver and laid it back down on the counter. We wandered back outside to our chairs. Once in them, we fell asleep from exhaustion. Later, I woke up to find Normaine gone.

She came back and sat down and handed me half of a cheese sandwich.

"Eddy," she said. That was all.

Geena and Cowboy Johnson took turns minding the store. We watched him teach her how to gas up the cars and trucks, run the store, and make change. Sometimes Geena gave Cowboy Johnson instructions, and he left and came back later with boxes of things and odd pieces of small furniture for her.

Before long, we wobbled past a couple of former junk chairs, newly repaired and painted with dark purple skies and blue stars and green plants growing up their legs. They were beautiful! A couple more chairs with bold patterns painted in flamboyant colors on them came along. An old pink lampshade became strewn with bells and delicate pink shells. Clay bowls bore little clay people climbing out of their interiors and lounging on their sides.

I felt a thrill of pride in Geena's artistic abilities, but I couldn't do a thing about it. This time chose me, I never chose it. I was helpless before this thing until it ended.

We sat on the porches and walked by everything in the store and slept on the air mattress each night. Then one morning, I sat up and felt the change in the air. It was cooler. Normaine wasn't beside me. She was sleeping less, getting up and fixing herself food before going to the porches.

I fingered my hair. It needed washing. My fine, naturally curly brown hair was short when we started this trip. Now it was almost long enough to tie back. I stood up and yawned. I was thirty years old, five feet four, and weighed plenty. Surely that was big enough to at least whip somebody.

It was a lot richer having a companion when doing whatever it was we were doing. Where the hell was Normaine?

I got up and trudged through the sliding glass doors into the store. Geena was on the left, sitting at a table, making a clay lizard. Normaine was on the right side, sitting at her table, braiding a rag rug. Colorful, long rows of strips were laid out beside her. "Huh?" I said, peering left and right at them before I made my way through the store and out to the porch. They ignored me.

I grew restless. I could not stay content without Normaine by my side. It seemed like there were a lot more people stopping at the store, instead of just the occasional traveler. They were noisy, too. They stomped up the steps and passed me by as though I didn't exist, interrupting the quiet I needed. This was not working for me.

I decided to go to the back porch, where it was quiet. I wandered through the store and watched Geena sell a purple clay lizard and a turquoise blue lampshade to a mother and her little boy. Normaine was chattering with a woman showing her pieces of colorful, textured used clothing. They ignored me. I wandered past them through the curtains and sliding glass doors.

I slid them shut behind me with relief. Too much noise for me! I stopped at the refrigerator and pulled out a couple of cheese slices and folded them into a slice of light bread, and headed for the back porch. Settling into a rocker, I ate my cheese sandwich. The crows watched me with knowing eyes, but then, most everyone knew more than I did these days. I tossed the bread crusts to them and went to sleep.

Early one morning before the store opened, I was snoring away on the front porch. I opened my eyes from napping to find an old geezer bent over me. The snore I was in the middle of jerked to a loud stop. I slowly reached up and wiped the drool off the side of my mouth. The old geezer peered down at me with bright blue eyes and nodded magnanimously.

"Yep. The desert will do that to you, but you'll come out of it. Happened to me onese't, too, only up in the mountains, and I learned a lot from it. Don't worry. Your time will end, and you'll learn stuff, too."

He didn't explain what "it" was before he ambled on into the store.

"Argghhh?" I responded, wanting to know what he meant, but I was unable to articulate the words before the screen door closed behind him.

Yeah, right. A prophet in the form of an old geezer prospector dispensing words of wisdom out on the porch of a godforsaken renovated former church, now a desert store and gas station, with me being a mostly catatonic doorstop on its front porch. What the hell had I come to? I shook my head and went back to where I was. In a little while, I felt Geena grab something out of my hand. Then I remembered the leftover remnant of a cheese sandwich.

"Mama! You've got to throw away what you don't eat, so the crows don't peck your hands!"

Geena helped me up and guided me indoors and through the store and down onto the Hideous Green Sofa in what once was Cowboy Johnson's living quarters. Until we took it over. Where was he sleeping these days? Alone, I hoped. How long ago was that? What month was this?

"Here. Sew this into something."

She thumped a cardboard box of stuff down in front of me. I peered into the box. It was filled with pink organza. She watched me and waited. I knew her potential for waiting forever, so I gave up. A long time passed. Then I stabbed the air with one word.

"Tutus?"

"Sure. Whatever."

She turned and left. I watched her leave. Instinctively I knew that this time was over.

I sat on the Hideous Green Sofa day after day and sewed miles of pink organza into tutu's, and slowly came out of that faraway place. One day the psychic pain was gone.

Another day, I was sitting on the front porch, taking a break from making tutus. I was napping and thinking about how much easier life was back when I was in my trance state, which Geena called my stupor. I didn't have to work near as hard as I did now.

My thoughts were interrupted when the old geezer prospector clomped up the front steps and woke me up and looked me over without mine or anyone else's permission for the second time.

"Well," he drawled, as if to console me, "you'll learn more later."

With that, he clapped me on the shoulder, throwing me straight out of my pity party. I glared at him. How rude! He laughed at me and sauntered on into the store. I squinted up at the hot blue sky.

"Thanks a hell of a lot!" I muttered, wallowing in self-pity and personal importance. At last, there was something concrete to complain to God about.

"You couldn't send me a motherly or a fatherly person to replace my lousy parents. No one with sympathy or a shred of kindness. No, not you! No, you send me a beat-up old geezer prospector who laughs at me, whacks me on the back, and as much as tells me I'm STILL missing the boat!"

I looked around for the mule the old geezer surely tied to a post somewhere, but all I saw was a gorgeous canary yellow 1946 GMC half-ton EC101 pickup truck parked by the gas pumps. The gorgeous truck stood out like a neon sign in the desert. I felt a strong urge to pose by it. Where was the owner of the truck? Pictures of tan, lithe young men in tight jeans with windswept, longish hair, carelessly cut and framing handsome, perfectly tanned faces, insouciantly posing by the truck, poured through my mind. How long was it since I posed by the Merc'?

I was trying to heave myself out of the rocker when Normaine ambled out the front door, followed by Geena, Cowboy Johnson, and the old geezer. The screen door shut with a bang behind them. In their hands were tall stacks of the pink tutus Geena ordered me to make. I watched them parade carefully down the porch steps and over to the gorgeous yellow truck. The old geezer opened the passenger door and solemnly laid his stack of tutus on the passenger seat. The rest of them handed him their tutus, and he added them to the stack. When they were done, they all posed by the truck and grinned up at me.

Back up the porch steps, they came. Cowboy Johnson stopped by my rocker.

"You," he said. I squinted up at him, trying to figure out the nuances in his voice but gave up. He turned to Normaine.

"You tell her, Normaine."

"Come on, William, there's more stuff," he said dryly to the old geezer.

The old geezer shook his head and grinned at me, his shoulder-length white hair and sharp chin moving silently. He followed Cowboy Johnson into the store.

Normaine put her hand on my shoulder. "We're going to a ballet concert in Pistachio Pico tonight!"

She waited for my response. I peered up at her, mouth agape.

I said, "Tutus? Beer?"

"No, dumbass. The town. Pistachio Pico. No beer."

Whose truck?" I gestured toward the canary yellow pickup.

"William's."

She waited while an astounded expression worked its way across my face. Then she smirked.

"William Thackery Makepeace."

With that said, she pranced into the store. I watched, open-mouthed, as the old geezer prospector came back out of the store, his hands loaded with the last of the pink tutus. He ambled over to the gorgeous canary yellow truck, loaded them in, hopped in the driver's side, and drove away without a backward glance. I stared out across the empty desert but didn't see a damn thing that would explain any of it to me.

After supper, Cowboy Johnson closed the store. All of us and some locals filled the old geezer prospector's cab and truck bed. The old prospector dude drove slowly toward Pistachio Pico, giving us the chance to admire the setting sun while drinking cold sodas from the cooler Cowboy Johnson had put in the back.

Eventually, he parked in front of a large white metal building on the edge of Pistachio Pico. A gaily painted sign above the door announced this was the newly built "Community Center."

Cowboy Johnson helped us "ladies" out of the back of the yellow truck. Inside the building were at least a hundred folding chairs with dark red padded seats. They were divided into two sections with an aisle running between them. The folding chairs faced a stage with a dark red velvet curtain pulled across it.

People filed in and took seats. The old prospector led the way down to the front row. Cool air swirled over us. I listened to the people laughing and talking. Then a portly red-haired man strode up on the stage and began a long speech thanking the old prospector, alias William Makepeace, for donating this fine new "Community Center" to the town.

Turns out, the old geezer had friends whose daughters and granddaughters wanted to take ballet and dance lessons. There was no place to learn or practice close by, so the old geezer had this building erected and hired a couple of instructors to come out from Albuquerque every week.

Before I could think much about that, the house lights dimmed. Stage lights came on. Classical music filled the air and out pranced dozens of happy little girls aged anywhere from four to ten, doing their own versions of pirouettes in ballet shoes. All of them were wearing the pink tutus I made over their leotards.

I sat there in stunned silence. My heart began pounding. I was trying to catch up with the world again. Silent tears ran down my cheeks. No one looked at me. Normaine was sitting next to me. She handed me a small white towel and whispered, "Dumbass!" just as I was thinking about sobbing out loud. That shut me up quick.

We stopped at a taco place after the concert, then climbed in the back of the truck and rode home under the stars. Normaine grabbed one of my hands and massaged it.

"Why are you massaging my hand? I'm not having a cramp."

"To relax it from all those tutus you made."

I started crying.

"Shut up, Dumbass!" she reprimanded me sharply. "Tonight is a nice night. Just look up at the stars."

I stopped crying and looked up at the stars. She was right.

"The stars are like children dancing up there, too, right, Dumbass?"

She was trying to tell me something. I didn't get it, but I nodded anyway. That night, instead of falling off the world into a deep and unrelenting sleep, I stayed awake. Later, I slipped out on the back porch and sat on the steps to watch the stars dancing in the night sky above me.

The heart cannot thrive on reason alone. It needs more. Essential, unseen reasoning and the hope it carries is necessary to add to the heart's path of endeavor so it can love more fully. Maybe I would learn to love better now than I could before.

The next day, Geena brought me a box of blue organza to sew into tutus. I went outside to the Merc' and posed by her before I went up the steps and back into the store, back to the Hideous Green Sofa, sat down, and began to sew.

Chapter Twelve

Stinky old smelly
love on wheels
Yeah baby!

The air was heavy with the scent of dust and cactus acids the morning Eddy Savingo, and his three sisters showed up at the desert store. The wind chimes Normaine made from everything she could get her hands on were hanging from nails around the edge of the porch and everywhere else. They chimed and screeched and honked and wailed in the hot breeze, stirring them every now and then.

I was sitting alone on the porch when I saw Esmerelda coming down the highway. Who could ever forget her? I watched, open-mouthed as she swung jauntily into the parking lot. The man driving her spun Esmerelda off the highway in one smooth motion. Then I realized he was towing what appeared to be a large silver toaster behind him. With the top down and Frank Sinatra blasting on the radio, the man fishtailed Esmerelda to a smooth stop directly in front of the front porch steps.

I stared at the driver. I assumed he must be Eddy because he looked sort of like the man Normaine described, at least after I removed the many smarmy "love" adjectives like "cute" and "fantastic" she used when she used to talk about him.

That was before our trip up north. She hadn't spoken his name since the phone call awhile back.

Evidently, he was a closed book to her. Right about now, I was thinking that she might want to rethink her position.

Three women rode with the man. They were wearing black sunglasses and black scarves over their hair. One rode shotgun, the other two in the backseat. They appeared to be female Mafia members. They looked extremely devout and very anti-social. Nervously, I looked for their guns. They had either come to pray for us or kill us. Maybe both.

The dust settled. The man snapped the radio off while I peered at the toaster. It remained blindingly silver in the desert sun. On its side was a long silver label that read "Airstream." The man stepped out of Esmerelda and shut the driver's door with a flourish. Then he posed beside her. The three Mafia sisters got out and posed beside her.

Huh? They knew about posing? Maybe they couldn't help it either. Maybe it was brought on by the presence of that gorgeous pink piece of mobile art on wheels they were riding in.

The five of us stared at each other. I had the advantage in any staring contest right now—I was still practically catatonic. I sat like a statue, my eyes the only thing moving, sizing them up. All four of Esmerelda's passengers were simply beautiful. All four had neatly rounded figures with black hair, dark eyes, and intelligent faces with perfect features set in tan, creamy skin. None of them were taller than my own five foot four. The man was dapper. The women were chic. The man wore a black, curved mustache. His chin was strong. He wore a short-sleeved, fitted white shirt, black slacks, and shiny black loafers. His snug-fitting shirt showed off his barrel chest and muscular arms. His thick black hair was rolled up into a pompadour; the back brushed the top of his shirt collar.

The women wore black slacks with white blouses and sensible black shoes. Everything fit their trim, rounded, very bosomy figures perfectly. No matchstick thin ladies here! I watched the ladies remove the scarves from their heads and smooth their thick black hair into higher and firmer French twists. While the women smoothed their hair, the man pulled a silver-edged comb from his pocket and began to comb his black hair into an even higher pompadour.

Each of the four sets of expressive, large black eyes watched me intently while they groomed themselves. Evidently, this was going to be a formal occasion, but nobody knew what to do next. Somebody needed to make the first move. They waited for me to make it. They didn't know I was asleep at the wheel, so to speak. Only I knew that me making the first move just wasn't going to happen. I sat there and waited while we stared at each other.

Suddenly, the waiting was broken by the sound of laughter coming from inside the store. It acted like a prod of lightning to me. I staggered to my feet as the man raced up the steps with cat-like grace, as light on his feet as thistledown. He grabbed my hands and looked at me with sparkling black eyes. Then he kissed the backs of my hands. His mustache tickled, and I jerked them back. His aftershave wrapped itself around me, a sturdy smell with a hint of blackstrap molasses or licorice in it.

"I'm Eddy!" he said.

"Oh."

That was all I could get out. The women trooped up the steps behind him and lined up in a row. Each one of them forcibly grabbed me and hugged me, one after the other. They smelled strongly of black licorice and leather. I felt like a clay doll, ready to be molded into whatever it was they wanted me to be.

"Hello! I'm Algestine!"

"Hello! I'm Aleda!"

"Hello! I'm Alena!"

Each one announced their names and nodded and smiled before quickly scooting rocking chairs into an even line with mine and sitting down.

"Would you mind going in and telling Normaine that Eddy is here to call upon her? And please tell her that he has brought his three sisters as chaperones." Eddy spoke formally as his hand swept out to include his sisters. "Algestine, Aleda, and Alena." He put his hand to his mouth in a deft aside. "Our father's name was Alistair." Then he shook his head, bowed it, and looked down mournfully at the planks on the porch. "And I am a junior. Eddy is a nickname."

The sisters broke out ornate fans with silver handles from somewhere and began fanning themselves and rocking. I set out on my mission. I wandered around the porch until I found the screen door and finally managed to open it. I stepped inside and meandered down the long room until I came to a stop in front of Normaine's work area.

Geena and Cowboy Johnson were perched on corners of Normaine's worktable. They were all laughing about something. They stopped talking and looked at me. I waved my hand at the front door and clutched my heart with my other hand.

"Eddy!" I whisper-shouted. Normaine looked at me, dumbfounded.

"No, Dumbass!" she hissed.

I nodded and pointed at the front door again. "Algestine, Aleda, and Alena!" I struggled with the names.

"His sisters are here?"

"Sisters. His father was an Alistair. He is, too," I blurted out. "Eddy, I mean. A Junior... Mafia!"

Cowboy Johnson and Geena slid off the desk corners. Cowboy Johnson spoke to Geena in an urgent low, voice.

"Geena, would you go get the frozen Pepperidge Coconut Cake and cut four pieces for our guests and put them on the 1880 Havilland Desert Rose dessert plates? The plates are in the closet by the dresser."

I watched him while he thought about it for a few more seconds.

"And could you add the mother of pearl James Dixon and Sons 1900 silver dessert forks to them while I procure the Galway crystal tumblers for the accompanying drinks?"

Geena nodded and dashed into the back room with Cowboy Johnson right behind her. I watched them go. Geena knew about that kind of stuff? Fancy dishes and glasses? From where? Was there still more stuff in that damn closet beside the angel topped dresser? Did that closet door somehow open into the Twilight Zone Warehouse of Good Housekeeping? Did Betty Crocker have a giant test kitchen hidden in there? Or Ann Pillsbury? Did he carry their genetics?

"I gotta' think." Normaine's hoarse voice interrupted my ruminations. She stood up and walked past the curtains, through the back room, and out the back door. I followed her. She hesitated and looked around, as though she would never see things in the same way again. Then she walked down the porch steps with me trailing her.

There were bridges to be crossed. Silence was deadly in a situation like this. Hope needed holding out. I knew this if nothing else. Since I was still practically speechless, I wondered how it would happen. By the time she walked around to the front of the store, Eddy and his three sisters held fancy plates with slices of frozen coconut cake glistening on them in their hands. Fancy cut glass tumblers of tinkling ice-cold tea sat on the porch floor beside them. They laughed and talked and ignored us as though we weren't there. I tittered. That's how! How ingenious of Cowboy Johnson!

Normaine kept walking. She circled the store, taking her time, staring at the scene on the porch, walking past it until I lost count, wandered over to the front steps, sat down, and waited.

Each time Normaine circled the front of the store, Eddy and the ladies were eating and laughing and talking with Geena and Cowboy Johnson. Expensive plates and forks and clinking glassware and ice made rich, satisfying social sounds, supplying the backdrop necessary to fill the silence until Normaine decided what to do.

A new place needed to be reached, and Cowboy Johnson was providing the best ritual he could on the spur of the moment. His fine dishes, cutlery, and glassware elevated this meeting to a higher level. They indicated that they would live in wonderful places. They would always have bounty. The laughter and chatting meant they would be accepted and appreciated as a couple by all involved here today if her decision went that way.

I watched Cowboy Johnson serve Eddy and the three Mafia sisters cake and soda, then chips and salsa off dainty Wedgewood plates with crystal sauce holders. Next came hot dogs and potato chips served on Dresden plates with French stemware. I wondered about that damn closet again. Geena and Cowboy Johnson ate with them just to be sociable. Geena was kept busy running in and out of the store.

A customer stopped briefly in front of the gas pumps, watched what was going on for a few seconds, then took off without gassing up when I mouthed "Mafia!" at them.

Eddy Savingo and the Mafia sisters stopped eating when Normaine wasn't in sight. As soon as she came around the front of the store, they became over animated and happy despite their sweat-soaked clothes and muted groans of repulsion toward any more food when she was out of sight.

Geena came out carrying piles of leftover pasta piled high on Cowboy Johnson's Villeroy and Boch plates.

"Desperate times call for desperate measures," Cowboy Johnson responded grimly to the chorus of groans that greeted the pasta.

Suddenly, Normaine rushed up the steps and threw herself into Eddy's arms. The old rocker he was sitting in broke, and they crashed to the porch floor. They both started laughing. Then everyone else laughed, too.

"Thank God! No more food!"

Geena set the plates down on the porch. The three Mafia sisters began fanning themselves madly, pleased with what was taking place. Normaine and Eddy got up and walked down the steps, talking rapidly, ignoring the rest of us.

I stacked the plates, went inside, and made my way back to Cowboy Johnson's living quarters. Lovely, fragile dishes and glasses were piled everywhere. Who would have thought the King of Spam owned lovely dishes? Was he as lovely inside as his dishes? I suspected he was. Let's face it. He had to be, or he wouldn't have these fine and elegant things. Knowing that made me feel funny. And lonesome.

I was happy for Normaine but scared for her too. Would I always feel this way about every man and woman in a relationship? Would I always look to the patron saint of Olympic Converse running shoes— the best of quality footwear—when it came to escaping the clutches of a man?

Normaine could have her man, but I couldn't. She could circle the place where dark dreams lived, where too many bright dreams died, leave that graveyard behind, and carry her courage back out into the sunlight. She'd been through a lot more than I ever did. I was a coward.

I washed the dishes carefully, dried, and stacked them on the counter. No way was I opening that closed closet door to put them away. Then I mopped and bleached everything I could find while I cried inside.

By that evening, the silver "Air Stream" trailer was parked on one side of Normaine's little pink trailer with the two tan tents on the other side of it. That night we held a campfire. We ate spaghetti and more cake, and the three Mafia sisters and Eddy Savingo danced around the fire. They were all light and graceful on their feet and full of happy vitality. But at one point, Normaine stood up and shouted, "Eddy Savingo! I'm not leaving here!"

Beautiful, dapper Eddy just looked at the ground and nodded his head sadly before he danced again. The next morning, I watched Cowboy Johnson make plans to go to Duke's Hardware for another outhouse and shower rig. "Damn! It's beginning to look like some kind of village around here! A regular desert oasis!" he said. I could tell by the satisfaction in his voice he was happy about it.

I sat on the Hideous Green Sofa that day, sewing tutus and thinking. Well, I was back. From wherever the hell I'd been. Nobody noticed. But then, everyone kept me at a distance anyway. I was used to it. That's how people always treated me. I lived life like I was watching it through a window. That's the way it still is. Karma, I guess. The happiness I yearned for was not available to me. It needed to be pursued, and I couldn't do it. I would have to give up hope and accept less and go forward. Still, I wondered about the dishes.

Inevitably, change came, blowing in like the wind, bringing with it the attendant ups and downs, leaving dust in the cracks of the store and us.

Geena made more clay lizards and painted them. Normaine made more wind chimes. I sewed tutus while Eddy and his three sisters consulted with Cowboy Johnson and made mysterious trips somewhere. Who knows where they went? I didn't ask. Word spread, and more tourists began stopping by to meet the artists living at the store. Normaine and Geena got cards made up; their work sold like hotcakes.

Then trouble came in the form of Beauty. Cowboy Johnson hired the old prospector's grandson Ray to help out. Ray was tall and slim. He was graceful, with dark hair and eyes and even large white teeth. He was a beautiful young man with the majestic aura of a young lion. He posed naturally and constantly, as a beloved only child does. Ray lived out on the old prospector's ranch with his mother. He attended Pistachio Pico High School and drove a fire engine red nineteen fifty Ford F-3 pickup truck.

The first bad thing that happened was Geena developed a crush on him. The second bad thing was he liked her back. "Just as a friend," he said when I bristled up. Neither situation worked for me. They were both just babies!

I felt useless. This place was driving me nuts! This damn love stuff was going too far around here! Why, we could start a soap opera at the store!

"Days of Desert Store Love" or "Restless Desert Love"! Normaine was doe-eyed over smooth Eddy Savingo and was planning on going on the road with him. He was a trucker, after all. But he couldn't go without wedding vows between them, and she wouldn't go with them—a lover's stalemate.

To get away from the love vibrations running rampant in "Cowboy Johnson's Love Nest in the Desert," I moved into the tent next to Normaine's trailer. Eddy Savingo was staying temporarily in Cowboy Johnson's quarters. Geena moved into the other tent. Meanwhile, my days of hanging out on the front porch were over. Eddy's three Mafia sisters claimed it. They were living in the silver toaster, and they needed to spread out, so they took over the front porch.

They held court there, fanning and knitting shawls and chatting with customers, waving at the sparse traffic. Soon, their shawls joined the artistic items Normaine and Geena advertised for sale. They added mittens and hats with flowers to their offerings of shawls, and people bought them because the desert winters could dip down into the twenties and linger there.

It wasn't long before some of the older local men started hanging around. Then the sisters invited them to our campfires. Next, the old geezer prospector started sitting on the front porch with Algestine, the eldest of Eddy's three beautiful Mafia sisters. Then the old geezer started coming to the campfires and dancing with her and said I should start addressing him as William Makepeace, a name he said he had taken when he lived on the "mean streets of 'Frisco back in the day."

Whatever that meant. Basically, I was to stop calling him the old geezer prospector. Before long, I was calling him both William and the old geezer prospector, whichever name fit the occasion for me. Though I was willing to change, I could be stubborn about some things.

The smell of gasoline and the scent of acrid desert dust and old cactus juice were not the only smells wafting through the hot desert air surrounding the store. Emotions each have their own smells, and I have always been able to pick up on them. Everywhere I went, there were new hopes and romances blossoming, giving off their strategic smells as they wended their way determinedly toward the success of their venture.

William Makepeace and Algestine emitted the combined fragrances of dark red roses, hidden forest violets, and spearmint when they were together. A musty, damp, modest smell.

The Savingo sisters were busy putting out feelers to attract "special" friends using a rich, fragrant bouquet of black licorice, lemon, and dark chocolate scents combined in their auras.

The cheerful and laughing scents of vanilla, daisies, sweet basil, and tobacco trailed Eddy and Normaine everywhere.

Geena smelled of cinnamon and dandelions and of innocence waking up, which I was trying to stop, while the object of her rising hormones, Ray, emitted enough varieties of musky chocolate love and cuddle hormones when he was around her to stock a chemical factory for eternity.

I stayed as far away as I could from Cowboy Johnson, so I wouldn't pick up his scent. I already knew it to be citrusy with slight sage accents hidden within a deep, shady green forest smell, cool and waiting, and react to it, maybe by swooning or grabbing him and kissing him.

The whole damn place reeked like a week-old combo plate piled high with "love" emotions trapped in a hot, smelly cafeteria. But I consoled myself with the thought that at least the "love" smells around here weren't of the negative variety, the rotted, putrid kind that sent me running for cover, while those around me who couldn't smell emotional odors worth jack, reacted to me like I was nuts.

Those smells were one of the reasons I had trouble getting close to people. Since humans use "manners" all the time, so they don't learn too much about each other, everybody holds on to at least a moderate amount of negative emotional smells. Being a Sensitive with keen olfactory perceptions like Geena and me, made surface relationships almost impossible to maintain.

I avoided Cowboy Johnson like the plague. He nodded absentmindedly at me whenever I was in his range of vision. Suited me just fine. I was busy worrying about Geena. How could I get her out of here? She seemed to think this was a forever situation. Young love could hold on damn hard. Her crush on Ray didn't help our future shine any brighter elsewhere. She had to start school very soon, and I needed to find us a place to live and get a job.

I was afraid she wouldn't budge, and I was right. I cornered her one day while she was putting the finishing touches of paint on a clay Gila Monster; her tongue stuck out in concentration.

"Geena, Normaine is going on the road with Eddy, and we need to get back on the road ourselves and find us a home so you can go to school."

She stopped working and looked up at me.

"Nope. I'm not leaving here."

I sighed gustily as though I carried the weight of the world on my parental shoulders and watched her thin shoulders hunch against my next words.

"I need a job. And you need a home. You have to go to school."

She answered me quicker than a sin committed on a hot Saturday night under the burnt-out lights beneath the faded scoreboard in an unused outfield on the edge of a nameless small town. That told me she'd already given her answer some thought. Probably long before I did.

"Ray has to go back to school too, so he can drive me back and forth to Pistachio Pico. You can take his place at the store because there are no other jobs around here unless you want to be a migrant worker or a prospector."

I slapped my butt down hard on the chair across from her.

"I'm not working for Cowboy Johnson, and you're not hanging out with Ray!"

"For God's sake, Mama, we're just friends!"

"No! I mean it!"

Her voice took on a bitter, adult tone I never heard before.

"I'm not you, Mama. I'm not leaving. This is my home now. If you go, you go without me. I'm an entrepreneur, for one thing. Cowboy Johnson says so. The money I make will put me through college.

I'm older than you, Mama, and always will be. It's too hard on you to figure this stuff out and do it. I know you love me more than anything else in the world. That's all that matters. Not who is the boss."

Her voice wavered and filled with tears. She wouldn't look at me. She fussed with a paint box instead.

"Please let me tell Cowboy Johnson you will work here, and let me ride with Ray to school. He's got two other kids paying him for rides, too. I will pay him every week for a ride."

Involuntarily, I nodded. Geena never said "please" to me. She must really want this. Stunned, I stood up and wandered into Cowboy Johnson's quarters to make myself a cup of tea. This conversation didn't go at all like I planned. I didn't get to be the masterful mother, fixing the world, making it right for my child. Was Geena twelve or fifty? Was she my child, or was a Muse slipped in on me on a dark and stormy night?

Whatever the answer was, I admitted to myself that I was relieved. Being a mother was never my strongest role. I didn't know what role was my strongest, and probably never would, given the way things usually went for me. But knowing she was right made me sad in a new way. My instincts told me this was the end of our old relationship. Geena was a teenager now, and I was no longer the wounded mother trying to escape with a little wounded daughter from a dreaded Monster and people who didn't care if we lived or died.

Lovely, thoughtful Geena had pulled us both past all of that with her strength and wisdom and anchored us to a bunch of misfits that loved her and maybe me too. She was a young woman now, with a voice of her own—a smart, sensible voice.

No more looking back. My heart shattered, but I stood it, and sipped my raspberry tea. Its pink fragrance was consoling. Geena would lead the way for us. And I would let her. I carried my tea with me and went back and sat down across from her again.

"What's the plan? And if I ever say you are in danger, will you listen to me?"

She laughed, nodded in relief, jumped up, and hugged me.

"They love you too, Mama. Especially a certain one."

She arched her eyebrows at me and waited.

"What?" I said. I didn't understand her. The changing of the guard had been successful. I stood up and went back to the kitchen and set my cup down. I walked out to the Merc' and got the map out of the glove box. I folded it into a neat square and hid it under the carpet in the trunk. It would stay there, ready to go again, just in case we ever needed it.

Then I went to find Cowboy Johnson. He would know what to do about changing our names. Geena couldn't go to school under her real name. If it could be fixed, then we wouldn't have to stay lost anymore. I found him out at the gas pumps. There were four of them now, green and white, sparkling with newness. He was wiping the eternal, infernal dust off of them. I placed my hands on my hips and studied him. Men! Out polishing gas pumps, cars, trucks, motorcycles, anything that had an engine, and could run! I shaded my eyes with my hand. The sun was directly overhead. Noon, maybe. Why wasn't he inside eating a bologna sandwich and sucking down a cold orange Nehi? Well, at least he was under the shade roof over the gas pumps.

I started wandering over to him, zig-zagging as I went. This might be a long trip. Suddenly my stomach felt funny. Maybe because I didn't eat any lunch, I reasoned with myself. That was all. But my Sight was muttering all kinds of things I didn't want to hear. It tended to do that in peak moments, mostly when I shot myself in the foot, not literally, of course, or was getting ready to make yet another big mistake.

I circled the gas pumps a couple times, watching Cowboy Johnson all the while. He ignored me in favor of the gas pumps and kept on rubbing them down. I guess he was getting used to me being kind of odd at times. That thought stopped me in my tracks. I didn't want to pursue that kind of thinking any further. I rushed over to him and skidded to a stop in front of his back. He started to turn around, but before he could, I grabbed his shoulders. He stood still while I fired questions at his back.

"Geena said you two talked and she said you said we could stay and she asked me if we could, and I said yes but only if it was okay with you but we have to change our names 'cause she can't go to school under her old name of they might find her! Can it be done?"

He nodded his head yes and slowly turned around.

I gulped. Tears sparkled in his eyes. They began to run down his cheeks. He ignored them. So did I.

He tossed the rag he was polishing the pumps with aside. I watched it fall into the red dust as he put his hands on my shoulders and cleared his throat.

"Yes. I can help with that."

Held captive by his hands on my shoulders, I studied him. His tears stopped, but mine just started. Yes, he was definitely a man of few words.

"Thanks," I answered, twisting out of his grasp, realizing too late that maybe I had gone at this thing all wrong. His peculiar reaction made me realize that he thought he was making what he sort of considered to be a permanent contract with me and my girl. A contract of protection and relationship. Long term. Like a marriage thing. I realized I had just proposed to him.

"How about Jones or Smith or Johnson for a new last name? I vote for Johnson," he drawled out loud and slow as though he wanted the whole damn world to hear, while I rushed up the front porch steps. What did he think this was? A marriage proposal? I wasn't even divorced! I stared at him while I grabbed for the handle of the screen door frantically and couldn't find it. I figured Geena was still at her worktable, so I bawled out, "Geena! Get your ass out here and talk to Cowboy Johnson! You started all this, now he wants us to have his last name!"

I burst into tears, found the handle, jerked the screen door open, and fled into the store just as Geena rushed past me and out the door, bawling at the top of her lungs. I heard her steps pound across the porch and down to Cowboy Johnson.

I ran through the store and out the back. I ran and walked and waited. Pretty soon, I accepted that I was going to be Mama Johnson. Legal but not married legal. Probably pretty soon. Oh hell. Speaking of hell, it sure was hot! I peered up at the sun and turned to head back to the store. It was past dinner time. Geena could fend for herself today, I thought huffily, after causing all this trouble. My Sight began soothing me, informing me that there would for sure be chocolate cake around the campfire tonight.

Chapter Thirteen

Up Fargo 'way
when da' sun shines bright
dere's jis't way too many long ass days
an' jist' ay too few dam' hot sweet long dark nights.

At the campfire a few days later, Normaine and Eddy made an announcement.

"We're going on a road trip!"

"When?" Aleda questioned sharply from the corner stump she sat on. She was holding court in an ankle-length purple silk dress, a purple comb quivering high in her elaborately styled black hair. She was surrounded on both sides by adoring local men.

"We're leaving next Monday!"

Dapper Eddy, who managed to be handsome no matter what the situation, and Normaine, who had become beautiful because of him, planted themselves meekly before the firing squad and stared at the ground. The firing squad consisted of Eddy's three Mafia sisters, Aleda, Alena, and Algestine. They glared at him. Could Eddy charm his way past them? Would they hang him at high noon if he couldn't? Ride him out of town on a rail? Tar and feather him? Tell his Mafia godfather on him? Make him wear white for the rest of his life?

If anyone could get past his sisters, it was Eddy. His dove soft, rather mournful voice and kind words smoothed life into a sweet syrup easy to take. And they were forced to admire his perfectly maintained cleanliness and upright bearing. He could wear a gunny sack and still be beautiful. So could each of the Mafia sisters. He was a manly man. Though small and round, there was nothing vulgar or obtuse about him. But the Savingo sisters had very strong standards. They would have the last say.

"And just where do you think you're going?"

"Up Fargo way," Eddie replied in his most gruff voice.

"Why an extended" trip?" the sisters asked.

"Because we want to get to know each other better as friends."

Eddy rolled his eyes at Normaine and tried not to smirk out of respect for his sisters who were acting more and more like Catholic school nuns tapping long, heavy rulers in their hands every minute.

"And we can assume that this is going to remain a platonic relationship until after wedding vows have been taken?"

They both nodded vigorously. They knew better. We all knew better. Normaine and Eddy couldn't keep their hands off each other and made numerous nightly trips into the desert. But in order to save face and help the three Savingo sisters maintain their high standards in front of the rest of us, amid much eye rolling, Normaine and Eddy pledged to stay just platonic friends.

The old geezer prospector was sweating. "Whew!" he said when the interrogation ended. Nobody else dared make a comment.

Eddy and Normaine sat down, drank some water, and stared at the fire while the Savingo sisters glared at them. Finally, the sisters withdrew their glares, picked up their fans, and went back to talking with the eager, but now subdued gentlemen they'd invited to the campfire.

Early Monday morning, Normaine parked Esmerelda in the shade up against the little pink trailer. I posed by her, then by the Merc' parked tight up against her.

Give me the car keys, Normaine!" I demanded with a grin. Then I sobered. "I think you're right to do it this way, Normaine."

"Yeah. I know. I can't marry again. Maybe never. And Eddy knows it. And he loves me anyway. Without that paper."

"Glad you're taking this chance. You deserve it. Now give me the keys to Esmerelda!"

She handed them over with a grin, then sideswiped me with her next words.

"Your turn will come with Avery someday. And I hope you get up enough guts to look past your fear and see him for the good man he is like I have my Eddy."

I shook my head, thinking of Cowboy Johnson. I was honest with her because we'd been through a lot together.

"There's somebody else I already like," I said slowly, thinking of Cowboy Johnson. The man whose name she said would have to look elsewhere. She started to object, but I stopped her.

"Don't change the subject. We're talking about you."

"Dumbass!"

She shook her head. I hugged her as hard as I could, then we laughed. What was happening now was a long way from what we believed would be our future back in that trailer in Wyoming.

The old prospector and Algestine drove Eddy and Normaine to Santa Fe in the old geezer's canary yellow pickup truck. They were sitting tight up against each other when they got back from Albuquerque. A piece of paper couldn't have fit been between them. I stood on the front porch glaring at them, my hands on my hips. They ignored me. Shouldn't they have to submit a medical report to somebody before each date? Maybe a medical exam three days in advance of dinner together? I shook my head in disgust as I muttered dire warnings of impending doom to myself.

"Damn! Is there something in the water here, or what? All of these people finding their "true loves" here! I know it was once a church, and now it's a store, which is okay, but damn, it's turning into a holy "love" oasis!"

I made smooching sounds and batted my eyes at the air. Just then, a voice filled with laughter interrupted me.

"You want a beer? Take the edge off?" Cowboy Johnson's familiar voice offered.

"I need a road trip, not a beer!" I muttered testily.

He swept his Moose lodge cap off, bowed, and pointed to his dusty green El Camino.

"At your service, madam."

"Oh no, you don't! I'd probably end up bearing your triplets six months from now, the way things are going around here!"

He grinned at me and waited. When I realized what I said, I felt my face turn brick red. I ran down the steps and around the back of the store. After involuntarily posing by the Merc', I jumped in and started her up, raced around the store, and back out onto the highway. I didn't give a damn where I went. Just anywhere. I needed to run.

Smutty, hot thoughts of Cowboy Johnson and me fooling around with each other out in the desert somewhere, and me needing every second of it raced through my mind. Yeah. I realized I was a needy Mama and would have to watch myself very carefully.

You'd think with as much negative sex as I was forced to have with the Monster, that I would have no libido left. Ever. But that damn sex thing kept coming up for me. Around Cowboy Johnson, that is. I was ashamed of craving his good thoughts and sweet kindness and gentle touches too. Maybe it was just my body knowing he was good and kind and clean about sex and life that attracted me to him.

I sighed at the remembered scent of cool pines with just a hint of citrusy sage he carried. Sex sure was powerful stuff, for good or bad. Thank God I never designed it and didn't have to be responsible for it!

After miles and hours, my need for flight passed. I returned home to the little desert store with orange and green gas pumps—the former little white church where people once confessed their sins and were slain in the spirit. The place that was fast becoming a hotbed of love, a desert nest of love. And I was stuck here because of Geena. But it was a place where even though I lived on the periphery, I still got invited in sometimes—a place where no one tried to hurt me or my Geena. It was enough. I could be at peace with it for now.

*

Geena started school in Pistachio Pico. Ray picked her up each morning. The cheerful greetings from the kids riding in the cab and in the back of his truck started my day off with a smile. At least they weren't alone together, and they would be supervised during school time. I could relax my vigil for a few hours.

I needed the time to focus on my new task. At first, my emotions on how to work with Cowboy Johnson in the store veered sharply back and forth like a drunken, speeding, chain-smoking, mountain woman navigating steep mountain passes loaded with switchbacks and hairpin curves at high speeds, while ignoring the numerous flashing yellow road signs that screamed in loud black letters, "Slow Down! Danger Ahead!"

Cowboy Johnson didn't seem to notice my condition. The days flew by, and he let me figure out what was needed. He went on about his business while I picked up the slack. Sometimes I ran errands. Other times I answered the phone and ordered supplies. The old geezer prospector dropped by regularly and inspected me.

"Want to become a Catholic?" he asked me.

"No. William Makepeace. I don't."

He sighed.

"Algestine is making me become one again. I was one in my younger days, you know. Choir boy and altar boy and all that, you know."

"No, I didn't know. Why are you doing it if you don't want to?"

"True love and old bones, my dear."

He shook his head and ambled off. I rolled my eyes skyward.

"See, there it is again! Another one bites the dust! Why doesn't anyone stay the same after they fall in love?"

In my spare time, I cleaned up Normaine's empty trailer. Normaine never noticed dirt. Aleda and Alena eyed me the whole time but didn't offer to help. They viewed Normaine's trailer as a den of iniquity. Anyway, they were busy with other things. I didn't want their help. I missed Normaine and the little girl I once thought I was raising. I was confused. I ran away so many times for her. And now she didn't need me to do it anymore. But my body was used to it and still built up adrenaline I had to work off by jumping in the Merc' and heading out—any place—until it drained away.

My illusions of being a successful mother were remnants I deliberately left lying in a tangled heap in a lonesome corner. I did not want to examine them. The talk about staying here left me no choice. I had to learn to befriend Geena in new ways instead of trying to do my old un-needed version of mothering her again. I took solace in the fact that I at least got her away from the Monster. In that way, I considered myself as a Heroine. I was lucky. There are a lot of women and kids that never escape those kinds of men.

Normaine and Eddy called every few days.

"We're out on the west coast! Eddy says it's our honeymoon! Eddy got me new front teeth, and they fasten right in! But don't tell the Mafia sisters we're anywhere except up around Fargo way, okay?"

"I won't, Normaine. I'm so happy for you!"

"We'll be home for Thanksgiving! See you then! Big hugs to everyone! We love all of you!"

Geena was making new friends and doing well in school. All seemed to be well. I stored the fear of being discovered by the Monster in the back of my mind and gave up thinking about divorcing him. That would only stir him up, and he might find out where we were. If I could just get Geena through school, then I could divorce him with no problem.

I kept on sewing in my spare time. I finished the blue tutus and started making white angel wings out of tulle for the little ballet dancers to wear in their Pistachio Pico Christmas play.

We had a lull, with everyone wandering around like a herd of cattle. We were all sort of between things. It was a good time, though short. We enjoyed about two weeks of it before the Mafia Sisters took over Cowboy Johnson's oven and began baking fruitcakes. They started out small, but in no time, fruitcake starters bubbled and simmered everywhere, emitting troubled bowel sounds and loud, medieval, alcoholic burps.

I listened while Algestine explained to Cowboy Johnson that they brought plenty of fruitcake with them, but they ran out and needed to make more.

Before long, I heard the Mafia sisters grumbling to Cowboy Johnson about his oven's limitations. Next thing I knew, Cowboy Johnson, William, and the three Mafia sisters were holding long meetings in the back of the store.

I watched them make drawings and hold meetings with tall, solemn men that came and went, carrying briefcases full of papers. I wasn't curious. I didn't care. I liked being left out of whatever it was they were doing. I drifted along, tending the store, making change, and pumping gas while they roamed in and out.

Then one day, Geena brought me up to date in a few short, enthusiastic sentences.

"We're building an eight-room motel out back where Normaine's trailer is, maybe more! And a restaurant and a bakery for the Mafia sisters to run! Maybe a gift shop, too!"

She made an "L" shape with her hands to indicate the positions of the new buildings. I nodded and smiled.

"Good."

I didn't ask her where we were going to live. I just assumed we were going to move on. Then Geena turned and left, tossing more words back over her shoulder at me, instantly changing my lethargic, pity partying "I don't care" attitude once and forever.

"Cowboy Johnson says we can pick out the rooms we want to be ours. He's going to build them special for us. But they need to be located beside of the bakery or next to the restaurant, and we need to choose our places soon, okay? I want ours to be next to the bakery because bakeries always smell so good!"

Stunned, I turned away. Tears filled my eyes. Names and a place. Now we would have both.

I went to William for an explanation. It was time for me to rejoin the world of Cowboy Johnson's desert oasis.

"Well..." he pushed his battered cap back on his head and scratched his head.

"You finally interested, huh?"

Dry mouthed, I nodded.

He seemed to know what was wrong with me without asking. He held his hands out and made an L shape with them.

"There's gonna' be two long, one-story buildings making an "L" shape. This one over here," he indicated the fingers on his right hand, "is gonna' be the long one. There'll be eight motel rooms in it. The one that's a little bit shorter will be double-wide. In the front will be the restaurant, bakery, and gift shop combined. Behind them will be the living quarters for the Savingo sisters and you and Geena."

"Bein' this is the desert," he swept his hand out to indicate the world around us, "we'll have deep wood shade porches runnin' along the front of both buildings, and we'll have shaded parking....and bein's as we all gotta' go ever day..." he grinned at me, "located at an astute distance behind the motel will be four more outhouses, courtesy of Duke's Hardware Utility Sheds, limed and cleaned daily, each one serving two of the motel rooms. There will be shower sheds at each end of the buildings. Each room has to have a front and back door. There'll be a small porch off the back door with a trail leading to the outhouse."

He peered at me like he was looking for an opening of some kind.

"Geena recommends whitewashed rocks and strings of lights with flamingos and red peppers lining the path to the outhouse after dark. What do you think?"

He watched me waiting for my answer, but I didn't have any. I turned away.

"I don't know."

I threw the words back over my shoulder. It seems we had a future here, no matter what I did or thought about Cowboy Johnson.

More of the motel plans came to me in bits and pieces. A laminated brochure from the nearest laundromat fifteen miles away would be posted in each room, advertising their laundry services. Cowboy Johnson planned to continue living in the store. He didn't want to change the store at all. He liked it the way it was.

When the plans were finished, the workers came and moved Normaine's trailer, the two tan tents, and the silver Airstream toaster around to the side of the store. Then they smoothed out the sand behind the campfire area and set to work.

Mozart, rock and roll, blues, and country music wafted through the air while the three Mafia sisters baked, and I sewed. I served in the store and pumped gas and watched the work on the motel progress each day.

William supervised the motel building. He consulted blueprints and hired eager locals who were anxious to get any work they could. Geena and Ray and their friends hired out to work on weekends and after school.

Cowboy Johnson and William hired just about anybody who asked for work, so the motel went up fast. The wood framing went up almost overnight, followed by thick insulation, then thick, creamy stucco exteriors.

Before long, the basic work was done, and the inspectors came and went, approving the careful planning of the water supply and the electricity.

Each motel room had its own air conditioner and heater, which could only be changed and turned off and on with the motel manager's key. There were no televisions, just a shelf of good books in each room.

The Mafia sister's restaurant offered spaghetti and lasagna along with breads and fruitcakes. Both the restaurant and bakery menu and hours were subject to change at any time. Campfires would be held once a week for motel guests.

All of this was explained in the "green" brochure handed out to each guest at check-in, along with one white bath towel and one washcloth per person per day with detailed instructions about how to use the community sinks out back.

One night we were all gathered around the counter in the store. Cowboy Johnson was trying to define the rules for customers. Each of us chimed in with different ideas, depending on our upbringing. It was chaos because we all grew up with different rules we didn't like. Mostly, we didn't like any rules. He listened to us. Then inspiration struck him.

"Okay...I got it! Why don't each of you make the rules about one area and let it be your area to patrol without any interference from anyone else."

A long silence followed his suggestion as we each thought it over.

"Geena, how about towel patrol?" he said. She giggled.

"I know I can handle that. And washcloth and soap patrol."

"Okay."

"Now let's talk about the money. All the money from our new ventures will go into a community pot, accounted for by a bookkeeper who will give us weekly reports for the time being. The mortgage and expenses get paid first. Each business will have a separate report. Then the rest gets divided up between us. You are now all equal shareholders in our new enterprises.

This is a complicated structure right now, so all of you shareholders will have to be patient as it is sorted out and made simpler. There will be no cheating anyone out of anything, so if you have a problem, better bring it out in the open as soon as possible.

We are putting together a new family of shareholders in this little forgotten corner of the world, this little third-world desert country of ours, so just keep that in mind, and let's take care of each other."

We stared at each other in surprise. None of us ever expected to be shareholders in anything. We donated our enthusiasm, work, and time, but no money. Making the misfit motel and the rest of it possible was an old geezer prospector driving a snazzy canary yellow pickup, who was taking lessons in being a Catholic again, definitely one of the religious corporations he couldn't abide, and the mysterious Cowboy Johnson, who now wore caps with meaningful logos instead of cowboy hats.

The glue holding us misfits together was this good energy place, a little desert store and gas station that was once a church where people danced in the spirit. And two oddball men who held their secrets tighter than a mother holds her babe to her breast in a gale-force wind while crossing a skinny rope bridge strung between two tall cliffs with water boiling far below.

Sure, us misfits still went off on our flights of fancy every now and then. But Normaine tenderized turkeys less often, and Geena quit biting her fingernails to the quick and muttering while hiding under her cascade of brown hair. And I finally asked for chartreuse tulle to work on.

We had black or blue or brown or green eyes, and we were short and thin and fat or old and young and middle-aged and different shades of stupid and smart. No matter. We had the same heart beating in each of us, trying to lead us into a better life, and now we were leaders of a desert empire. Shareholders. A bunch of misfits. No more dead ends, or dead beats, or old age or painful memories to keep us from it. We were all errant, footloose believers in Magic with next to nothing in social skills. We were a bunch of nomadic misfits living out in the desert, and now we owned a motel.

"Let's paint the outside of the motel Miami blue!" Geena shouted, dancing across the former church floor. Everyone joined in the dancing. Now us misfits owned a motel that would be painted Miami blue.

*

Normaine and Eddy came home for Thanksgiving. They drove in one afternoon while I was sitting on the front porch. Everyone else was out back at the construction site. Their eighteen-wheeler looked new. It was long and silver with miles of chrome and a shiny purple sleeper cab. I didn't know much about semi-trucks, but I knew this one was expensive.

I jumped up and opened my arms. They opened their doors, started shouting, jumped down, and rushed me. They wore matching black leather pilot's jackets and red toboggan hats with a ball on top that flopped to the side on their silly, loveable heads. Normaine smiled a blinding white, full toothed smile at me so I could admire her new teeth. She was beautiful! We grabbed each other.

"Where the hell have you been? You've been gone too long! Some honeymoon!"

"What honeymoon?"

They rolled their eyes innocently at each other, smirking.

"We just been up Fargo way."

"I got to stay right here and mind the store. Go on out back, and see what's going on!"

They rushed into the store. Pretty soon, I heard shouts of joy coming from out back. I smiled in contentment. Yep. They were home. So was I.

The next few days flew by. Suddenly Thanksgiving Day was upon us. Cowboy Johnson turned over the preparation of the bird to William Makepeace, thus keeping the bird safely out of Normaine's tenderizing reach. He invited all the motel workers, and I watched while he made a lot of bow tie pasta. There was something meaningful in that, but I couldn't figure out what it was. Heck, I was still busy trying to figure out the meanings of his cap logos.

Normaine and Eddy poured sauerkraut over two huge pans of brisket, then covered the pans with foil and placed them on the edge of the campfire to simmer all night the night before.

They planned to nurse the fire through the night while embellishing the meat with wine and beer at strategic moments. I was sitting with them at the campfire, pouring beer over brisket, when inspiration struck me like a bolt of lightning. I jumped up, shoved my half-empty beer bottle into Normaine's hand, and ran off to find Cowboy Johnson. He was in the store, sitting at the back counter, studying a piece of paper. He looked up and watched me as I skidded to a stop in front of him. I grabbed his arms.

"It's called green organic architecture that you're doing! Incorporating Nature! Like Frank Lloyd Wright! He built a place not far from here just over the border in Arizona! We should go see it before we build any more!"

I grabbed his thick, strong hands and tugged him to his feet, not paying attention to the fact that I hadn't touched him in a very long time. The faint scent of sage and cool forest pine began embracing me, slowly giving me notice of his divinely smelling presence while I babbled on. Without thinking, I began massaging his hands.

"I can see it all now! Canvas and wide, covered, shady places, and amazing colors instead of all dust and rocks and scrawny vegetation!"

He watched me while I chattered on. I found myself staring at the insides of his arms and smoothing them. They were soft and warm. His skin would never break out. It wasn't thin and sensitive, like mine. He probably never broke out as an adolescent. I straightened the imaginary collar on his tee-shirt, patted his chest, and turned and ran like hell for the back door. It slammed behind me as I raced off the porch towards the campfire. I didn't look back.

"Told you," Normaine said smugly to Eddy, as I rushed the stump where they sat. "Didn't I, Eddy?"

I blushed and sat down.

"A little encounter with romance?'

"Shut up, Normaine!"

Geena and her friends sang and danced around the campfire while the brisket simmered. Geena showed them the latest insects she collected, then they moved up the back steps of the store as One and returned in a few minutes, arms piled high with Cokes and Lay's Potato Chips and Milky Way bars—a teenager's idea of God's food.

The old geezer prospector, William Makepeace, spirited the sturdy bosomed, prudish natured Algestine out to his ranch to help prepare the turkey. I sighed. Who knew what they were doing out there? I'd actually watched him blush when I caught him staring longingly at Algestine a few days ago. What the hell was he thinking to blush like that? Did old people still have sex? In slow motion, with many rest stops? Well, hell. I was young. Sort of. So, what the hell did I know? Enough to go back and paw Cowboy Johnson a little bit more, please, a small, yearning voice inside me pleaded.

It grew late, and most everyone else left the campfire. Geena and her girlfriends went to sleep in her tent. Normaine and Eddy were cuddled up to each other, watching the fire. I stumbled to my tent and fell into a deep sleep. My last thought was that this was the weirdest night I ever spent before a Thanksgiving Day. Sleeping under the stars in a tent pitched on the sand with a bunch of snoring nuts. And the best.

Chapter Fourteen

Hey baby, I want to know
if you'll be my girl.

Early the next morning, we set up long tables on the motel porch beneath the shade roof. Before long, there were beat up, dusty cars and old trucks parked everywhere. Everyone brought food to share. It looked like an old geezer prospector's convention was taking place. I wondered what stories the old geezers could tell. Was there still a "lost" gold mine out there somewhere? Had "Gold Dust Annie" had been their girl and abandoned them for another prospector that struck it rich? Surely there was a love story in there somewhere, after all the "love" scents that were still permeating the air around here.

Speaking of which, the guilty parties soon arrived, looking sedate and saintly. William Makepeace and Algestine Savingo had finally spent the night together. Hand on hip, I studied them. God knows what they did, it couldn't have been much, weren't they too old? Maybe just a little groping and sweet, gentle words?

I was sure the other two Mafia sisters would turn into a firing squad as soon as they saw them. I smirked at the old prospector geezer as I trailed them around the back of the store. They were headed for the food tables, their hands full of turkey, their faces full of modesty.

But the two Mafia sisters acted as if there was nothing unusual about their having stayed alone and together all night. They came and took the turkey from them and placed it on the table. Then they all hugged.

Cowboy Johnson was watching me again. He stood near me, holding a bowl of yellow corn, and he knew exactly what I was thinking. I glanced at him and blushed in mortification and deep confusion. He sat the bowl of corn down, turned to me, grabbed my face, kissed me quickly and thoroughly, and drew back.

"Want me to tell you a bit about older birds and bees sometime?" he offered.

"Hell, no!?"

I tried to shout, but it came out as more of a hopeful question. Everyone burst into laughter. The old geezer prospector and Normaine slapped their legs, they laughed so hard. Then when they got their breath, they started all over again. I couldn't see what was so damn funny. I stood there in righteous indignation until I realized that they wouldn't quit as long as I was there. I stomped away.

Cowboy Johnson left before me to bring out more of his fancy plates, endless glasses of different heights and shapes, and more silver cutlery from his merciless, fancy schmancy, never-ending mystery pantry.

After the food and turkey were properly admired, Cowboy Johnson stood up at the head of the table and tapped his glass. The fifty or sixty people gathered around us went quiet.

William Makepeace said a short prayer of gratitude, and Aleda Savingo gave a prayer in Latin. Then the two Savingo Mafia sisters went and stood on each side of the old geezer prospector and their sister Algestine, boxing them in like they were the innards of a tasty sandwich.

"We have another announcement to make, don't we sister Algestine?"

The two haughty sisters spoke sweetly in syrupy voices, intermittently shooting glares at Eddy and Normaine. I watched William the Dude. He didn't look like a Dude right now; a Dude should look like he was in charge of his world. What he looked like was an old man getting ready to faint. The old geezer prospector was sweating bullets. Cowboy Johnson appeared at his side and shoved a cold Black Label into his hand. William tilted it up and downed all of it while the ladies waited patiently. They knew they had him now, no hurry. As soon as he finished, they announced,

"Our sister Algestine Savingo is now engaged to be married to William Thackery Makepeace! Isn't that wonderful? A winter wedding and very soon, yes? Would Christmas be soon enough for everyone? After all, none of us are getting any younger."

The sisters smiled at each other with fake daintiness, like sharks putting on their bibs when their intended prey had given up. I was horrified. Everyone else gave forced laughs. They liked the three Mafia Sisters about as much as I did. Emma and Ray were in Europe. Of course, they waited until they were away to snare the father and grandfather.

Algestine took William's arm and led him off. She sat him down at a table and strolled off to fix a plate of food to fortify him.

"Whew! I'm glad that's over!" he said to anyone listening. There was a smattering of sympathetic laughter, muffled and quickly ending when Algestine returned with a plate of food.

I looked at Cowboy Johnson. So that's why he made the bow tie pasta! That's why so many people were here. I turned in a circle, not knowing what to think. Just then, Cowboy Johnson brushed by me and murmured, "I told him I didn't think it was a good idea, but he was hell-bent on doing it. I hoped til' the last minute he wouldn't."

I nodded and sighed. He took my hand and led me to the store to gather more "condiments." I let him.

The campfire stayed lit until the wee small hours of the next morning. Geena and her girlfriends piled into her tent. A bunch of people piled into mine, and we all went to sleep.

The next morning, amid mixed feelings about the engagement announcement that nobody talked about, everybody went home to make their own breakfast, leaving us misfits on our own for the rest of the holiday.

I had gone to sleep mulling over the idea of going to Scottsdale to tour Taliesin West. There were tours available, but I didn't know if they would have any during the holiday weekend. It was a long trip. I didn't want to go alone, so I moseyed toward the store in the early morning light like I didn't have a care in the world. I wanted to use the phone when

Cowboy Johnson wasn't around to find out about the tours.

I found him out front, gassing up his El Camino and the old geezer prospector's truck. I fixed an innocent look on my face and opened my mouth to ask about using the phone to make a long-distance call. He interrupted me.

"Get ready, we're going away for the weekend. Alena and Aleda will watch the store for us while we're gone. We'll be back Sunday, so pack for two nights on the road."

I stared at him.

"Where are we going?"

"To tour Taliesin West. I'm glad you thought of it. I've never seen it. It's actually a necessity, isn't it, before we go any further?"

He grinned at me.

"I already called. Yes, they do have tours today and Saturday."

I stared at him. My heart realized he understood what I never seemed to be able to put into words. He included me as no one else ever did. I hugged him and ran my hands along his jawline. He kissed the tip of my nose in response and pulled me into his arms. I melted up against him quicker than hot butter under a glaring noonday sun. I snuggled up under his chin, my favorite place in this world. From here, I felt loved, sheltered, and protected. We breathed in the early morning air together and listened to the waking up voices of our misfits. I said the words I'd been thinking since the moment we met.

"You are my, mine, and theirs, a most unlikely hero."

Tears filled my eyes, and I began to tremble. Afraid I couldn't keep to my feet, I jerked away and rushed back to my tent to pack. I always went into action when any tenderness of the heart pulled at my safety. Geena was the only exception. Running kept the pain at bay, for who knew how many times a heart could stand to be broken before it killed its owner?

When I came back carrying my knapsack, the back of William's truck and Cowboy Johnson's El Camino was packed with workers, coolers, sleeping bags, and Geena and her friends.

Algestine sat in the front of the canary yellow pickup, stuck to the old geezer prospector's side like a piece of grim, licorice smelling Velcro.

Geena and her friends crammed into the front seat of the El Camino with us while Cowboy Johnson pored over a map. They shouted enthusiastic directions at him until he held up a hand.

"It's okay. I know the route."

I rolled my eyes over at him.

"I bet you do."

At that point, Geena and her friends shouted, "Euww!" and hastily climbed into the back of the El Camino to get away from us. After they settled in, we followed William the Dude out onto the highway. He turned the radio on and found some soft music.

"I'm thinking a couple nights in a sleeping bag under the stars will be just the break we all need from school and work. What do you think?"

I nodded and yawned behind my hand. If I wasn't driving, road trips always put me to sleep. I scooted across the seat and laid my head on his shoulder. He never said a word. But sadly, a short time later, I had to move away again, for my hands had a mind of their own. They wanted to make their own voyage of discovery, and Cowboy Johnson was the new land they wanted to explore. I had to move away just as I was beginning to understand the deep urges that drove the exploring and claiming of unknown lands by determined explorers and to understand just why it was they wanted to plant a flag and claim what they discovered as theirs. But the only place we were headed on a voyage of discovery was across the Arizona border.

We stopped outside of Scottsdale for the night. We made a campfire and roasted hot dogs and counted the stars. I had dibs on Cowboy Johnson's front seat for my bed. Some of the kids slept in the back of William's truck and others in the back of Cowboy Johnson's El Camino. Cowboy Johnson and the old geezer prospector and the rest slept on the ground beside the campfire.

The next day, we took the tour of Taliesin West. What an amazing, innovative, gorgeous place it was! We took notes, and the day flew by. We spent that night around a campfire, singing and sleeping under another starry sky. We got back to the store, and everybody scattered. Monday would come soon enough, bringing the responsibilities of work and school with it.

We all examined the motel with fresh eyes after the trip. Cowboy Johnson and William called in the architect again and had him draw up the changes we decided on. Before long, there were interesting angles and fieldstone and canvas incorporated into the long buildings. The angles of roofs changed, and the slant of the sun was considered in where to put the windows and how to shade them.

"Hey, you," he said, a few mornings later, to get my attention.

"I observed your awe for Taliesin West, and I think we should incorporate something sacred here."

I stared at him in surprise.

"Maybe a garden chapel in the center of the motel? It could serve as both a vegetable garden and a garden for our souls, thus being both practical and lofty. I want you to design it."

I just nodded and walked away. But I loved the way he thought of me. Nobody I knew ever thought what I liked could be sacred. Was he a disguised priest, trying to make a place to give a wayward, road-weary sinner an unforgettable religious experience? Would he let me wear his varsity cross from his God college and yell, "Go, God, Go?" to cheer him on? Or was he having me design the chapel so if it turned out ugly, he could blame me? I turned on my heel and strode back to him.

"Ah, but what about the roofline? It can't stay long and low like the motel rooms. All chapels have pointed ceilings, don't they?"

"You mean vaulted ceilings. Want stained glass windows too, do you?"

I nodded.

"What about the religious Mafia? The three sisters? What if they try to take it over?"

He looked at me a minute and shrugged.

"I guess you'll have to figure out what to do about that yourself."

Changes were made, then changed. But the changes were simple and sweet, and we let each other have what we needed, though we didn't always understand it.

The garden chapel was finished a month before Christmas. The inside walls were waiting for paint or whatever I wanted to do to it next. The Mafia sisters looked it over and decided that we would hold Algestine and William's wedding in it as soon as a fount for Holy Water could be put in. We substituted a portable birdbath from Duke's Hardware for the fount and didn't tell them it would be moved and called upon to act as an actual birdbath later.

The little white store that was once a church had a sanctuary again. The new sanctuary was supposed to be for everybody, but I knew it was for the hitchhikers and runaways of which I was a member. My prayer for every nomad and wanderer stopping here was for them to have access to a good pair of long-lasting Converse shoes, a few bucks and a 1949 Chrysler Country Convertible, or a red 1934 Hudson Eight Convertible Coupe, maybe a silver 1951 Hudson Hornet, or a 1949 black Coupe De Ville, any one of the amazing land yachts that could easily double as home to their travels. Many misfits had been captured and domesticated, but we had escaped through using land yachts. We would always find a way to escape, that's what we did best. Escaping from the Shadow.

We roving misfits loved our land yachts. They gave us the freedom of movement to flee bad situations. Land yachts were the precious something we held on to when there was nothing else. Every one of us converted our dependable, beloved vehicles into security blankets on wheels. I kept chicken noodle soup and a can opener stashed under the front seat of the Merc'. A spirit catcher hung around Esmerelda's rearview mirror. Stashed in her glove box was a little brown teddy bear belonging to her son.

Eddy's handsome father's purple silk tie was wound around the rear-view mirror of his eighteen-wheeler. Cowboy Johnson had a soft, old ladies white lace handkerchief tucked neatly into the glove box of the El Camino. Who it belonged to, no one knew. William the Dude carried a brown, intricately carved cane behind his truck seat. He said it came from a Scottish ancestor's home who used it to kill snakes.

Since all of us knew well what it was to be bedless and unwanted at one time or another without a vehicle to sleep in, we would keep a permanent altar in the new sanctuary for both the known and the unknown Gods surviving in people's hearts, with an eye towards the unwanted misfits, for we needed them in our lives to keep us limber, laughing and able to move on. They carried the precious, secret alchemy that kept us darkly flexible towards the shoe falling and the car not stalling. I looked around the garden sanctuary and smiled.

When I went outside, Normaine was waiting. She glared at me in stony silence.

"What's wrong, Normaine?"

"Aleda and Alena say you are building them a church so they can oversee everybody's ways and keep em' on a Godly path, including every person that rents a motel room."

"What? No. That's silly."

"Is it? You might want to tell them that."

"Normaine, I go to the round church so the devil can't corner me. I bet you're just fed up with their religious B.S. Our sanctuary is going to be a place where anybody can come and be at peace or sit around. It's a sort of Holy room with a garden in it. Whatever. It is not a regular church."

"Then, you need to straighten them out!"

I watched her stalk away and shuddered at the thought of confronting the Mafia sisters. Would they perform an exorcism on me to cure me of my blasphemous ways? Would they insist I eat their fruitcake? Did I need to find a new hideout?

William had it worse than me. The Mafia sisters kept his feet to the fire. They kept the old prospector geezer busy training to be a dedicated Catholic again. He told me one day that the only reason God made Sunday was Algestine. That she was in training to kick the Devil out of Hell. He sounded so despairing, I didn't know whether to laugh or cry.

He drove the three sisters to Albuquerque each Saturday so they could attend mass at Saint Anne's Catholic Church. The drive was over an hour each way. I could tell the three sisters' holiness was wearing on him. His jaunty step became hesitant, and the gorgeous blue light in his eyes dimmed. I disliked the religiously cruel Mafia sisters more each day.

Normaine and Eddy left on a short trip. They promised to be back before Christmas for the wedding. I planned to concentrate on finishing the sanctuary before the wedding, but the three sisters got busy and filled it up with crosses and candles and their many treasured religious objects. I let them take it over without a word of protest.

Cowboy Johnson asked me about it.

"What do you think?" he asked.

I shrugged.

"I don't mind. I need time to talk to you and William about how to put it together better anyway."

"You don't mind all that religious stuff being in there?"

"It's fine until after the wedding. But eventually, I want something for everyone to admire, to be in awe of, in the sanctuary. That's religion to me."

I grinned at him and thought to myself, "Maybe we could put a statue of you in there."

I clapped my hand over my mouth to keep from saying the words out loud. Cowboy Johnson grinned at me.

"What didn't you say?"

Out loud, I said, "What about stained glass windows set in a new way? The colored lights can play over the vegetables and flowers and small trees? Dance with them? A waltz, maybe?"

He lowered his lips to my forehead for a second and touched my hand briefly, and I didn't pull away.

"Yes."

Then he said, "The Mafia sisters are religious zealots. I don't mind them wearing medieval costumes, drinking red wine constantly, praying all the time, and working their fans hard enough to stir up a tornado, but that damn fruitcake smell is everywhere! It smells like I am running a saloon instead of a store."

He sighed.

"So, You... That's where I am at with it. Maybe add to the brochure about the sanctuary being non-denominational? Maybe the sisters could found their own church somewhere? Not here, of course!" he added hastily, turning away. We were always so busy.

Algestine and William were to be married on Christmas Eve in the garden chapel. For his beloved, he'd chosen a rigid, fanatically religious, haughty fruit cake maker no one liked, one that was fast becoming a crowing rooster that never stopped when it came to him. It was obvious to all of us the aged spinster Algestine was planning on having a religious husband who would follow His and Her instructions, live sparsely, and stay small. I didn't like that for the William Makepeace I knew, and neither did anyone else. That is, with the exception of her two sisters.

The first week of December sped by like a gangster fleeing the law in a bullet-riddled, rusted out, fast-moving, silver spiked, hub capped 1935 Ford. Cowboy Johnson took to hanging out with the old geezer prospector all the time to help him get through his wedding jitters. He plied him with beer, wine, platitudes, and music. He took him for long rides and listened while William bemoaned his upcoming fate. Then Cowboy Johnson came to me for help.

"Can you help with William? He's having trouble getting through this."

"You're kidding. I thought you knew him from the time you were both knee high to grasshoppers."

"I can tell you what I know, but there are some pieces missing because he's a bit older than me," he spoke tersely.

"William is from California, same as me. I met him at school. He married Thelma, and they had one daughter, Emma, Ray's mother. William brought Emma back to the ranch after Thelma and their second child died in childbirth. He raised Emma alone."

"When Emma grew into a young woman, she met a no good handsome actor named Barron Swift. Their brief marriage produced Ray, after which event the erstwhile actor moved on, leaving no forwarding address or tracks to be traced."

"Emma and Ray live with William out on his ranch not far from here. The three of them have lived together ever since Ray's father left, two of them without the benefit of spouses or dates. No others for them. Ever again. That's what they say. Or said."

Cowboy Johnson shrugged. I did too. I already knew most of what he was telling me.

"But of course, there have been women along the way."

I peered up at him. I could tell he didn't want to tell me anything more. He must have trusted me a hell of a lot to have confided in me as much as he already did.

"Can you tell me more?"

I said it that way so he would know that I understood his hesitation in spilling his guts to a goofy, silly psychic woman who he must have suspected, kind of liked him. Did he think I might swoon and beg for a ring? Grab him and plead the fifth amendment after I ran my hot hands all over his body or blackmail him into submission if he confessed to knowing more?

"Well, there was Andrea. William lived with her for a long time. I still don't know why they parted."

He shrugged, and that was it. I thought it over. Men. They all seemed to be scared of emotions more than anything else. They weren't afraid of guns or fast cars or of drinking each other under the table while arm wrestling and cursing in loud voices in old smelly bars. In wars, they shot each other without hesitation. They skydived and flew planes and conquered worlds. But let a teeny tiny little emotion get near them, and they grew shortsighted, terse, surly, and regressed into one syllable explanations like "ummph", just like ancestral cavemen.

It was becoming obvious that I wasn't going to get any more out of that less than silver-tongued savage, at the moment, at least, Cowboy Johnson.

"So, William hasn't gone forward. He's somehow managed to put his life on hold. Sounds like Emma has, too. Sometimes fears get the best of us and hold us hostage in a dark cellar with no windows and bars. Of course, the prison never looks like that...it could look entirely spacious."

I swept my hand in a circle to indicate the vastness of the desert around us. Cowboy Johnson looked at me, and I realized he knew I was including myself, too. Time to shut up and change the subject.

"Well, maybe Ray knows what happened to Andrea. If they were married, they are either divorced, or she's dead unless William is hell-bent on committing bigamy."

I waited for him to say something, but that was it. Finally, he said, "I'll do that right now."

He put his cap with its meaningful logo back on his head and turned away with purpose. I shook my head. Men. Give them something to do, and they stop thinking. I called after him.

"Ask Ray about everything, not just Andrea!"

"Now, why didn't I think of that?'

"Because you're a man!"

He grinned at me.

"Somehow, I know you know that."

"What?" I pretended I didn't know what he was talking about.

Chapter Fifteen

Gimme' a' little dat' hot coffee baby,
and some of that fine fruitcake, honey

    Later, Cowboy Johnson told me that William the Dude suffered from arthritis bad enough to wake the dead, and over time, he became very superstitious about it. He came to believe that admitting it out loud would jinx him even worse. He blamed the arthritis for his white hair beginning to thin, and for not being able to toss back a six-pack at will anymore.
    When he couldn't stand the pain any longer, he went prospecting in the desert, using the excuse that he was a prospector at heart when what he really wanted to do was to find a place away from people so he could vent his frustration and anger from his never-ending arthritis pain. His prospecting trips sometimes lasted a week. That's how bad it was. Then one day, he ate a meal at the store, and the pain lessened considerably for a couple of days. He became determined to track down the source, so he hung out at the store. He didn't find it until he bought one of Algestine's fruitcakes. He took it home, ate it, and was suddenly pain-free. He kept his secret. He tried out the other Mafia sister's fruitcakes, but they didn't work. Each of the sisters made their own secret recipe, but only Algestine's fruitcake stopped his arthritis pain.

So he started courting the source of his newfound bliss and eventually convinced himself that they should marry. His thinking was good for business; to secure the source, but not for his personal life.

I thought about Algestine's fruitcake. Could we bottle and sell it as a new medical wonder? I pictured a traveling wagon and a medicine show in which the Mafia sisters wore black and cracked long, black whips to make their audiences part with their nickels and dimes.

"What's the Catholic thing about?" I asked him to hide my impish thoughts.

"William's family was and is solid Catholic, and he was very devout as a boy. When he moved away, he dropped Catholicism like a hot potato he couldn't get rid of fast enough."

"There's another thing you should know." He said. "But it's a secret. Can you keep a secret for me?"

"Yes," I answered without hesitation.

"A few years ago, I came up with an idea of how to help William with his pain. I did it, then I told him about it. When the pain got too bad, he was to use the excuse of going prospecting, then he was to head over the ridge behind Washman's Draw and do what he needed to do until he felt better. It worked for a long time."

"What did you do?"

He looked at me and shrugged. Then he said in one long breath, "I cut out six wood cactus, painted them red, hauled them over the ridge and propped them up in buckets of sand and secured them with posts. I...ah...in effect...made a red cactus desert." He spread his hands out.

I covered my mouth with a hand to keep from laughing. He warmed to his subject, once he got past his first words.

"I'm pretty good at making up stories. I told him the red cactus were there to eat his anger and pain. I told him his anger and pain was a great delicacy to them. He was to shout and holler at the red cactus, whatever he needed to do, and he could shoot them, too. And he did. I told him they loved it all. He said his visits to them were successful. They cut a week's pain down to three days. He pitched a tent and stayed right there until he was done. When the next buildup of pain came, he just visited the red cactus desert again. Now he has found Algestine's fruitcake."

I went to Geena.

"He's old, not dead, Mama, and his name is William the Dude, not the old prospector geezer. He's just trying to make amends to his mostly dead family for leaving them, and he's trying to get close to them again through religion while he is still alive. Also, he loves Algestine's fruitcake because it keeps him loaded most of the time and free from his never-ending arthritis pain. You know, like marijuana does for some people? He feels like a young Dude again when he eats her fruitcake. And she has a never-ending supply."

I pictured a bubbling, evil-smelling, tortured mass of rising dough.

"You mean like a fountain of youth sort of thing? He's hooked on Algestine's fruitcake?"

"Yeah. That and the family thing. He's got a lot of money, and Ray's mother is a famous recluse artist. She spends her time painting and drawing and uses a lot of different names, and she has money, too. Emma knows Georgia O'Keefe."

I stared at her, stunned.

"Georgia O'Keeffe? The artist?"

"Yep."

She skipped away, leaving me standing with my mouth open like I was trying to catch flies. I told Cowboy Johnson what she said, and we agreed true love might just survive on a doughty load of fruitcake soaked in enough booze, along with a strong dose of religious guilt.

Now we needed to find out all we could about Algestine. Our available resources were the two Mafia sisters because Eddy wasn't home. He and Normaine were "up Fargo way" again. The sisters would not be easy to interrogate, so we would have to double team them. We were under pressure to do it soon because the wedding was only two weeks away.

But before we could get to it, Normaine and Eddy came home wearing matching outfits. Long, slim, black wool coats with wide lapels, black cowboy boots, and Trilby hats. They were beautiful. Normaine explained as she hugged me.

"Boston. We been to Boston."

Cowboy Johnson drew me aside.

"Let me talk to Eddy and see what I can find out before we tackle the Mafia sisters. He might be easier."

That night Cowboy Johnson and Eddy climbed into Cowboy Johnson's dark green 1959 El Camino carrying a case of beer, and a grocery bag of God knows what else. They took off in a cloud of dust, veered out onto the highway, and set out for Washman's Draw.

Late that night, Cowboy Johnson's dusty green El Camino came drifting slowly back and forth across the highway. I watched them from the front porch. The El Camino was barely moving. The guys were singing a mournful dirge that was all the rage when it was written and sung back in seventeen fifty-nine, then re-sung in modern times by that most languishing and despairing of mournful country singers, Hank Williams. The El Camino finally lurched to a stop in front of the porch.

"Howdee!" Cowboy Johnson swept off his cap in a salute to me. He was wearing the cap with the smiling moose on it. I, who tended to search out the meaning of things, was never able to figure out the meaning of his moose caps.

Normaine ran past me and down the steps. She jerked open the passenger door and started kissing Eddy.

"Got any left? Gimme' some!"

She laughed and grabbed the long neck bottle he handed her.

"Only one left, Babe. And you got it all now."

Eddy leered at her as she helped him from the El Camino and half carried him around the corner out of sight.

Cowboy Johnson grinned at me like he was waiting for me to run down the steps and start kissing on him, too. And maybe help him out of his El Camino. And maybe smooth his straight brown hair before he put his moose cap back on. Well, he had another think coming. But I couldn't help myself. I ran down the steps, shut the passenger door, and leaned through the open window.

"Did you find out anything?"

He studied me with glazed eyes and finally managed to speak.

"About what?"

"So, you can sing better than you can talk right now, huh?"

He leered at me like a lovesick dog and began to serenade me.

"Oh my darlin', Oh my darlin'..."

I interrupted him.

"We'll talk later. "

I turned from the truck window and stomped around the store like a mad, righteous housewife whose husband has come home late and drunk. Then I slowed down and sighed. I wondered. Maybe I was more invested in that green-eyed, brown-haired fool of a Cowboy Johnson than I was willing to admit.

I slept a troubled sleep, filled with dreams of being jilted at the altar by Cowboy Johnson. The next morning, I arrived early for coffee at the back door of the store. I banged self-righteously on the door and waited a long time before it opened. He'd pulled on jeans and a white tee-shirt. I marched past him to the stove and made a pot of strong coffee while he took two aspirin and huddled on the Hideous Green Sofa, groaning every few seconds. I carried a cup of coffee to him. It was thick as mud. He took a wary sip.

"Oh my God! Did you have to make it so strong?"

I bristled.

"Dragging God into it, huh? Well, God don't listen to nothing or nobody until Sunday afternoon. He's too damn busy procreating or meditating or golfing, or whatever the hell He does, and today is only Friday."

I had no other pearls of biased, applicable wisdom to apply to the situation, so I finally said, to keep from inflicting more double negatives on a doubtful subject, "I'll just come back a little later."

"Yeah."

I slammed out the back door of the store, filled with seething, confusing emotions, mad at him all over again. It was road trip time. I needed to run. It took me a while to tear Normaine away from Eddy's clutches and get us on the road. She climbed in the Merc' and promptly fell asleep. I glared at her. What the hell was wrong with these people? Screwing like a pack of dogs, then sleeping in, all lovey-dovey. Still, they were speaking a language that broke my heart, one that I didn't dare go near. I drove hard and fast for a long time. Finally, Normaine woke up enough to complain.

"I'm hungry."

I swerved the Merc' into a U-turn, squealing the tires and laying rubber, and headed back the way we had come. Normaine ignored my ugly mood. I could tell she was doing it on purpose. I felt wounded and all alone. Like always. I stood it as long as I could before I pulled off the blacktop, rammed the Merc' into park, and covered my face with my hands. I started sobbing.

"I'm so alone! Not a friend in this world! I don't know how to have relationships!"

She steadily ignored me and watched something out the window. Finally, I blew my nose and got pissed off enough to ask her what the hell she was looking at.

"That cat. The mountain cat that's been running alongside us for hours. I bet it's tired."

She motioned out the window.

"You've caused it to run until it is exhausted."

She accused me.

"What?"

She took a deep breath and deliberately didn't look at me, as though I was despicable.

"Life proves itself to life. There are no exceptions. You, in your Dumbass life, have believed a bunch of bullshit you never bother questioning. And you drag it out, and offend God... Alone, my ass!"

She glared at me.

"... and all the people around you, and the lovely animals from the kingdoms, by asking them to smell your bull crap, and be offended, too! I don't know where you got that stuff from, but you better evict it from wherever it is stored in you. That's a broken record you better stop playing! We know God didn't put it in there, so guess who that leaves? You, Dumbass! That's why I can have Eddy. Why I can love again. Through every bad thing that's happened to me, I know I'm not alone. Nothing is. Are you just plain dumb or what? Beings from the plant kingdom and the animal kingdoms and all the others that watch over us are always with us. We eat em', fool, and sleep on em' and shelter under em'. That's why we can exist, Dumbass!"

She shuddered.

"It's a group effort. And when you kick them out by believing your "alone" bull crap, you become a creep of the lowest order, and it sets you back. My advice would be to be very careful and fight that bullshit persuasion. Get over yourself, okay? I want to go back to the store now. I'm done."

I started the Merc'. We rode back to the store in strained silence. I intended to drop Normaine off and go off somewhere and lick my wounds, but Eddy and the three Mafia sisters were waiting for us on the front porch.

Eddy raced down the steps.

"Cowboy Johnson took William to the hospital in Pistachio Pico with a heart attack! He drove Esmerelda! Aleda and Alena are gonna' watch the store for us! I waited for you!"

Algestine started down the steps, taking her time, doing it her way. Eddy grabbed her arm, hurried her down the steps, and pushed her in the back seat of the Merc'. He jumped in after her.

"Stop your crap, Algestine!" he shouted at her. A shocked and offended expression came over her face, but she wisely kept her mouth shut and settled into the corner of the back seat farthest away from him.

I fishtailed the Merc' out of the parking lot, leaving tall dust plumes behind along with the shocked faces and loud, angry voices of Alena and Aleda. I guess they expected to have their way in this, too. But William belonged to us first, and he would always be ours, even though they thought they owned him now.

I flew down the highway. We rode in stony silence. A few minutes later, I squealed into the small parking lot outside the six-bed hospital in Pistachio Pico.

Geena was sitting in the cheerful little yellow waiting room. She jumped up and ran to us.

"He came up onto the front porch, and grabbed his chest and fainted. There's no ambulance close by, so Cowboy Johnson took him. He knows C.P.R."

Geena explained importantly to us.

"William the Dude was breathing, so he didn't have to kiss him or pound on his chest. We put him in the back seat of Esmerelda and took off!"

We waited for what seemed like hours before Cowboy Johnson appeared, looking exhausted.

"William is sleeping. They've done some tests, but it doesn't look like a heart attack. They say his heart is strong as a horse's. That it was probably caused by some kind of stress he's under. He should be able to go home in a little while. I've called Ray and Emma. They should be here to pick him up pretty soon."

He glared at Algestine for an instant, then grinned at Geena.

"Young lady, you did a good job opening the car door and getting William into the back seat."

She strutted over to him, and they hugged. Algestine spoke up.

"I told him he has to stop eating so much of my fruitcake even though he loves it so much! I will stop him from eating so much of it. That was probably what caused this!"

We all shot her dirty looks and turned our backs on her. Just then, Emma and Ray hurried in.

Emma strode over to Algestine and planted herself directly in front of her. Slim, dark, and small, always a lady, she swayed back and forth, like an angry, tiny, determined boxer finding his footing.

"How much for your fruitcake recipe?"

She spoke to Algestine in a loud voice filled with contempt.

"I will pay whatever it is you want for it."

I watched Emma. She had the Sight. I didn't know what kind or how she used it. She was always too polite and reserved to allow any observation of it. She was extremely private. Maybe she kept her Sight under control and saved it for her painting.

I watched her aura grow larger. Reds and yellows began to streak through it. There was no black in it. That was good. No chronic hidden diseases of the mind or anywhere else. Just plain, old warrior red mixing with mental body yellow. Someone was in for a tongue lashing.

Algestine grew pale under her olive skin. I could see she wanted to step back, it would have been the natural thing to do, given what she was being confronted with, but she was Mafia proud and stubborn and stood right where she was. She didn't answer Emma's question.

I cocked my head in silent admiration. She was one obtuse woman. They became locked in a silent battle.

Emma's aura was growing larger. She was moving past a tongue lashing. Soon she would take some kind of action. She began to raise her hand to slap Algestine. Algestine was an old lady. Emma and I were young. Whatever happened, hitting her would be wrong.

Hastily, I used my Sight and blew Lawrence Welk Music Hour bubbles between them. Lots of them. So many they could barely see each other. Bubbles were one of the best emotional shields. They are spheres holding Light. Low, negative energies are raised to a higher level of vibration, whether they want to be or not when bubbles are around. Nothing could get past the power of a bubble, for about ten minutes. Emma looked at me. She knew what I was doing. She finally lowered her hand and turned away. Algestine retreated to a window and stared out into the bright sunshine.

The confront lasted less than a minute.

Emma came over to me. "Bubbles?" she said to me, amused, in a low voice.

I said, "William is okay. He will be out soon. He is physically fine. They said it was stress-induced."

She raised her voice, so it carried through the little waiting room.

"You know, I've given this situation much thought. Something or someone has been keeping my father stressed out for quite a long time now. This caps it. Enough! I think I'll take him away for a while. On a long trip. Right away. Today. We'll go to the Jesuit retreat he likes so much. He has good friends there. Or to the Trappist or Buddhist monastery in Oregon. He has good friends there, too. He has family and friends all over the world of different spiritual persuasions that have his back. Who appreciate that he understands that many fine, upright, good people have grown past the archaic idea that serving a particular religion makes them better than anyone else."

Algestine kept staring out the window.

William walked into the waiting room. Emma and Ray hurried to embrace him. The three of them ignored Algestine and went out the door together, arms around each other. She didn't try to follow them. She knew better. Normaine and Eddy hurried out to Esmerelda in the parking lot, leaving her on her own. She rode back to the store with Cowboy Johnson, Geena, and me. Nobody spoke. When we got back to the store, she rushed away with her sisters. The air was heavy with their unspoken anger.

Cowboy Johnson came up to me.

"Want to go for a walk or a short ride? Get away from it all for a little while?"

I nodded. We grabbed a couple of beers and took off in the EL Camino, leaving the others to mind the store. When we reached Washman's Draw, he pulled over and shut the engine off. I opened a beer and waited.

"I want to talk about William. Okay?"

I nodded.

"When he stepped up on the porch and clutched his heart, he gave Algestine the worst look a person can give another. He said to her, "Your crosses are killing me." like it was the strongest fact ever stated by a human being since we were put on Earth."

He stared straight ahead, an angry look I rarely saw on his face. I carefully placed the beer in its holder and waited.

"Then William clutched his chest and started to fall. I grabbed him and tried to lay him down on the porch. The three sisters jerked out their god damned crosses and started praying. Next, they rushed him. He wouldn't let me lay him down. He wanted to get away from them. Me and Geena carried him to Esmerelda, put him in the back seat, and ran away with him. I've never hated their way of practicing religion as much as I do right now."

He turned and looked at me, his green eyes flint and steel.

"William is like a brother to me. I don't want this marriage to happen. I'm afraid she will kill off the only family I have left from my younger days."

He shook his head.

"You don't know what we have been through together!"

He hit the steering wheel in frustration.

"Thing is, when William gets an idea in his head, it's hard to get it out. The stubborn old fool insists on marrying her, and I have not been able to persuade him otherwise! He knows none of us like her, and nobody wants this marriage to happen. He knows why, and he knows better, so I can't figure out what the hell is driving him to jump off the cliff, so to speak."

He took a long breath.

"When Eddy and I came out here, I tried to question him about his sister's past. His rebuttal was to try to question me about mine."

He looked at me and grinned.

"We both kept drinking instead of telling until we both became two tight-lipped, drunk as a skunk guys."

I laughed.

"Have Emma and Ray talked to William?" I asked him.

"Yes. But they haven't gotten any farther than I have with him."

He shook his head. I got out and walked around to the driver's window and held out my hand.

"Let's go for a walk, okay?"

He studied me a minute.

"You mean, let's go see the red cactus, don't you?"

"Caught!"

I laughed, careful not to touch him, or I might get steamed up in another way. Then we would have two steamed up people who were steamed up for reasons that didn't match. We walked over the ridge together. The red cactus desert appeared in front of us. I stopped and looked them over carefully with my Sight. There was no question that this man had cemented some badass warrior energies into this place.

"Good job," I said.

I left him to it and walked back across the ridge. I went to the El Camino and drank my beer, leaning up against the car.

I opened a beer for him when he came back and handed it to him. To take his mind off his anger, I stood under his chin and pulled his arms around me. I said, "I've been afraid for him for a long time, too."

"Why?"

"I'm afraid because he's a practicing, ordained Dudeist from his Frisco' hippy days? He practices his own internal religion. When I talk to him, he's as tender with me as mist...his voice. It's kind of high and mild.... laden with overlooking bygones. I think he starts over with who she is every day. That's how he can stand it. That, and her fruitcake. Maybe it's the fruitcake more than her."

Cowboy Johnson laughed and kissed the top of my head. I wanted to kiss him back in the worst way, but couldn't. It wasn't time.

Chapter Sixteen

We need a gunslinger
somebody tough to tame this town
-John Fogerty

A few days passed, and William began courting Algestine again as though nothing had happened. We watched Algestine put away her guns. One of the three Mafia spinsters had got her man, and she intended to keep him alive, whatever it took.

There was no more talk about religion or crosses or judgments. They hastily removed all their religious objects from the garden chapel. They realized they'd dodged a bullet. They calmed down and grew almost peaceful about their religion and their fruitcake. Algestine became less rigid. No more deadlines or religious ultimatums for William. I wondered how long it would last.

Cowboy Johnson tried to talk William the Dude out of the wedding, but William was determined to go through with it.

"Sure, you don't want to put it off? At least until you feel better?"

"I'm going through with it. Appease some old ghosts, maybe." William the Dude answered enigmatically. Everybody decided to give up and have a good time. We would have to leave William to his fate.

*

The temperatures dropped down into the mid-thirties the morning of the wedding, a few flakes of snow were drifting down. I watched the snow through one of the stained-glass windows in the chapel while Geena taped up white paper flowers and Cowboy Johnson hammered nails in walls at the direction of the two Mafia sisters. White flowers bloomed everywhere amid makeshift benches, stumps, and chairs.

Cowboy Johnson turned on heaters to keep the chapel warm. There was standing room only, and people were standing outside. William was well-liked.

When all was ready, the music began. Geena strolled in. Wearing a simple pink dress, she tossed flower petals around the perimeter of the chapel. The priest followed her and took his place at the front of the sanctuary. Next came Emma, purposeful and dignified in beige. Aleda and Alena followed her, proud in dark purple with high lace mantles and pearls, looking like nuns in disguises; escapees from a Mafia convent. Cowboy Johnson and Ray took their places beside the priest. All was ready for the entrance of the bride and groom.

The wedding march began. The wedding couple strolled in, holding hands. To prop each other up in case either one or the other fainted or died? To propel each other with gentle tugs down the aisle to their doom?

Both the bride and groom wore white. Algestine wore a simple A-line, ankle-length white dress with short white heels. A tiny white lace veil sat atop her head. William the Dude wore a white linen suit and spats. On his head sat a Panama hat that looked vaguely familiar.

The prospective bride and groom were so pale, I wondered if it was their corpses getting married. How would we be able to tell them from the snow outside or the white flowers inside? Maybe we could find them when they spoke. Either way, we would have to keep an eye on them, so we didn't lose them.

The two Mafia sisters dabbed delicately at their eyes using tiny, purple lace handkerchiefs. The priest married the couple as fast as possible, gave them a quick blessing, and rushed away. I watched him leave. Why was he in such a hurry? Maybe he thought marrying corpses to one another was a sin? Did he hurry because they were so old he feared they might not make it through the wedding ceremony?

We caravanned to the reception at the community center in Pistachio Pico. Cowboy Johnson and I squeezed into the back seat of Esmerelda with Geena and Ray. Esmeralda's top was down. Our own version of a sleigh ride began. A few large snowflakes drifted lazily down through the air. We turned our faces up to catch them on our tongue.

Yes, everybody should have a good experience in the back seat of a land yacht like Esmerelda. I speculated on whether there were more babies made in back seats of cars than in beds, but couldn't figure out how many cars versus beds there were.

Not one to miss an opportunity, the mayor of Pistachio Pico had the tiny ballet dancers flitting about the hall when we got there. They were wearing the blue tutus and white angel wings I made. I felt smug this time instead of crying.

The celebration actually started a week before the wedding. Trucks, vans, and cars were everywhere. Briskets, hams, chickens, and sundry other items were kept roasting out back of the community center for days.

Someone put a fruitcake instead of a groom's cake on the wedding table. Everyone laughed when the groom refused to eat any of it. But some of us got the message. I hoped Algestine got it, too. Undertones. Would there always be undertones at every wedding I went to? Many of the reasons for getting married were as old as human beings were. Possession of another, legal rights, disguised hate, needing protection, or money, love might be somewhere in there, but not always.

William the Dude and his new bride left the party early. They were going to Santa Fe to see a play and do some shopping. Their plan was to live in one of the guesthouses out at the ranch until they decided whether they wanted to travel or not. Emma and Ray were leaving on an extended tour of Europe in a couple of days. I'm pretty sure that was happening with the purpose of avoiding the newlyweds. William said maybe they would build, but for now, they planned to play it by ear.

The rest of us ate and danced until after midnight, at which time I let Cowboy Johnson nuzzle my neck. At that hour, all I could do was turn into a pumpkin, right? We made our way home under a starry sky, the top still down on Esmerelda. We wrapped up in shawls and blankets and didn't hurry for our sleigh ride home. It was done. For better or worse, William Thackery Makepeace, William the Dude, was now married.

*

"Merry Christmas!" Geena shouted the happy words at me the next morning. I climbed out of my sleeping bag and slipped into a sweater, jeans, and boots. There was a respectable amount of snow on the ground. Geena wanted to make a snowman, but the snow was too thin and powdery.

"Come on! Let's make Cowboy Johnson fix us breakfast!"

"I don't know, Geena. He might still be sleeping."

I looked around the tent. Dust and hope filled it ever since Cowboy Johnson and Geena put it up. Summer and fall were past, now a thin snow lay across the sandy desert outside the tent. This was our first Christmas away from Monster town. We'd been gone for seven months. They were the best months of our lives.

I didn't have any idea what to do about this new kind of Christmas. I trailed Geena up the porch steps to the back door of the store. Alena and Aleda were frying bacon and eggs and making toast. Cowboy Johnson was nowhere to be seen.

"He'll be back soon. He's running errands," Aleda said comfortingly to me in response to my looking around. Did everything have to lead back to Cowboy Johnson? And why did she have to sound as if she was consoling me? Miffed, I went to the table and sat down, munched a piece of bacon, and sipped orange juice. Then I heard Geena shout.

"Oh, goody! He's brought us Christmas presents!"

My hand froze in the act of delivering a bite of delicious, crispy, buttered toast to my mouth. I didn't get him anything! Or Geena! Or anybody! Loaded with guilt, I scuttled out the back door, hurried to my tent, and started sorting through stuff, tossing it everywhere. Nothing. Then I stopped. This was the first Christmas at the store for all of us misfits. Whatever happened, it would be okay because we had each other. How long was I gone?

I ran out of the tent, up the steps of the back porch, crossed it, opened the door, and stepped inside. The heat, carrying breakfast smells hit me. Eddy was wearing a black top hat, a superman cape, and big plastic clown shoes. He and Normaine, who was wearing a feathered headband and holding a yellow rubber chicken and a spatula, were capering about. Geena was lolling on the Hideous Green Sofa, wearing a tiara with a giant pink boa wrapped around her neck. Aleda and Alena were wearing huge black sunglasses, nun headdresses, and holding rubber newspapers.

A red sack trimmed on the top with fuzzy white stuff lay empty on the floor by Cowboy Johnson's chair. Normaine danced up and handed me my unfinished glass of orange juice. I looked around cautiously. My Sight was a zealot about Christmas. It usually brought on healing situations and forced me to participate in them. Sometimes they worked out, sometimes they didn't. Therefore, I was a bit leery of any do-gooder Christmas plot.

"He's out front, helping a man to fix his car," Geena said comfortingly. I stared at her. Why did everyone assume I was constantly searching for Cowboy Johnson?

I looked around again. Simple bookcases full of books. A Reader lived here. One filled with Goodness, like Will Parton was. This was not a spiritual wasteland filled with purposeless wanderers. On the contrary, this church, now a store, was filled with spiritual warriors of all kinds.

Eddy pulled me into a dance and whirled me around with Normaine keeping time by slapping the rubber chicken with the spatula in lieu of a turkey and a knife. "Drumming!" she yelled briefly towards me. Some warriors!

Voices and laughter washed over us. Somebody put a ham on to roast, and the Mafia sisters brought out a variety of fruitcakes. Later, while the ham was cooling, Normaine stirred red-eye gravy while Eddy manfully crushed and generously buttered and fluffed potatoes.

After dinner Cowboy Johnson played both his ukulele and his harmonica for us. I was impressed. Was he a maestro in disguise? Did he lead a Philharmonic orchestra in his younger years? Where were his tuxedo and Hawaiian shirt? Did he know how to hula? Or row a canoe?

I forgot myself and murmured the questions out loud. Everyone laughed and waited for the answers. He told no one much of anything about himself unless you counted the probability of the old geezer prospector, William the Dude, the old Dudeist Priest who was honeymooning somewhere in Albuquerque with the third religious Mafia woman. I wondered how their Christmas honeymoon was going. What were they giving each other? Handshakes for presents? Evidently, they both still believed in Santa Claus, or they wouldn't have married when they both had one foot on a banana peel and the other in the grave.

I wished I hadn't asked my questions out loud. He paused and looked up into the air as though he were plucking something out of it.

"I studied music in college."

Then he went back to playing. After a while, he went to the Victrola and put on Christmas music. Geena pulled me to my feet to dance. The little desert store filled with the cozy warmth of companionship and laughter as us Christmas hams danced to the music of Deck the Halls.

*

Christmas vacation passed. School began again for Geena. Ray was being tutored for the duration of his trip with his mother. The old geezer prospector and his bride returned from their honeymoon and settled into the guest house out on the ranch. They took up exactly where they left off, with William the Dude and Cowboy Johnson supervising the last of the building and running the car garage beside the store.

Things went on as before. Algestine and her sisters knitted, prayed, baked, and watched the men working from the front porch. I worked on the sanctuary and did whatever else I was called on to do.

By spring, the building was done. The garden chapel was lush with plants under gorgeous, colorful stained glass windows. Arranged around the sanctuary were rockers, benches, tree stumps, homemade throw pillows, shawls, and wind chimes. Geena's clay statues of Elementals peeked from the plant beds and played by the birdbath.

The long, deeply shaded motel porches held new and old rockers, tree stumps, painted chairs, and textile throw pillows. Normaine's colorful rag rugs dotted the blue painted, planked floors. Intense blue, amber, and yellow knit shawls lay draped across the backs of rockers in front of each room, courtesy of the Mafia sisters. The windows of each room were framed with shutters painted the cooling, bright, turquoise of Miami beach waters, on special from Duke's Hardware paint department.

The doors to each room were painted blue, green, rusty red, orange, yellow, lilac, purple, or white. Matching colors repeated themselves in paler shades in each room, creating a soft, colorful, cocooning effect. The back doors were painted a softer shade of the same color and framed with lights. The sheets and towels were plain white so they could be carried to the Laundromat in Pistachio Pico and washed and bleached.

The restaurant, bakery, and gift shop were housed in the other long stucco building. The gift shop was filled with fruit cakes, rag rugs, clay lizards, shawls, and wind chimes.

The Mafia sisters had taken over the designs of the restaurant and bakery. Cowboy Johnson and William the Dude were glad to leave them to it. Our new quarters adjoined theirs. Cowboy Johnson built Geena and me two large rooms with separate entrances and connecting doors. We both chose the cool turquoise water colored shutters, and the almost white wood planked floors that matched the motel rooms for our porches.

Geena painted her room pink and green. Before long, it overflowed with plants, insect collections, and lizard skeletons. She kept her workspace in the back of the store and made more clay lizards, little clay people, and other things, while Normaine wove more rag rugs and made wind chimes on the other side of the room.

My room was white and spare with a twin bed in it. I had just a few clothes, and I didn't want any more. I unloaded almost everything out of the Merc's trunk into the room. But not everything. I left a few of my things in the trunk as travel insurance – who knew what might happen? Life rarely did what you expected it to when you were a runaway.

I stored my suitcase under the bed. It held an emergency flashlight, chicken noodle soup, and a can opener. There were pieces of me I'd been robbed of through different degrees of neglect and violence from the time I was a child. I would never get them back. Those parts stayed ready to move on in case the robbers showed up again and tried to force me to do their wishes.

Maybe someday those parts could put down roots. I sure hoped so. I wanted to be enough for Cowboy Johnson, but I knew I wasn't yet, so for now, that was on hold.

I did take one of the rugs Normaine offered me. I placed it on the floor by the window and sat my favorite old rocking chair from the front porch on it. Because I love to read so much, I asked the old geezer prospector for leftover planks from building, and I used bricks and the planks to make bookshelves near my rocking chair. I hung sheer curtains over the windows to soften the sunlight because I needed to be able to see outside.

The psychology books referred to this need as a "womb with a view." I added shades I pulled down at night. The window opened easily if I needed fresh air or an escape route. It had a good lock on it. I closed the shutters each night and pulled the shades. Geena closed hers, too. No Monster would ever jump through our windows and terrorize us again if we could help it.

Chapter Seventeen

Put up yo' big sign baby
cause da' people
de's a' comin' in

We needed a sign to go up by the store to direct people back to the motel. We held a meeting to decide on a name. William the Dude didn't want his name on it. He shoved his hat back on his head and grinned easily at us.

"I mean, I got that community building over in Pistachio Pico named after me, for one. That's enough."

Ray interrupted. "Whatever it says, I vote for a tall sign with a dancing girl in neon with an arrow pointing back to the motel."

"No! No!" said Aleda and Alena in shocked disapproval. Ray ducked his head, blushed, and grinned at them. Everybody started talking at once. I listened, and when I'd heard enough, I interrupted them and stated the obvious.

"Let's not waste time, okay? How about Cowboy Johnson's Desert Oasis?"

There was a moment of silence before they all roared with laughter. I stared at them, puzzled.

"We can write Store, Gas, Motel, Restaurant and Gift Shop in smaller letters underneath Cowboy Johnson's Desert Oasis," I added helpfully. They roared with laughter again.

"What's so funny?" I asked again. Cowboy Johnson interrupted their laughter.

"I like it. We'll do it. Only the sign has to be homemade. No neon around here unless it's a beer sign," he grinned. "Besides, the rewiring is done. I don't want to even think about more right now," he groaned loudly. They laughed. I tilted my head and looked at them. Their laughter held a relieved timbre to it. Secrets. All of us misfits kept secrets.

Geena, Ray, and their friends painted two big square boards glaring white. Using stencils to make the black lettering, they made the signs. The motel workers mounted the double-sided sign high up on a tall pole just past the store.

The sign read, "Cowboy Johnson's Desert Oasis." Beneath, in smaller letters, the sign read, "Gas, Food and Rest." I shaded my eyes and looked at it. It couldn't be seen clear to Philadelphia. Chicago, maybe.

The workers put a driveway in at the foot of the sign for people to turn into the unpaved parking lot, and we were open for business.

*

Everybody settled into their new routines. Geena got out of school and spent her summer making things and examining the desert around us for insect life to impale and preserve in her collection boxes. Ray went with her on her treks into the desert, but he was more interested in the rock formations and the layers of sand. Sure he was. I believed that like I believed the store was oceanfront property.

Normaine and Eddy spent most of their time on the road. They called us every few days to tell us where they were leaving from and where they were headed next.

The old geezer prospector, William the Dude and his lady Algestine began traveling with William towing the silver "Airstream" toaster behind his canary yellow 1946 GMC truck.

The two Mafia Sisters stayed busy running their thriving businesses, praying, knitting, and entertaining their boyfriends at night. Ray dutifully drove them to church once a week. There was a steady stream of business at the motel and store. The customers liked the idea of keeping everything simple and "green". They said it was restful and harkened back to a better time.

Cowboy Johnson hired a lady and her friends to clean the motel rooms, wash the linens, and do odd jobs. Ray and Geena worked in the store. Things were going smoothly. All of us misfits were making a bit of money. That was good. We settled into our desert oasis. It was our new home.

*

Now that we'd put down roots, I felt it was time to let Bud Spencer know Geena and I were safe and doing okay. I couldn't bring myself to talk to him, so Cowboy Johnson called back to Monster Town for me. I stood next to him while he dialed the number on the rotary dialer.

"Hello? I'm calling on behalf of an old friend of yours. They wanted me to give you a message. Are you alone?"

There was a silence while Bud answered him, then Cowboy Johnson said, "She said to tell you that we made it. We got a good new home now and good new friends. Her new last name is Johnson. She said for you to take down this phone number for emergencies and to memorize it and destroy the paper you wrote it on so no one else up there ever gets a hold of it."

He gave him the store phone number and started to end the call, but I grabbed the phone away from him.

"I love you, Bud!"

I bawled into the receiver loud enough to wake the dead. Bud spoke calmly.

"No paper. Just tell me where you are. I need to know."

"Near Pistachio Pico, New Mexico. At Cowboy Johnson's Desert Oasis. Food. Gas. Rest."

"You'll always be my little Map Girl," Bud said. I hung up and grabbed Cowboy Johnson, wet his shirt with tears, wrinkled it with laughter, and ran away.

*

Time flew by. Geena was in then out of high school until she was ready to be a senior. That summer, our easy time came to an end, but out of it, we got a big gift. We got Timmon. It happened at the Fourth of July campfire. Eddy, Normaine, William, and Algestine were home. The men were crazy over fireworks, so we moved the fire farther back from the buildings so the men could set off bigger rockets.

Armed with a long list, snacks, and beer, they drove an ungodly distance to purchase fireworks that "blew up better." They returned close to sundown with the back of the El Camino loaded with boxes of fireworks.

Geena invited her friends to the campfire. One of them was her new friend Leeza. Leeza had stayed overnight with Geena a couple of times. She was small with short, curly brown hair and watery blue eyes. She was quiet and seemed sad and secretive. I didn't want to ferret out her troubles. She was just a young, average girl, but mostly because her secrets might be too much like Geena's secrets. Underneath, I feared that was the reason they were friends.

Leeza brought her youngest brother Timmon with her. Timmon was as tall as Leeza, though he was just ten. He was a handsome boy with thick blond hair, a straight nose, full mouth, and wide blue eyes. The two of them huddled together, sad and silent, perched on an end of one of the logs circling the fire pit. Once in a while, they smiled. They were hungry and ate seconds and thirds of everything in sight. I turned away from the thought that they might not have eaten recently and busied myself with keeping an eye on Geena and Ray. They were both bursting with hormones and the primitive urge to do the "wild thing." I lectured Geena at what I intuitively felt were the right moments, and so far, it worked. I hoped tonight wasn't going to be yet another night of lectures. Between Normaine and me, we managed to keep the steam in the kettle lowered, but the kettle was obviously singing again tonight. Ray and Geena left to take Leeza and Timmon home.

"If you're not back in a reasonable amount of time, we'll come looking for you," Cowboy Johnson said with an apologetic grin. "We wouldn't want you two to have a flat tire or get caught in a dust storm. Something you couldn't handle."

We all knew what he really meant. I studied Ray. His mother's refinement was evident in him. Ray welcomed whatever life brought him. He would always be a little swarthy and elegant, no matter what he wore or what the situation was.

My Geena stood next to him, carelessly elegant too, with long brown hair, slim, tan legs, and a mile of freckles across her turned-up nose. She casually held her own in life and was one of the prettiest girls in school.

They left, and we turned back to the campfire. We were all warbling out a questionable rendition of "Home on the Range" awhile later when Ray came running across the sand to the campfire.

"Listen. We didn't take Leeza and Timmon home. We couldn't. So we brought em' back. We gotta' help them!"

Cowboy Johnson was on his feet.

"Are they hurt? Do they need first aid or a doctor?"

"Nope. They're in trouble all right, but it isn't that kind!"

We were all on our feet by then.

"Where's Geena?"

"She's out front with them in the car."

We all started for the car, but Ray stopped us.

"Wait! Before you go, you need to know that last night, their oldest brother, Gary, and a bunch of his no-good friends forced themselves on a girl out back of their house."

"Where were their parents?" Cowboy Jones asked in a cold tone of voice.

"In the house. They locked the girls up when they tried to call the police and turned out the lights and hid under a window until it was over. Then they let the girls out and told them not to tell anyone. Their parents are hiding Gary from the cops and the girl's brothers. The girl's brothers want to kill him. The girl is hospitalized. She may still be there. I don't know. Their parents are defending the Gary guy. They're saying he didn't do anything wrong, that she was asking for it."

"Where is this Gary guy right now?" Cowboy Johnson asked in a cold voice.

"He took off for a few days with his pals, but who knows when he'll be back."

Ray turned to go back to the car and swept us along with him. The car seemed like a million miles away, but my legs stopped trembling as we went. I was never much of a heroine, but I drove a twelve-year-old in a getaway car from an ongoing crime scene. It had to be enough.

We surrounded Geena's car. It looked dusty and tired in the darkness. The windows were down, and I heard Geena saying something about our family being fun. I snorted. Eddy was still twirling his mustache. Normaine was chanting a Native prayer under her breath. She'd taught me a few Native phrases, and the chant sounded like the one in which certain people got scalped and consigned to hell. I wobbled around the car and stopped by Geena's window.

"They are not going back there, Mama!" Geena shouted the words at me in anguish.

I sighed. I'd hoped she would never come across anything reminding her of the bad parts of her past. But whatever we call the force that runs the big show, it also runs our pitiful little human lives, and it brings us what it does for its own unexplainable reasons. It was the Boss.

I felt the collective energy gathered around Geena's car. None of us were ever kept safe and secure. We owned that in common. Not a damn one of us trusted the universe or God or the mouthy preachers running their religious corporations. That's why we were living out here in a forgotten, godforsaken patch of desert in a little store, trusting each other only, living in a former little white church that would someday crumble into ruins and probably take us all with it. What was the point of life? Nothing. Yet we would do everything we could to survive, as though it did matter.

Cowboy Johnson and William the Dude helped Leeza and Timmon out of the back. I opened Geena's door. She jumped out and hugged me, then raced around the car to Leeza and Timmon. We all clumped together in a bunch and wound our way up the front steps and into the store. William and Cowboy Johnson led Leeza and Timmon into the back room where everyone clustered around them.

"Geena, go lock the front door. Ray, go put the campfire and lights out and when you come back in, lock the back door behind you," he ordered.

We waited until they returned from their errands to talk. We listened to Leeza and Timmon's story and sent Leeza off with Geena to get some sleep. Ray took Timmon and holed up in motel room number four with sodas and snacks. Eddy and Normaine escorted them to their rooms and locked their doors. When they came back, we began the task of figuring out how we were going to handle the next few hours.

"We can't send them home, not for one minute. You heard what Leeza said about her brother and his friends eyeing her."

"We'll need a lawyer. And we can't reach one until tomorrow because of the holiday. Probably in the afternoon. The ones I know tend to sleep in," William said sheepishly. "They're old, like me."

"I'll keep watch, William. You go get some rest," Eddy said. "I'd almost relish a run-in with those bums!" He grabbed the shotgun Cowboy Johnson kept propped beside the closet door.

"It's loaded," Cowboy Johnson said, handing him a box of shotgun shells.

"We should leave all the lights out. That way, they might think we're all in bed. And they won't be able to see us, just in case they decide to take a pot shot at any of us."

The lights went out. Cowboy Johnson and William walked away, strategizing in low voices, with Algestine trailing them. Normaine went with Eddy.

I settled into a corner of the Hideous Green Sofa and stared into the darkness. It was almost three in the morning. Eddy was on the front porch with a loaded shotgun, Normaine by his side. Odds were Leeza and Timmon's family wouldn't show up this late at night, but who knew?

I dozed off, and immediately my Sight started sending me signals, pointing the Way, reminding me of how Darkness can sometimes restore a path Light cannot travel. So what if my getting to the stage of sleep, REM or something, that my Sight required to get its messages across to me, involved me snoring and drooling? It didn't care that I wanted to be a dainty, pretty sleeper in front of Cowboy Johnson these days.

I awoke to the smell of coffee. Cowboy Johnson, William, Normaine, and Eddy were sitting around the table talking in low voices. Someone had covered me with a blanket. I threw it off, went to the table, and sat down.

"I dreamed last night," I said, interrupting them. "I'm going to call their mother."

They stared at me, digesting my announcement. Then Cowboy Johnson stood up and dusted off his hands like the matter was finished.

"I'll get you the phone book."

I carried the phone book to the counter in the store, looked up the number, picked up the receiver on the old black phone, and dialed. The phone rang and rang. I waited. As though I was right there with her. Though I didn't know her name, I knew she was wringing her hands, wanting to answer the phone, but afraid to. The man was at work. I didn't know where the others were. Just gone. She picked up the phone after twelve rings.

"Hello?"

I caught my breath. Damn! This woman knew things in the same way I did! I never met another that carried my kind of Sight. She knew it, too. But this one was lost. She was off her Path. And there was no one to remind her of the Right Way until this instant. The silence ran down the phone lines, back and forth between us while the recognition took place.

I finally said, "They are here. Safe. At the store."

Her voice answered, hostile, tense, and scared.

"He was already passed out before they were supposed to be home last night. He had to work today. I don't know what he will do tonight."

She spoke clipped and quick and low, as if any second, he might walk in the door. Suddenly, she opened a psychic door and shoved me through. I almost fell into a swoon as from afar, I watched her mother and father and a bunch of kids back in West Virginia crying over the taking of their fourteen-year-old prized daughter and sister, Mina.

"She's mine now," the man stated smugly. "She's been had thataway, so she ain't no good to any other man now. Used goods. She ain't worth much, but I'll take 'er off yer' hands."

Weak in the knees, I sank down on a barstool. Cowboy Johnson held my back, and the rest circled me. I don't know how they got there, but it was a comfort.

I heard her screams for herself and her children in my head. She dialed up the psychic sound until I ordered her to stop it. Before she could pull another stunt like that, I stepped in and did business my way. This was familiar ground to me, and she needed to learn that fact fast. I was thoroughly grounded in this Way, if nowhere else. I held the power here.

"Let me sort this out for a minute." I laid the phone down and turned to the anxious faces around me.

"Okay. Mina is Leeza's mother. There are seven children, three boys, and four girls. He won't come after the girls. Just the boys. He sees the girls as subhuman. Slaves. Two of the boys are like him. There is no going back for them."

I paused.

"She wants us to take her and her kids out of there, but that is impossible because much of the die is already cast. Only the three girls and Mina can get out. And only if that church over in Albuquerque with that homeless shelter will take them in."

"What shelter?"

"The Church of Pentecostal Ruptures or something like that! I know things, remember? We have to hurry. The man wants his boy back, and he's going to act soon."

I picked up the phone again.

"Listen to me, Mina. You stay out of this for now, until we get Leeza and Timmon settled. Then we'll figure out your leaving. Meanwhile, don't say a word. And remember, your boys can't come with you."

I listened to her cry of protest without pity.

I shrugged.

"Tough luck. Sometimes we pay prices. It's just you and your girls. And you're lucky to get that much gifted to you after....!"

I caught myself. Now was not the time for a scolding about her psychic abuse of the Path.

"Wait!"

My mind was searching for something missing. Something important. It took a minute, but I finally understood it.

"The phone's in your name, isn't it?"

"Yes," she said reluctantly.

"Okay. What's he wanted for?"

"I didn't know he was."

"Sure he is, and you know it. Take a look. He's your man! You have to face the truth, Mina!"

After a long, sullen silence on her part, I ordered, "He won't be home until later. Go get his red flannel shirt. You know the one. It's never been washed. It's hidden in the back of the gun closet on the floor. Folded. You already know about it. Put your hands on it, and come back and tell me."

She went away and then came back. Her ragged breathing filled the phone. She spoke in a reluctant whisper.

"A woman at the side of a road needed a tire change, and he shoved her into the car and forced himself on her. There have been more. They have a description of him all over this state, plus the old car he sold." After a long silence, Mina said, "I can't do this anymore," and hung up.

The phone returned to a dial tone. I turned around to the waiting faces and repeated what she said. Cowboy Johnson and William began looking up the number of a judge they knew in Albuquerque.

The next night, at three in the morning, the man and his two boys drove in and stopped their old truck beside the gas pumps. They took a couple shots at the darkened store windows. Then they gunned the engine and sped out and got the surprise of their lives. The state police were blocking their escape. They arrested all three of them. The man went to prison, and the two sons that took after him were held without bail, awaiting trials for all the bad things they'd done.

Mina was set free, but she didn't like it. She didn't want to go back to West Virginia to her family. The other misfits began talking about moving them to the motel. That's what Leeza and Timmon wanted. I was against it for good reason. The biggest reason was that Mina lost her Way and aided and abetted the men with her Sight. That's how her man and boys got away with so much. Maybe, in the beginning, she was forced to do it, but later on, she saw it as her only power with the men. She believed it made them equal.

Then there was the Timmon problem. Leeza said he was already a drinker, that her father started him out young. If he stayed here, we would have to stop him. Maybe we could, but not if his mother and sisters were around. If they lived here, there wouldn't be a snowball's chance in hell of weaning him off the booze.

One night those decisions got made for us. Before the trial for Mina's oldest son came up, he broke out of jail at night, sneaked home, and set their place on fire, knowing full well that Mina and the girls were asleep in it. The house burned down, but they made it out alive, and it seemed to wake Mina up. She'd held a tight grip on her old bad life, and it took one of her sons trying to kill her before she was ready to let go and move on.

The three Mafia sisters moved her in with them against my protests.

"Mind your own business!" they ordered.

Mina's three daughters and Leeza moved into motel rooms seven and eight, two to a room, down on the end farthest away from the highway, next door to the Mafia sister's headquarters in the other building. Timmon stayed with Cowboy Johnson. The two Mafia sisters ignored Leeza and Timmon, but they made the three girls and their mother mind them. It wasn't long before Mina grew adept at making fruitcakes and rocking on the porch in the evenings while knitting.

Mina and I didn't talk. Our one conversation was enough for me unless she changed. Abuse of her Sight committed her to a lower way of life. What the reasons were didn't matter. It was so. She needed to learn that being a psychic doesn't mean that you get your way. There was a bigger reason Mina was stolen away from her family, but she refused to look at it and make a better choice.

Unfortunately, Leeza's sisters looked like their father. They were thin as whips with short brown hair, thin, puckered little mouths, sharp chins, and watery blue eyes that stayed wide open as if in perpetual surprise. Their thin bodies quivered, vibrating with an excess of a kind of energy unknown to me. God only knew what that was about. The three of them drew their words out in a learned, trashy way and esteemed the values and manners of lowlife scum. Their father's influence on them was strong. They stuck together and stayed away from the rest of us. At first, the three girls stayed in their rooms, but Geena's naturally positive attitude overcame their shyness, and they blossomed. She called it "blossoming," but I called it growing bolder. They nosed into everything. And Mina was lazy. Normaine was the only one that could handle them, so she took over. She'd seen all kinds of ugly before, and this one was familiar to her.

"Dumbasses!"

She called them down time and again, lecturing them on manners and not taking other people's things. But they were stubborn, and Mina conveniently looked the other way.

Ray and Geena seemed oblivious to the growing problems, so we left them out of it. The rest of us went about our lives, giving each other long, guilty looks filled with silent words. All of us wanted Mina and her daughters gone from Cowboy Johnson's Desert Oasis. But we wanted to keep Timmon and at first, Leeza.

About three weeks into our misery, Normaine and Eddy took the situation into their hands. On Sunday morning, Mina and her three girls were sitting on the front porch. Normaine and Eddy rolled up in Esmerelda. Her top was down, music blasting out of the radio. Normaine peered over her sunglasses at them.

"Dumbasses! Get in the car!" she ordered. The four of them filed down the steps and got in without asking any questions. Normaine and Eddy blew the horn. Cowboy Johnson, Geena, and I got up from our breakfast and went to the front porch.

"Bye Bye!" they shouted. That was all. They waved at us as we watched them drive away. At nine that night, we turned the store lights on. Cowboy Johnson, the two Mafia sisters, Ray, Geena, and Leeza and Timmon, and I waited on the front porch for Eddy and Normaine's return.

They rolled in about ten o'clock. Mina and her three daughters weren't with them. Eddy got out of Esmerelda and swaggered around her miles of gorgeous chrome and leather. He swung the passenger door wide for Normaine and bowed her out. Then they leaned back against Esmerelda, grinning up at us.

"Got a beer?" Eddy asked.

"Where are they?" Geena asked.

"Bring us a beer, and we might tell ya'."

Geena raced into the store and came back holding two long-neck bottles of Stroh's. She ran down the steps and handed them to Normaine and Eddy. Then she ran back up the steps and stood between Leeza and Timmon.

"We took them to that church place you mentioned over in Albuquerque. The Pentecostal Revival and Rapture Church. They all got saved and decided to stay in that shelter part of the church you mentioned before."

They grinned at each other.

"The four of them gave us messages to bring back. They said they ain't comin' back. You all are too bossy and look down on the ways they keep and they intend to keep their ways. They suit them just fine.

They said Leeza and Timmon can come over there too if they want to. But if they are going to keep on thinking they are big shots, to just stay the hell away!"

Cowboy Johnson tipped his cap back on his head and let out a low whistle loaded with what sounded suspiciously like relief. I turned to Leeza and Timmon, expecting the worst, but they wore looks of relief on their faces. The Mafia sisters huffed and turned away. Normaine watched us, waiting while we stood frozen on the porch.

"Dumbasses!" she shouted. She shook her head. "I'm going to celebrate!"

She headed toward the side of the store.

"Come on, Eddy!"

"Yes, love!" he said, ambling after her.

Geena ran down the steps.

"Where you going, Normaine?"

"Gonna' make a campfire for all you dumbasses!"

Geena giggled and motioned to us. That was all it took. In a flash, our combined guilt was over. Our low, bad time was finished. We were set free by The Pentecostal and Revival Rupture Church Shelter over in Albuquerque, a nice, long distance away. Us do-gooders could at last leave the situation to the Sheriff and God. Normaine and Eddy had sprung us from our trap of inevitable guilt, shame, and failure.

And so it came to be that four miscreants got shipped off to a more fitting place instead of becoming desert store misfits at Cowboy Johnson's Desert Oasis with us. Meanwhile, two more misfits joined us at the former little white church disguised as a gas station and store.

Chapter Eighteen

He's da' one ye' picked,
Yeah, he da' chosen one
Ya, dat' little son's a' gun

Timmon dreamed of becoming a baseball player when he grew up. He had a natural throw a major-league pitcher would envy. He was not left alone for a minute. Cowboy Johnson locked up the liquor and put locks on the beer coolers. We all noticed the locks, but nobody said a word. We took up drinking Nehi or Coke. It was what needed to be done for now. Cowboy Johnson unlocked everything each morning.

The Mafia sisters taught Timmon how to make fruitcakes without any alcoholic content. William taught him how to pan for gold, and over time, Cowboy Johnson would teach him to shoot guns, while Eddy would teach him to waltz properly and to be courtly to all of life, especially women. Normaine would fill him with Native American legends, offer to teach him how to take a scalp, and he would learn how to make rag rugs and wind chimes. Eventually, we hoped the emotional scars and bad habits we saw in him would mostly disappear.

Leeza would not turn to us like Timmon did. She wanted Geena. Even though Ray was around, we often had to pull Geena away from Leeza's emotional death grip and turn her life back into fun. I could tell Geena was tired of Leeza, but she kept a pity party going for her. Leeza knew it and took advantage of it.

She instantly turned into a black cloud of suffering every time Geena came near. She ignored the rest of us and was fine when Geena wasn't around.

Normaine and I took Geena and Leeza shopping in Albuquerque for school clothes. Leeza picked out the ugliest, cheapest things she could find, though I noticed her eyes lingering on finer things. When I started to put the clothes she picked back and get something better for her, Normaine stopped me.

"Don't put them back," she whispered behind her hand.

"Don't fix this for her. It's a game she's playing to keep you feeling sorry for her."

So we let her pick out shabby clothes, and she pouted while we picked out pretty things for Geena.

Out of desperation, we moved Leeza to motel room eight, closest to the Mafia sisters' headquarters so they could keep an eye on her. The sisters seemed easily capable of making a whole village do their bidding, so we took advantage of their propensity toward bossing the world around and gifted them with sullen, manipulative Leeza.

When she went looking for Geena to lay her pity party on, somebody put her to work. The Mafia sisters hired her to waitress for them after school and weekends and during summer vacation. She didn't like to work, but she knew she had to. She turned sour faces on us, but smiled and laughed with customers.

Then one day, Mina called the store.

"I want to see my kids!" she demanded.

Cowboy Johnson took Timmon and Leeza to visit Mina and their sisters on Sunday afternoon. I was sitting on the front porch of the store waiting for them, reading a magazine article featuring that awesome Burt Lancaster and wondering if he could make it rain in this desert, when Cowboy Johnson flew off the highway in Elsie, his El Camino, and lurched to a stop at the side of the store.

The three of them climbed out of Elsie. Their clothes were torn, and they looked like they had been worked over by a gang of hungry rodents.

"What happened?" I asked, jumping to my feet.

"Those good church folks and these children's kin got a mite overzealous and tried to "save" us," Cowboy Johnson answered cryptically.

"Go get cleaned up," he said and sent them on their way. He watched them leave before he climbed the porch steps.

"I need a shower. The sooner this stuff is off me, the better I'll feel!"

A few days later, Mina called again. I knew it was her before I answered the phone. She knew I knew, so she went off on religious a rant.

"You're a' keepin' my flesh and blood away from me! They are sinners! All of you are sinners! I want to see them!"

"I don't think that's a good idea after what you did to them last time," I said coolly.

She went off on her rant again. I yawned and examined my fingernails, and kept a psychic watch on her posturing. Then I felt someone come up behind me. It was Timmon. I sighed. I knew what he wanted. I interrupted Mina's rant.

"Okay. Enough! They will meet you one week from today, at the Taco Palace at noon. That's two miles from your church. Look it up on your calendar. That's seven days from today."

I hung up. Timmon touched my shoulder briefly in thanks, then turned and left. A week later, Mina and the sisters met Cowboy Johnson, William the Dude, Leeza, and Timmon at the Taco Palace. Things went okay, so they agreed to meet once a week on Saturday from noon until about four o'clock. Sometimes Mina and the sisters showed up, but mostly they didn't, so the visits stopped.

School started again. Ray and Geena's friends came by each morning and picked up Geena and Leeza. Timmon rode the long yellow school bus that stopped at the store for him. Mr. Shubert, the bus driver, said he was glad to pick Timmon up because of the donuts and coffee, but we knew it was because of Timmon. He had a soft charisma and light shining in him. God knows where he got it from. Mr. Shubert ordered fresh donuts and coffee from the bakery each morning. I watched Timmon's bright, innocent face light up each time he handed him the donut bag and coffee.

I decided that whatever one called the Force that runs the show here on Earth, it sure had a sneaky habit of planting Lights of Goodness in unexpected places. Many times, the people carrying those Lights had hell to pay, at least during their lifetime, because they were either misplaced or displaced Lights surrounded by Shadows.

We tried hard to do right by Mina and her family because she was a misplaced Light. But she chose a life of working for the Shadow. Those who toiled on the Shadow's behalf lived in fearful misery and hurt others. Some people liked hurting others, some didn't. Those who didn't, eventually left the Shadow lands and moved back into the Sunshine. Timmon inherited her Light. And there was plenty of sunshine for his Light to bask in at our little desert oasis.

Halloween came and went. We celebrated with a campfire and marshmallows. Then Christmas vacation came. On Christmas day, Cowboy Johnson gave me a quick kiss under the mistletoe, and I let him. The kids went back to school after Christmas vacation, and our days settled into their old routines.

Leeza stayed dour and unapproachable through all our celebrations. Then things changed again. A couple more months passed, and all of a sudden, Leeza bloomed into a nice person. She became interested in clothes, and her plain, sharp little face became animated, not quite but almost pretty with unusual good cheer.

We searched around for the source of this miracle and found him slouching in a back corner booth of the restaurant every night. He was dressed in the usual blue jeans and cowboy shirts common to these parts. He looked to be around thirty with greasy black hair in need of cutting, and small, calculating eyes.

Cowboy Johnson, Eddy, William the Dude, Ray, and the other men in our misfit family began taking their evening meals at the restaurant. They chose the tables closest to "Leeza's Chosen One" to sit at. Suddenly he was surrounded by a bunch of disapproving, adult men who watched his every move. They ignored the guy until Leeza came near him. Then they stopped talking and eating, openly watching and listening to him and her with disapproving frowns and glares. Of course, Leeza was furious. She tried to bring the subject up, but no one seemed to know what she was talking about.

The guy hung in there, trying to drum up his chosen jailbait until the two Mafia sisters salted his food so much he couldn't eat it anymore. We didn't see him in the restaurant after that.

Suddenly, Leeza got interested in helping us out by pumping gas. We watched as her Chosen One pulled up out front, and she ran down the front porch steps to pump gas for him. She hurried to his car window to take his money and leaned in to talk. He took off in a hurry after Cowboy Johnson stood up and started down the steps. Leeza gave us all black looks and stalked around the side of the store.

Leeza's chosen wasn't going to give up. If we stopped him where we could watch what he was doing, that was one thing, but what if he went to her school, or she slipped out to meet him? Child slavery has always been an evil in this world. And Leeza was a child even though she was seventeen. Would she be abducted like her mother was, only willingly?

We had to stop her. We hired a detective to follow him around, get his name, and run a background check on him. He was to make sure the guy knew he was following him. At the end of the first day, the detective called in to report that it took the dumb guy awhile to realize he was being followed.

Later that same night, Leeza slipped out to meet him, and they ran away together. The detective finished the background check on the guy and gave it to us. Her Chosen One was thirty-one and single, with no criminal record. That's all we needed to know. We dropped the matter with relief.

Timmon was too young to understand all the implications. He was sad, but he was one who never held a grudge, and he knew he had it good now. Lots of people loved him, so he left everything to us.

A couple of days passed, then our conscience got the best of us. Cowboy Johnson and I called the Pentecostal Revival and Rapture Church and arranged to meet Mina at the Taco Palace. We figured she would blame us for Leeza running away. But we felt we should tell her Leeza was gone. It was the right thing to do.

When we walked into the restaurant, Mina was sitting at a table in the back, watching us, looking smug. Leeza and her Chosen One were sitting across from her. Leeza was snugged up to him and looking adoringly at him.

"Boy, did we get duped!" Cowboy Johnson muttered and grabbed my arm. We did a fast U-turn.

"Ha Ha! You son's a bitches!" Mina shouted across the restaurant at us.

"Yeah!" Leeza's voice chimed in. "You put my daddy in the pen!"

"My sons are in the pen because of you!" Mina shouted.

We jerked the restaurant door open and ran out to Cowboy Johnson's dusty green El Camino, jumped in, and sped away. We tried to be either sad or mad after we got over being shocked, but instead, we laughed with relief.

"At least we don't have to wonder if she is with him against her will anymore!"

"Yeah, we don't have to hunt for her, or do anything... oh!...I'm so glad she's gone!"

I do not believe that our spiritual paths ever end. We are a part of an infinite universe. But pieces come to completion along the way, over and over again. This was a finished piece. Intense spiritual drives can and do manifest in both positive and negative ways. And who were we to tell God, that supposedly monotheistic deity who was probably too busy trying to sort out his and her multiple personalities or socks to pay much attention to us simple folks, what to do about Leeza? We would leave it alone.

When we got back to the store and told everyone what happened, we all shared in the catcalls, whistles, and laughs. Timmon was relieved that she was found and safe, but he didn't want to see any of them again.

"For now," we all cautioned him.

We all knew how fickle the Fates could be and how life could change in an instant. No preferred parking for this bunch of misfits. The Leeza incident changed all of us. We had become desert store gangsters. We had collectively become the Ministry of the Fence, defending our territory. We owned our own turf now, and we would fight to keep it. So what if it was a piece of unwanted, overlooked desert real estate, far from the benefits any polite social order might offer?

Our former church, now a gas station, grocery store, motel, restaurant, and much more, meant everything to us. It was our social center, our healing center, a place where both love and a few plants grew. We were misfit shareholders in what had become our own holy place. For the first time, a member of our misfit gang had committed treason and Exited Stage Left. Gone. By-bye. Good luck and good riddance! No more Shadow interrupting the practices of the tribe. We ate Pepperidge Farm cake and drank sodas to celebrate the delightful loss at our campfire that night then went on about our business.

Chapter Nineteen

The winds of time
are a' playin'
across da' desert
carryin' da' sand ta' othr' places

Time flew by. Ray started college at Colorado State University. He left with a load of his stuff packed into the back of his 1950 Ford F 3 fire engine red pickup. Geena drove the store car, Miss Gertie La Mars, to her last year in high school.

The old geezer prospector William Makepeace was lonely after Ray left for college, so he took Timmon under his wing. That comforted them both, and eventually, Timmon moved out to Ray's ranch to live with William, Algestine, and Emma. Then William took Timmon and Algestine to the west coast on a vacation. They liked it so much they decided to move out there. Emma stayed on at the ranch.

"Maybe I'll take up surfing again!" William declared, his light blue eyes twinkling. "Anyways, I'm tired of being a desert rat! Gonna' go try something new and old."

He built a large home in California, but Algestine was lonely without her sisters. Emma wasn't there to keep her in line, so she turned all her attention on William the Dude and Timmon. When the two men became wretched enough, we got a surprise visit from them. They were on a mission. They spent their time wheedling the Mafia sisters into moving to

California. The two sisters finally packed up and left with them. All the older, single men in the area were devastated and insisted the two sisters write to them.

More time flew by, and a day came when Cowboy Johnson and I were the only ones left at the store. I wore an apron that first day. I was dyeing some dark blue cloth to put away for Normaine to use when she came home.

I sat down beside him. He put his pen down and took off his black-rimmed glasses. He was bareheaded. I noticed that his straight brown hair was thinning on top. A spasm of endearment struck my heart, and I looked down at my hands to keep from looking at him. After a bit, I was able to look at him again. He never noticed. He was looking off into nowhere, just thinking, I guess. I imagined he was tired.

I'd known for some time that Cowboy Johnson was the glue holding us all together. I squinted at him. Did he know that? Did he know how valuable he was to this motley crew of dysfunctional, lost misfits? Was he able to cook soup? He'd never made any that I knew of.

I reached over and covered his hand with mine. Salt of the Earth. Stocky and sensitive and lovely beyond words. He squeezed my hand absent-mindedly, let it go, picked up his glasses and pen again.

I stood up and walked toward the front door, wishing I still smoked like a freight train. But I didn't, so I turned and stared at him awhile. He still didn't notice. I took his four square measure and placed it in my heart forever. It was free and easy. I'll never forget how he looked that day. Tired and happy and strong and willing to live life as it was.

I went out on the front porch and looked across the highway at the flat, space filled red and yellow desert sand. A stubby cactus was in bloom. There were yellow flowers on it.

The next day was quiet again. Nobody was around. Shortly after two, I got a cold orange Nehi from the cooler, opened it, and sat down beside him. I wanted to give my life to this man, but I thought I better start with a soda, so he didn't get scared off. I handed him the soda.

"Thanks," he said absentmindedly. I watched him and wondered what kind of little boy he once was. Was he filled with heartbreakingly sweet, untamed curious energy until older ways and new friends called him away from his steadfast beloveds? Was he a little boy who avoided embraces? Someone he loved had rejected him, I knew. If I had my way, that little boy's feet would never touch the ground again without a hand to hold him up. I would hug him until he was desperate for release.

I couldn't look at him any longer, or I might start a crying that could last forever. I touched his hand. He took off his glasses and laid his pen down and took my hand in his and held it. He rubbed it for a minute, then let it go.

I studied him like I did yesterday, and my heart finally made up my mind for me. I would surrender too. My father had finally surrendered. He'd accepted his personal defeat and learned to live again. The doing of it inspired a higher spiritual redemption in him. Not much, but any is good.

Sometimes God dresses up as a Monster to save our souls. Sometimes God becomes a Shadow character with the purpose of destroying the Monster in us or someone else. And we help God when we learn to draw snowflakes under our Shadows.

I would surrender now. I was taught from childhood that I should "know" all the answers in order to be safe. Someone would say, "You know better than that!" But I didn't know better than that. Never did. Still don't. I don't know why things happen the way they do or why my life has turned out the way it has. I don't know why I react the way I do. I don't know why I think the way I think. I don't know why I was always taught that the things that I do naturally, that my very nature, my Sight, was always wrong.

I looked at him. He was staring out at nothing, so I did too. Was he thinking the kind of stuff I was thinking? I didn't know. We stayed that way a long time.

Days passed without him noticing the state I was in. One night, I lay sleepless in my room on my demure twin bed covered with its white sheets, listening to the strains of the music on his gramophone floating through the air.

I sat up and looked around my sparsely furnished room. It looked like a nun's cell, though it didn't have a cross anywhere in it. I despised religious symbols, but I could tolerate them as long as they weren't in my bedroom. I sighed and dropped my head. For the first time since I ran away, I let myself remember the reason I couldn't stand crosses.

The Monster. That was why I didn't have a cross up where I slept. Ever since I was a little girl, I always found a way to go to church. My family never went that I knew of. I loved the cleanliness, order, and stained glass windows of churches. Every time we moved, I hunted up neighbors to give me a ride back and forth to whatever kind of church they attended. It didn't matter to me what kind it was, I just needed to go.

When I met the Monster, I was going to church with a Baptist couple. I was living with them because I was forced to leave home and quit school and go to work. But I questioned some of the church's beliefs, and the couple kicked me out. I found a babysitting job and rented a room from a cousin who took care of old people in her home. I helped her nights and weekends to pay the rent.

I was too young to take care of myself. I was at my lowest ebb when I met the Monster. There was no one else to turn to. I turned to him, and my life became a living hell.

One night when he was gone, I slipped out and went to a tent revival with the religious couple I used to live with, trying to get some hope back into my life. Somehow, he found out where I was. He came in the tent and strode down the aisle to where I sat up front. He grabbed me by the hair of my head and dragged me down the aisle and out of the tent. No one tried to stop him. Those good Christians believed I was his property. They let that happen to me. That was the night I gave up on both God and them.

I paced the floor, crying with misery. Suddenly, the story of Samson and his "friends" from the Bible flew into my mind. Samson's "friends" tied him up and tried to get him to accept abuse and a miserable fate. But Samson broke the cords his "friends" tied him up with and took out a whole bunch of the abusers with just an ass's jawbone. Well, I was an ass. And I had a jawbone. Several, in fact. Attached.

I would have to accept having to live my life out without the love I needed because of the abuse, just like Samson's friends. I had overcome the bad experiences I went through with the Monster in most ways, but not in the bedroom way. I had never finished the process.

I waited for my body to shudder with the remembered physical horror I'd been forced to live with, and the fear of dying.

I waited, but instead, a relentless, hopeful excitement coursed through me that would not be denied. The excitement was insistent and alive with sweetness. It didn't give a damn about the memories my mind was holding on to. It informed me that my cellular structure had changed many times since back then, with the help of good beer and good friends and just time. Also, I read somewhere that our cells are completely changed out for new ones every seven years, anyway. It was a guarantee.

Besides, it was time. I'd kept myself and him waiting long enough. I kept pacing, almost running, while the pink, warming up blood of new hope coursed its way through my body. Maybe I could do what Samson did. Set myself free from my old bedroom "friend", although I didn't plan on dying to get the job done. I planned to finally live. With a

Good man. In fact, a Reader. I walked the floor, thinking and drawing my thoughts together while my body tanked up on fresh, new hope.

When it was time, my Sight kicked in. I created a sphere of Light armed on the outside with sharp swords. I stepped into it and spun it to the right, then cut the bedroom memories with the Monster loose. Then I asked the Mother of Earth energies to complete the job and help me be whole again. SHE came and comforted me. At last, I felt the organic, biological changes taking place in my body as the old, bad, cellular memories released their hold on me and fled, leaving in their place, peace at last, and hot pink love and blushing joy.

When I was all pink and red and hot, I stepped out of the sphere and out of HER bosom, a cleansed, wild, organic cavewoman drooling for a sweet, hot time with her Good man. It was time for me to learn about a higher sexual vibration, to learn about organic spirituality.

I freshened up and changed into the pretty, thin white nightgown Normaine gave me years ago and combed my hair. She'd said I needed to be a "virgin" and start over with that man she kept trying to introduce me to. Well, that wasn't going to happen, because it was Cowboy Johnson I loved. But I'd kept the lace-edged, knee-length cotton nightgown anyway.

He met me at the back door like he did so long ago on the first night I met him. He took my hand and pulled me in. He ran his hands over my face as though memorizing it. He gave me a chaste kiss like the first one he gave me. But a lot of water had run under the bridge since then, over a decade of it, and I needed more now. I felt like an Ohio Blue Tip match that had been struck and was flaming high. It's a wonder I didn't burn the store down. We waltzed slowly around the kitchen while I wondered how to get that chastity belt off him.

"That's the first time I've heard you play that music since the night we met," I said helpfully.

He didn't answer.

"Why did you play it tonight?" I asked, fishing for more.

He didn't answer that question either.

It was beginning to dawn on me, while I flamed around the floor feeling like a hormonal nuclear weapon about to explode, that if I thought I was going to get a romance book answer out of my man, I was bad fooled. I'd read many romance books in my former life to keep hope alive, and in all of them, the manly heroes owned masterly gifts of gab. They were silver-tongued savages with just one goal in mind, to love their woman thoroughly and well, verbally and physically.

Did I really need to hear sweet, pining words from Cowboy Johnson? Yes. Was he able to speak in romantic situations? I hoped so. Did his courage go down the drain in romantic encounters? I hoped not. How come there were no nice, smutty romance directives for two mature older people waltzing alone in a little church disguised as a store out in a desert?

It hadn't mattered how long I'd waited until this very instant. I'd dawdled along, not learning who this man was because of the boundaries I set to keep myself safe from another unexpected Monster. I put those boundaries in place for good reason at the time, and I expected them to remain in place the rest of my life. No more men. Now those rules were gone, and it was time for me to claim this man.

I was thoroughly tired of holding myself back from whatever it was that lay ahead with this good man. All the times I desired him flew through my mind, leaving a hot trail of memories coursing through me. I'd put up a hell of a fight and lost. But my battle had taken away years from both of us. It had cost us both plenty.

Desperately, I began muttering, asking myself questions, and answering them to halt the inevitable flow towards the path we were taking. There would be no turning back.

"Was I having my first hot flash?" I asked myself.

"No. It's all love hormones, dear," I answered smugly.

"I'm too old for this stuff, aren't I?" I asked.

"Never!" I answered.

"Am I acting like a harlot in the Biblical sense?" I asked.

"I hope so," I answered myself.

I didn't give a damn about wanting someone in the Biblical sense. I assumed almost past forever that the Monster had ruined me for any other man. But he hadn't. I'd finally caught on. Better late than never.

I shuddered as a new question entered my mind. It was a question I dared not face before. Was the low life, painful sex with the Monster all there was to doing the wild thing for men? He was the only man I was ever with. Was I wrong to crave tenderness and cherishing with soft words and caresses? Were all the romance books wrong?

All of a sudden, I was stunningly terrified. I pulled away and ran to the back door, gasping for air.

"Whoo!" I said, fanning my face. I had to say something.

Cowboy Johnson stayed where he was. He didn't say anything. The music wound around us, holding us together in a kind protective cocoon.

Finally, I said, "I've never loved this way before."

"I have," Cowboy Johnson stated calmly.

I was flabbergasted. He'd loved someone else like I loved him? My heart broke. I began to cry. He didn't come to me and try to comfort me.

"What was her name?"

"Lola Smetzel," he answered without hesitation.

"You're kidding."

"Nope."

I wanted to laugh at her name. I giggled. A long silence passed. I didn't know what to say. Maybe I didn't want to know any more. Maybe I was getting myself into big trouble here. I sighed. He spoke again.

"It all began in third grade when I pushed Lola on the swings on the playground and saved my graham crackers for her."

I immediately felt better. A childhood sweetheart. How threatening could that be? I turned to head back to his waiting arms, but he stopped me with his next words.

"Lola never tasted graham crackers, you see. She was very poor. I didn't know the details and was too young to ask. She rarely brought any lunch.

Sometimes she brought a homemade biscuit to school. She was too thin. Her hair was short and brown, and she was pretty. What made her pretty was her eyes. She had expressive blue eyes with rings of gold around the edges. But the gorgeous part was the hope and light her eyes held in them. She didn't know about anything but poverty and survival, and yet I knew she had already risen above it somehow and would remain there. I'm not sure she ever knew that about herself. That was something I didn't know about myself at the time. She woke up that part of me and made it stronger each time she looked at me. Lola was just the beginning."

He waited a minute. Then he said the words I will always remember.

"You. You. You have done that for me, too. Each day I am a better person because of You. You are filled with Light and Sight and are as easily wounded as a fawn finding her way through the woods. You live in your own world, a Good world, and have strengths you have yet to discover. ...and you are cute, too." He leered at me, then he got serious again.

"I need you to know that I have loved many women in my life in many ways for many reasons, and most likely will love more of them. I also love William and other men and Geena. I will never stop loving in all the different ways life demands of me. You must not become possessive of my need to love, and demand that it all be turned towards you."

I was crying, weeping great sobs of relief from my soul.

"Never, never!" I whispered. "I love that you love many different ways. Wish I could."

"Well, let's learn more of it together." He looked away.

"But I need you to know that tonight is just for you and me. I can't stand to hear the words of what he did to you this night. I already have a good idea. Maybe I can stand hearing it another time. Maybe never. Maybe neither of us will ever need to speak of it. I just want to love you past everything else tonight in whatever way that has to be for us."

I stared down at the floor. Beneath was the Earth we stood on. The sleeping dragon beneath our feet had awakened us again from our past lives of sleep, and it was moving, turning over from that long sleep to lead the way into new adventures. This world was turning in circles, dancing, and the sun was shining, making flowers and velvety, cool darkness lay somewhere, feeding tall, waiting Shadows.

It was time for us to dance again, too. Like we always did before. Nothing could ever come between our souls for long, though it might take lifetimes to find each other again. I lifted my eyes to his, crossed the floor, and slipped into his waiting arms. A comforting darkness, filled with insights and warmth, a joyful path previously untaken and unknown, enveloped us, and we traveled where the red dragon led.

Chapter Twenty

Jis' da' two a' us
oh yea'!

    The next day, I sat beside him on the bench again. We sat together until one or the other of us was needed for something in the store or outside. We did this every day we could, for as long as we could, then we started taking long drives in Elsie, his green El Camino, in the evenings to get away from the store.
    That's what we did all through Geena's last high school year. After she graduated, she moved to South Carolina to go to college so she could become a bug scientist, a herpetologist, and pursue her interest in lizards, bugs, and such. Ray majored in archeology, then followed her to South Carolina. They eventually eloped and had Celia.
    We drove the Merc' to Carolina for Celia's birth. I watched Ray carefully. He had become stuffy about his new professorship at the University. He was proud and reserved, cautiously happy over the arrival of Celia. I tried to chalk the changes up to his nerves over having become a new father, but there was more.
    Ray wanted a nanny to start immediately, but Geena vetoed that idea. She intended to take time to be with Celia, so she took a leave from her teaching job, a decision that shocked and horrified Ray.
    The big house he chose for them to live in was too formal for us to enjoy. It was a place for well-shod

thinkers and intellectuals to gather in, to drink to drive and ambition, to one-up each other. Geena seemed to mostly ignore Ray's ambitions. She stayed simply happy with herself and Celia. Then William and Emma arrived, and Ray was kept busy with them.

On the drive back to the store, we talked about the situation. I stuck my hand out the window of the Merc' to catch some airwaves.

"I'm worried about Geena's biological father finding out about her and Celia. After all, she has married into a famous artist's family."

He glanced over at me. After a minute of studying over what I said, he spoke. He always knew what I was thinking.

"Maybe hire a detective to keep track of him?"

I nodded, yes. I hadn't thought of that. All I was doing was worrying in circles while he was problem-solving.

"Know a good one?"

"Nope. I guess the phone book will have to do."

I grinned at him. He would take care of it. I let my worries about Geena and Celia float out the window.

We searched until we found a detective about eighty miles from Ardenville. We didn't want anyone in Ardenville to know anything, but we also needed someone who could go there quickly if needed, without making a long trip to do it. We found Dan Swain. We chose him after we had a good laugh over his name. He had a smooth voice to match his name and the gift of changing his voice to suit any occasion. We arranged for him to report back to us every month by phone. Nine months later, he called again. I was nearest the phone and took the call.

"Hello?"

"Is this Map Girl?"

Both Dan and Bud Spinner had nicknamed me that to make sure they didn't slip and say my real name around anyone else.

"Yes, it is. Hello, Dan."

His voice turned solemn. Mournful and funereal.

"I have some news for you, but it's not about your ex. It's about your family. I thought you might like to know."

I blinked.

"Has someone died?"

"Nope. But your mom had a bad stroke, and they sent her home for your dad to take care of. Then that snowstorm came, and he was stuck in the house by himself with her. She ran out of her medications and had seizures. He made it out to the highway after four days of being snowed in to get her medicine. To make a long story short, he said he wasn't going through an ordeal like that ever again, where he couldn't get help for her or him. So, he moved them to Florida. Johnny on the spot. Faster than a speeding bullet. Quicker than a lightning bolt. Within a week."

Dan had a cliché' to suit every occasion.

"The rest of your brothers and sisters are heading down there too or off to other states. Your family is breaking up, Map Girl. None of them are going to be living in Ardenville much longer."

My head was spinning. I turned to Cowboy Johnson.

"Would you mind talking to Dan for a minute? I'll be right back."

Puzzled, he looked at me. Then he picked up the phone. I wandered out to the back porch and leaned against a post. So my family was fleeing Ardenville like I did. Didn't matter the reasons. It was happening. I guess life sometime evicts the bad parts too. Finally, my mother might get some much-needed rest. The shoe was on the other foot now. I would think more about it later. Now was not the time. I took a deep breath and went back in. Cowboy Johnson handed me the phone.

"What does it look like for my mother?" I asked Dan.

"Nobody knows."

"Okay... and my father is taking care of her?"

"That's what the word around Ardenville is."

Dan repeated what he told me. I thanked him for calling, and we hung up.

I tried to find meaning in his news, but couldn't. I felt a leaden sadness about Karma and what it does to people. I refused to let his news drag me into the past and lock me up there again. Sometimes freedoms are unwanted. Mine wasn't.

I looked at the positive. Maybe they would be happier in Florida. Maybe Mom would see pretty flowers there. And fishing. She loved to fish since she was a girl back in the hills, catching fish with her hands in the creek above their house. I shut it out of my mind and looked ahead.

A few months later, I got another phone call from Dan, telling me my mother had passed away. The stroke was too much for her. Well, for me, she would never be gone.

I asked Dan to send a huge bouquet of standing flowers to her funeral. He sent it with a ribbon saying "Spellbind's Child" with a red heart across it. No one knew who it was from. My memories of Mom and her great laugh and the way she was will always stay with me.

One night soon after her passing, the angels came and showed her to me. She was dancing with her ten-year-old school girlfriends in green, silky, tall grass beneath a railroad trestle. They were picking and eating tiny wild red strawberries.

She smiled at me in the dream. She knew. Even though we loved each other, it wasn't enough to keep us enduring the same bad situation together this lifetime. That's all it was. There was never any bad intentions or hate. Just a lot of love that couldn't happen this lifetime. Maybe next time. Sometimes situations break people apart. That's just the way it is.

Dan called out of schedule two more times in the next few years, once to tell me my father had passed away, and then my ex-husband from cancer. The frog prince and the perverted one were gone, too. He told me where my brothers and sisters lived now.

"Keep calling, won't you Dan, even though my ex is gone? I would like to keep track of my brothers and sisters and how they are doing. Just report in like you always have, if you would."

"Sure, Map Girl. I'll be glad to. No problemo. Easy as greased lightning. Fast as a running spoon, a galloping horse."

Chapter Twenty One

I'm a' comin' home
I' did' ma' time

Four years passed without a ripple on the surface of our lives. Most of our beloved misfits were gone. Geena and Ray to Carolina. William the Dude and Algestine, Timmon, and the two Mafia sisters to California. Normaine and Eddy were on the road most of the time, traveling the country. We might see them a few days every three months or so.

Then Geena and Celia came home to us the summer when Celia was four and filled up our lives again. Normaine and Eddy met them halfway on the long drive from South Carolina to the store and drove them the rest of the way home. Geena called us for help when she couldn't drive any farther. Ray was off on a dig somewhere and out of touch, so Eddy and Normaine, who happened to be home with us, went and got them.

I paced the porch all morning long, waiting, alternating between doing dishes and running out front. Normaine called me every night from the motels they stayed in on their way home.

I dried my hands on a dishcloth and watched them drive up to the store that first morning. Eddy was in Esmerelda. Normaine was behind him in Geena's Dodge. For once, I couldn't remember what year of Dodge it was, and I never forget land yacht statistics.

My girl sat pale and silent beside Normaine, her brown hair covering her face like dripping rain. They rolled to a slow stop. I ran down the porch steps, jerked the door open, and grabbed Geena in the death grip of a mother grizzly. Normaine stopped me with warning words about not scaring Celia. I turned to Celia. She was fine. I looked to Eddy for confirmation. Eddy smiled at me and nodded. He twirled his mustache and grabbed Celia's hand. I helped Geena out. We wandered up the porch steps and followed Normaine and Eddy into the store. Cowboy Johnson sat Celia on a stool at the long store counter and poured her a tall glass of cold chocolate milk.

"Now," he said to her, "What amazing stories have your Aunt Normaine and Uncle Eddy been telling you on the way here?"

Celia giggled. I guided Geena into the back of the store and down onto the Hideous Green Sofa. Normaine came in, and we went to cooking spaghetti. Lots of it. Geena ate and strayed back to the Hideous Green Sofa, landing there like a shipwreck on an island. We didn't ask her anything. We left her to find the way back out of where she was. We ate and laughed and talked and went on our way and let her be. We included her in our meals and sat near her while Normaine wove rugs, and I sewed pale green tutus for the spring festival in Pistachio Pico.

She slept most of three weeks away on the Hideous Green Sofa while everyone happily kept Celia's attention diverted to other things. Celia loved the campfires and wanted one every night. She ate hot dogs for dinner and Pepperidge Farm cake.

Cowboy Johnson ran and got his southwest geometric blanket from the end of his ugly cot, brought it out, and wrapped it around Geena's shoulders the first night she wandered out to join us at the campfire. I watched him, and my heart welled with splendid joy. That action told me more than any words could, of his great love for my girl. His girl too. I remembered him holding her in his arms years ago while scolding Normaine and me for not taking better care of her.

Slowly Geena came back to herself. She started making clay lizards and painting them again with Cowboy Johnson sitting nearby, doing his endless paperwork, or reading, his black frame glasses perched low on his nose. He was truly her emotional father. If he left, she got up and went to the Hideous Green Sofa and stayed there until he returned. His patience was never-ending with her, and as I knew, with anyone he loved.

One night Geena asked him for her old room back.

"Of course," he stated coolly, putting up a good front while I watched him tamp down his tears.

"It hasn't been changed since you left, anyway," I added casually.

We left her room the way it was, just locked the door when she moved away. That's what she asked us to do. We never knew why and didn't ask. She and Celia were staying in one of the motel rooms. She took Celia's hand and her door key and left.

We yearned to see Celia's reaction to the innocent, enthusiastic girl's room Geena left behind. Her bug collections and fringed lamps and the rest of the things she filled her room with were still where she left them. But we were wise enough to let them go without us.

That night, Cowboy Johnson and I went for a ride. When we reached Washman's Draw, he pulled over and parked. Then he turned to me and took my fingers in his hands. He brought them slowly to his lips and kissed them gently.

"You know, this is like what you and Normaine went through way back. Your little girl is going to come out of this just fine, too."

I burst into tears; he scooted me close and held me until I cried the tears out and could think straight again.

The next day I was able to care of business again. I called the doctor, and he came and examined Geena. He took some blood and went away. He came back in a few days and said Geena was anemic, that's what was making her weak. He said she needed to eat more meat. Geena was never much of a meat eater, and when she did, she was very picky about it.

I told Cowboy Johnson about the problem. He nodded wisely and strode off like a man on a mission. Next thing I knew, all the men on the place were in William's canary yellow truck. They roared off, packed in like sardines in a can, shouting and laughing. I shook my head. Men!

They returned a few hours later with barbeque grills, each one silver or black, each one the size of a small state. There were mysterious meats and spices and brines and smelly wood chips along with grills loaded in the back of the truck. They set up their grills out back in a long row, with picnic tables between them. Then, amid much beer drinking and laughter, they broke out their spatulas, meats, and other tools, and set to work, one barbeque grill per man. I shook my head as I watched them from the back porch.

From the minute the first piece of meat was ready to eat, Geena was constantly plied with a never-ending supply of delicious meats, a dozen different kinds, fixed a dozen different ways. Sometimes she ate some, sometimes she didn't eat any. But she grew steadily better and started smiling again. The delicious smells wafted through the store and out around the gas pumps, causing customers to salivate. They eagerly bought the extra meat and other food that the men "cooked off" every couple of days.

*

Normaine and Eddy stayed all summer that first year. Four-year-old Celia was kept busy learning to make wind chimes and rag rugs with Normaine, learning how to dance with Eddy to the music from Cowboy Johnson's Victrola, and having fun in general. Geena was working the clay again. She was teaching Celia how to make clay lizards and bugs.

But it was her grandmother Emma who won Celia's heart the day she began to teach her how to paint. Celia spent afternoons out at the ranch with Emma after her first painting lesson. The rest of us rested up during her lessons.

Celia and Emma painted together and rode all over the ranch. Celia loved the ranch. William the Dude stayed at the ranch so he could spend time with Emma and Celia. He left Timmon in charge of the three Mafia sisters back in California. They still made their fruitcakes, and he stocked us up with them when he came home.

William always left California with the understanding that he owed Timmon a long vacation when he got back. Timmon always headed like an arrow to Emma and the ranch after William came home. William told Timmon he could live on the ranch, but Timmon wouldn't leave him alone in California. Timmon told him he wouldn't last a day with the three Mafia sisters if he wasn't there. We believed him.

Our little Celia became the magic and glue that brought all us misfits back together again. Geena and Celia stayed all summer. They left for Carolina one week before Celia had to start school for the first time.

Ray was home in Carolina, and he arranged school for Celia. Cowboy Johnson was designated to put up with his huffy, demanding phone calls.

Geena never talked about the spiritual malaise that almost killed her that first summer. Instead, she came home and leaned on us for love, and got better because of it. Life isn't easy mostly and all of us misfits knew it. It was bigger than us and much more powerful. I will be forever grateful to the universe that my girl was dancing under the desert stars once again before she left for Carolina at the end of that first summer.

These days, my girl and I both dwell in the Light, in two different ways of Being, with two different philosophies on life. But since both places are far, far away from the towering Shadow of a Monster, it is an acceptable Fate. We won. I know this when I look up at the stars. They are full of mystery and wonder, and I know my girl is sleeping safe under those same stars, same as me. It has to be enough, though I miss her wild, sweet ways and laughter, for she has chosen to live by the ocean, far away from this desert.

*

Celia came home to us misfits every summer for eight years. Geena came with her most summers unless Ray became too demanding of her time. Ray was gradually growing more leonine and proud. Geena accepted him the way he was. There were rumors now and then of Ray's wanderings, and I instinctively knew they were true. My girl was a straight arrow, one who wilted under mistrust and lies. It would take time because of her great, pure love for Ray, but she would eventually sort it out.

At the end of those eight summers, when Celia was twelve, she began to travel with her parents, only coming back home to us for Christmas. The glue that had held us misfits together for eight bright and sunny summers was gone.

That time was over, and our beloved misfits scattered to the four winds again. Emma booked Normaine an art show in New York City at a famous art gallery. Normaine and Eddy moved to New York City, where they became a big hit with his Italian relatives and all kinds of artsy folks. Esmerelda, that wonderful work of art, went with them. William the Dude chose to stay in California the summer after Celia left. Emma began traveling in the summer too leaving the ranch for Timmon to take care of.

After a while, we closed the bakery and the restaurant and converted them into motel rooms, and hired help to run the gift shop. Eventually, we closed the gift shop too. There were no more colorful clay lizards and rag rugs and wind chimes, fruitcakes, and other enchantments to sell. We turned it into a motel room. Sometimes someone asked where the restaurant and gift shop were, so they could eat, and buy the famous fruitcakes, rag rugs and clay lizards they'd heard about. Then a time came when no one asked anymore.

But all our misfits still come home to Cowboy Johnson's Desert Oasis for Christmas, even though the black and white homemade sign out by the two-lane highway is dusty and faded now, and some of the small print is gone.

They come home, and we share our lives again for that little piece of time, and we remember what was, and the men take hold of their cojones again and make campfires and set off fireworks and grill all manner of things while the women's hearts are strengthened with the wisdom that comes from washing dishes by hand together and making fruitcakes, rag rugs, and painting clay lizards.

"Nothing ever changes around here!" they all exclaim in great satisfaction.

"I hope it stays this way forever!"

But our time together flies by, and the store empties out once more. The fake Christmas tree comes down and goes back in its box. Every one of our beloveds carry away the remembered courage and kindnesses us unwanted misfits have always given to each other, and they go back, renewed, to their far away dwelling places to share themselves with others that will never know us.

This little desert store remains our home and theirs. The store we grew our misfit roots in, and healed each other in, and had each other's backs. And still do, until the last one of us draws a final breath.

As for me and Cowboy Johnson, whose real name is Avery Mott Judson, not Johnson, like I assumed for so many years, and who still calls me "Mama" or "You", I never did tell him anything about the Monster. The Monster had become small to me. I knew now that there were millions of women and children who suffered through childhoods with Monsters and came out okay. They lived on and wrote and danced under the stars and sat around boardrooms, nursed others in hospitals, and some stayed at home. Evil can't stop Life from moving on. And Shadows and Light will always interplay their karmic roles in it. What has to be will be.

My body, mind, heart, and soul, all of me, shut the door to that place and threw away the key the second night we waltzed together in this sacred place, a little white church disguised as a store and gas station out in the desert.

*

These days, we still pump a little gas and clean a few windshields, and I still pose by the Merc' now and then, though I've lost my girlish figure. My Sight still tells me when a person has been sent here to be healed. Whether they are conscious of it or not is another story. Sometimes they rent a motel room and stay awhile. Others stay long enough to get hugged or encouraged to do certain long term silly healing things before they are on their way again. Those with spine troubles are Geena's specialty. Any bones. Sometimes my Sight directs me to simply clean people's auras.

A day came when I was sitting on the front porch. It was a quiet day with no traffic on the highway. I sat there, idly thinking, just letting my thoughts go where they would. I sank deeper into them, and then I remembered a thing I often studied on. My father and the frog prince. I often wondered about his favor with the Elementals. Today, my thoughts went deeper, leading to new realizations. They told me that my father had always had a bunch of pipedreams, and I had inherited them through his genetics. Like him, I had a genetic grid of them encoded around my chest and back. Suddenly, I understood that his pipe dreams had allowed him and his generations before him to survive. They had protected him from realities that would have killed him. They had given his life meaning.

I had inherited them. They had kept from seeing too much just as they had him. They had protected me and kept me distant from life. My father and I were both full of pipe dreams that could never come true. He genetically wrapped me up in them way back then. He loved me in that way, the only way he knew how to love anybody. We'd stood there in the sunshine, father and daughter, and talked the language of dreams about a frog prince for a brief moment. I agreed with him and kept the grid in place until this very moment.

The inherited grid of impossible dreams fell away from me. I heard them clink and clang as they hit the ground. Evidently, I didn't need them anymore because my dreams had come true.

I thought I should be scared to death, but I wasn't. I felt like a huge burden was gone. I felt empty and scared and adventurous. I was in a new place with my Sight, one destiny provided me. I could breathe better now. I suspected for the rest of my life.

"Thank you, Father," I sighed.

*

Summers, I keep the sanctuary filled with blue morning glories winding their way around sweet peas and turnip vines like he did. I tend the past by growing them, and green beans from seeds I bought through a catalogue that advertises "Tennessee Wonder Beans" in memory of my mother, father, and family. And once in a great while, I sit down in one of the rocking chairs for just a few minutes to remember the good parts and the strengths I gained from my family. But there is no going back. Just forward.

Other times I look around this place and remember the two tan tents and the little pink trailer, and the laughing, tall, brown-haired girl and the rest of us who ended up being held together by Cowboy Johnson, and my love for him flies up through the air and falls down in pieces like the pure white snowflakes us misfits learned to draw while bowed low under the weight of our Shadows before we came here. Now we are all snowflake artists out in the world, bending beneath Shadows, practicing the geometry of doing Good.

And it all happened because each of us stopped for gas out in the desert in the middle of nowhere, at a little white church that had been converted into a gas station and grocery store with a simple, black and white homemade sign nailed to its side reading "Gas and Groceries."

A small sign that would eventually be replaced by a bigger sign reading, "Cowboy Johnson's Desert Oasis."

Look for the next books in the Desert Oasis Series!

Book Two
The Red Cactus Desert
Geena and the 59' Dodge Lancer

Twelve year old Geena escapes the clutches of her Shadow-tainted father and the town that supports him. Fleeing south with her Mama in their 57' Mercury, they stop at a desert store in New Mexico where she meets Cowboy Johnson. Having inherited the Sight from Mama, she knows the store is her new home, and he is her good, new father. Now she has protection and a family—and love at first sight—when she meets Ray Makepeace. More misfits settle into the store. But families carry both strengths and weaknesses and the misfits have plenty of both.

Geena and Ray's love is in for a bumpy ride. Normaine won't marry beautiful, dapper Eddy. Mama is terrified of returning Cowboy Johnson's steadfast, calm love. William the Dude Makepeace makes troubling decisions based on his arthritis.

Still, love will have its way, traveling the many paths it takes to stay true to the soul each misfit carries. Interspersed here and there are children's stories currently being made into children's books. Geena's coming of age story is an inspiring tale of innocence and courage.

Book Three
The Three Cactus Limbo
The Gift of the Three Magi and Map Girl

Bud Spinner, a fear-filled reclusive garage owner, a shy inner-knower of hidden goodness in people, helps Map Girl and Geena escape Ardenville with cash and a map. Bud secretly writes auto manuals, banking the money in another town. Bud, Ben, and Andy, the two other fear-filled recluses in town, find each other and become fast friends. Bud repairs cars. Ben reads science fiction. Andy fishes unsuccessfully.

They appear to be boring, aging bachelors to the town citizens. Unknown to themselves as well as the town, they are able to detect good and evil, hidden emotions and intentions in others. Constantly overwhelmed by their gifts, they stay extremely resistant to the ills of the outside world. Their solution is to hide.

Overwhelmed by Nature and the unknown, as well as people, they've never traveled anywhere. They buy a cabin and settle for weekends away from Ardenville. But Dan, a private eye hired by Mama to keep tabs on her ex, ejects them from their cabin, causing them to flee Ardenville in their classic cars with a gift for Map Girl.

After visiting Map Girl, Miss Emma, a world famous artist, and her father, William the Dude Makepeace, talk the three into staying at a remote monastery. From there, they await their first Christmas with Map Girl at the desert store.

www.ingramcontent.com/pod-product-compliance
Lightning Source LLC
LaVergne TN
LVHW041956060526
838200LV00002B/45